ENDURE AT THE END OF THE WORLD

A POST-APOCALYPTIC ADVENTURE

M. P. MCDONALD

MPMCD PUBLISHING

ALSO BY M. P. MCDONALD

THE MARK TAYLOR SERIES

Mark Taylor: Genesis

No Good Deed: Book One

March Into Hell: Book Two

Deeds of Mercy: Book Three

March Into Madness: Book Four

CJ SHERIDAN THRILLERS

Shoot: Book One

Capture: Book Two

Sympatico Syndrome Series

(Post-Apocalyptic Survival Novels)

Infection: Book One

Isolation: Book Two

Invasion: Book Three

Sympatico Syndrome World

Alone at the End of the World: Book One

Endure at the End of the World: Book Two

Suspense

Seeking Vengeance

Noah Boyle unloaded the last of the supplies Leona had packed. Dr. Turner seemed to have a lot more medical gear than Noah had expected. There were vials of medications, syringes, IV bags, needles, tubing, and boxes of bandages. It looked like enough to equip a small clinic. Noah looked up from the box to the kids racing toward the pasture to see the goats Jalen had found while Noah had been away.

Their numbers had doubled with the addition of Ethan O'Connor, the young teen who had tried to defend Cassie Boyle against Noah. Noah chuckled at the memory, although it had been terrifying at the time. The kid had guts, that was for sure. He'd only met Cassie Boyle and her two children, Bella and Milo, a few days before Noah had arrived at his former sister-in-law's house, but he'd been ready to defend them with his life. That made him just as much family, in Noah's book, as blood. There was no question that he was welcome to join them when Noah had invited them to come to the farm. The more people they had contributing, the better everyone's chances were for survival. Of course, right now, half the group was under the age of fifteen, but Noah was glad of that. It meant hope for the future.

Jalen and Ava had been excited to find out Noah had brought Milo, Bella, and Ethan with him, and it seemed like they'd all made friends within minutes of meeting. Jalen and Ethan already seemed to have hit it off, and Ava had talked a mile a minute to the other two, telling them all about the farm. Bella showed her the box of Barbie dolls Cassie had allowed her to bring, and Ava had squealed like the little girl she was. The only one left out was Milo, but Ethan had called out to him before Jalen had pulled him away to see the goats. Milo's face had lit up at the invitation to tag along with the older boys, and all three had raced down to see the goats in the pen.

"Did Jalen tell you how he found the goats?" Dexter exited the house and stood on the back stoop, his hand shading his eyes as he looked past Noah to the pasture with the goats.

"No, not really. He just said something about finding them on a back road."

Dexter threw back his head and laughed as he hopped off the stoop to stand beside Noah. "Yeah, well, it was a back road that led up to a farm a mile or so west of here. I'd told him not to go that far, but you know Jalen..." Dexter shook his head. "Anyway, that mama goat was bleating her poor head off because the baby was tangled half in and half out of a car down in a ditch. The window had been partly down, and that silly little kid had gotten her head stuck in there."

"Really?" Noah slammed the tailgate closed and leaned his backside against the top of the stoop. "Talk about good timing."

"Sure was. And ever since he saved the little one, it's been trying to follow him around like a lost puppy."

Noah smiled. "Your son is a good kid. He's like a real-life hero to that baby goat."

"He's so proud of that animal you'd think he grew up raising goats for the 4-H club."

"4-H... huh." Noah crossed his arms and toed a weedy tuft of grass that had sprouted in a crack in the pavement. "I remember going to school with kids who grew up on farms. The 4-H club was a big deal to them, but I didn't understand. I wasn't mean or anything, but I'm ashamed to admit that I secretly thought they were dorks. I'd bet if they survived the virus, they're doing better than most."

Dexter sighed, his tone wistful. "Do you think our lives will ever be even close to what they were before?"

"Like before? No. But I hope we create a new normal that isn't so bad." He gestured to the kids. "For them, this is the new normal. Ethan and Jalen will have memories of what life was like before, but the other three are already adjusting to this. In a few years, the time before will be just a fuzzy memory."

"Yeah. You're probably right." Dexter peered into the boxes at Noah's feet, nodding approval at what he saw. "I suppose it's a good thing too. Those kids will be the ones who'll have to carry on when the conveniences we still have are long gone." Dexter nodded to the truck. "Like, how long can we keep finding good gasoline? That stuff degrades, and we'll be lucky to be driving much of anything in a few years if we don't find an alternate way to fuel the cars."

"I guess you have your work cut out for you, then." Noah lifted one box and nodded for Dexter to get the other. He headed for a small outbuilding. It would make a good clinic for them. He hoped they wouldn't need something like that, but he was realistic. They were alone and working on a farm. Things happened. All they could do was be prepared. Leona had gone into the house with Cassie and Vivian, unpacking and getting everything settled, so Noah and Dexter left the boxes on a dusty counter in the building. The place would need a thorough cleaning before any type of treatment could be done here, but he hoped it would meet Leona's needs.

Dexter set his box beside Noah's and brushed his hands off. "What did you mean when you said I had my work cut out for me? What work?"

"Hey, you're the engineer. It'll be your job to find us a way keep the cars and tractors going."

Hands on his hips, Dexter gave Noah a skeptical look. "Really?" He laughed and shook his head. "Why didn't I go into medicine like my mother wanted? I could be like the good Dr. Turner and have a nice little building set up all for me."

Grinning, Noah clapped Dexter on the back. "Come on. We've got bridges to build."

"Not that again! I wish Vivian had never gone on that rant." Dexter bowed his head in mock despair.

"What rant?" The door opened, and the three women joined the men in the building. Leona stopped to look around while Cassie sent Noah a tentative smile and nodded. He assumed it meant she was happy with the farm.

Dexter shot Noah a panicked look. "Uh, nothing, babe."

"I heard my name mentioned in the same sentence as a rant, so you better spill it... *babe*." Hands on hips, Vivian cocked her head, waiting.

Noah took pity on the other man and volunteered. "He said 'ant,' not rant. We worried about ants finding their way into here." Noah looked at the counter and smacked an imaginary ant, hoping his gesture fooled the woman.

Vivian dropped the pose and grinned, shaking her head. "I don't believe a word of it, Noah. But even so, we'll kill the fatted calf for your return."

"Fatted calf?" Cassie shot a look at Noah, her expression horrified.

"Just a figure of speech. You know, from the Bible," Dexter explained.

"Oh. Good." She wiped her brow and chuckled.

"Um, you know, we will be butchering our own meat though, right?" Noah crossed the short distance between them, searching Cassie's face. How did she expect them to eat?

Waving a hand in front of her face, Cassie nodded. "Of course. I know it's not like we can run to the grocery store, but I'm not sure I'm ready to eat a little calf. Maybe an old steer?" She offered them all a helpless shrug. "What can I say? I'm still getting used to this new normal."

Vivian put an arm around Cassie's shoulders. "It's all good. I had to learn how to fish, of all things. Me... fishing." She snorted and shook her head. "Crazy times."

Leona nodded. "That it is. I brought some dried venison with me, so we'll have a little meat stored. It's not a lot, as some dogs got to my drying rack, but we can put it away as insurance for the winter."

Dexter's eyes widened. "Venison? How did you get it?"

Leona smiled and cocked her head. "I hunted it. How did

you expect I got it? At the local grocery store?" She winked at Cassie, and Noah grinned.

"Damn, Dr. Turner. You sure do have a lot of skills you bring to the table." Dexter elbowed Noah. "I think she might have more skills than you do."

Noah laughed. "I have absolutely no doubt that she has more skills than I do. I've been the recipient of both her hunting skills and her medical skills."

Dexter and Vivian exchanged confused looks before Vivian said, "What happened?"

Noah opened his mouth to speak but then held his hand out toward Leona. "You should probably hear the story from Dr. Turner."

Vivian raised an eyebrow. "Oh, believe me. We will. But why don't we save it for after dinner around the fire? We should probably be getting dinner started, and while we don't have an actual fatted calf, we do have a mess of fish from the pond and fresh eggs from chickens, and we discovered a farm not too far away if you cut through the fields."

"Did they have something good there?"

"Sure did. A big old garden. Some of it had died and was all weedy, but we salvaged some fresh peas and weeded the best we could. We got a bowl of new peas from it."

"Fresh peas? Wonderful!" Cassie clapped her hands. "I was working on a few gardens back home but hadn't been able to harvest much from them except some rhubarb and strawberries. I guess they'll rot in the ground now."

"We put in a garden, too, but it was so late when we got here, not much we'll get but a bunch of pumpkins and squashes this year. And there's corn, of course. Loads of corn, but we think most of it is field corn. We only found a small field of sweet corn." Dexter motioned to the building counters. "Anyway, what do you think, Leona? Will this do for an infirmary? We can put in more shelves and get a generator to run a little power here when needed."

Leona moved to a dusty counter and ran her hand over it. "Of course, I'll need to clean, but this will do fine." She moved to a stainless steel table pushed against the side of the wall. "Where did this come from?"

"When Noah told me you were a doctor, I remembered seeing this in a veterinarian clinic when we were looking for medications for the animals not long after we got here. I took Noah's truck and ran down to get it. I also grabbed a bunch of instruments. I have no idea what they're for, but maybe you do." He moved to a cabinet and opened it. "Voila!"

"Medications?" Leona turned from examining the steel table. "Did you find any?"

Dexter shrugged and nodded. "Some, but other than a few basics, like antibiotics, we didn't know what they were for, or how to dose the animals, so we just did our best to give them clean water and food. A couple of the goats had sores on them, so we dabbed them with antibiotic ointment and kept them as clean as we could."

Leona nodded. "I'm not an expert on animals, but that's what I would have done for a person."

ONCE EVERYTHING WAS STOWED, they sat down to a relative feast of fish, coated in cornmeal and flour brought by Cassie and fried in a large cast iron skillet salvaged from the farmhouse.

"This is delicious, Noah." Cassie took a bite of her fish. "How did you manage to keep the oil at the right temperature?" She eyed the large fire the meal had been cooked over. It had been hard enough making the biscuits, but at least she had been able to use a heavy Dutch oven heated in the embers. She was a bit amazed at how well the biscuits had baked. They weren't her best, but she felt with practice, they'd be better.

While Noah had told her he had a propane stove, they were using it sparingly, mostly when it rained. They had scrounged up as many tanks of propane as they could from backyard grills, stores, and gas stations where people used to exchange them for new ones.

Noah shrugged. "I've been getting a lot of practice. Vivian here is quite the fisherwoman these days."

Vivian preened as her husband raised an eyebrow. "Um, excuse me... I caught one of the fish."

"The littlest one, Daddy," Ava piped up, much to everyone's amusement. Dexter leaned over and gave his daughter a pretend scolding, much to the little girl's amusement.

Cassie glanced at Bella. She sat next to her new friend, her eyes wide, seeming unsure if Dexter was teasing or really angry. It broke Cassie's heart to see her daughter so confused by normal father-and-daughter interaction.

"And, who made this delicious salad? I don't think I've ever had such an unusual bowl of greens."

Ava's hand shot up. "I made it!"

"You did not. I did most of the work." Jalen rolled his eyes at his sister, who stuck her tongue out at him.

"I did so. I found and picked the dandelions and the chickweed. You only picked the lamb's-quarters."

"Lamb's-quarters? Chickweed?" Cassie pretended to be horrified. "Is there a little lamb in here?"

"No, silly. It's a plant!" Ava giggled again, and this time, Bella gave Cassie a tentative smile.

"Well, whoever picked them, they are fantastic. Where did you learn about these plants?" Cassie was curious. She knew about dandelions, of course, but the other two were a mystery to her. The leaves looked vaguely familiar, but torn up for salad, she wasn't sure what they would look like growing in the wild.

"Noah showed us where to find them. He showed us a lot of stuff when we were in the forest."

Cassie turned to Noah, who sat at the other end of the two picnic tables they had pushed to form one long table. He sat beside Jalen and said something she couldn't hear, but whatever it was made the young man's head dip as though trying to stifle a laugh.

Catching Noah's eye, she lifted a forkful of salad. "Where did you learn about these? Are you one of those preppers?"

Noah threw his head back and laughed. "Not hardly. I'm a chef and use a lot of these in the kitchen. I did have a friend a few years ago who was really into foraging for natural foods, and she showed me some of them, and in the Army we had to learn some survival skills. I guess I learned more than I even knew."

"Well, thank you to your friend." She'd meant it in a light-hearted way, but Noah's expression turned bleak for a moment before he took a bite of his fish, and she could have kicked herself. Whoever his friend was, she was probably dead now. Had they still been close? How could she have been so oblivious?

"Cassie, these biscuits are fantastic." Dexter held one up. "Vivian said it was your first time using a Dutch oven to cook them, but I'd have never guessed."

She gave him a weak smile. "Thanks."

After dinner, a few more chores were completed, and then they gathered around the fire.

At first, there was just small talk about the meal and chores to be done over the next few days, but when there came a lapse in the chatter, Vivian turned to Cassie and said, "So, how in the world did you survive over a month by yourself with two little kids?"

Cassie sat on a wooden Adirondack-style bench on one side of the fire. Matching chairs were on the opposite side, and various lawn chairs filled in around so that everyone had a place to sit. Her kids had sprawled on the bench, one on each side of her, their heads in her lap, their legs curled up. They were probably sleeping, but she couldn't see their faces as she absently stroked their heads.

She drew in a deep breath. "This is going to sound so stupid, but we were saved by a nasty stomach bug and cupcakes." Looking around at their faces, she saw the confusion on Dexter's and Vivian's faces. Leona knew some of the story already, and Ethan, of course, had already learned it.

"Those must have been some pretty bad cupcakes." Vivian made a face and sat back.

Cassie laughed. "No, the baking was fine. I had a big order I was trying to complete, but wouldn't you know it, the kids got a stomach bug. They were puking out of one end and... well, you get the idea. Anyway, I was so busy caring for them while trying to complete the order at the same time that I didn't have time to listen to the news or watch television. The little snippets I heard I applied to the kids' stomach flu, and I shrugged it off. I thought it was the same thing."

"You didn't go on your computer or anything?"

Dexter sounded skeptical, and Cassie couldn't blame him. Even to herself, she sounded like an oblivious idiot. With a shrug, she spread her hands. "I've never been a big computer person. I used it as a tool for my business, mostly. Other than my business, I don't—didn't have social media. Too many creeps would send me disgusting pictures or messages, so I just deleted my personal page. Plus, when I'm baking, I listen to music. I know enough about tech to download playlists and connect to my Bluetooth speakers."

She didn't intend on sounding defensive but was afraid that was how it came across. Where was it written that everyone had to live their life online? She glanced at Leona, relieved to see the woman nodding.

Vivian leaned forward, her expression worried. "Baby, it's fine. We're not trying to interrogate you. We haven't talked to another soul other than Noah here for weeks. He's your brother-in-law, so you must know he's not exactly a chatterbox."

Cassie nodded and glanced at Noah. He sat back in a lawn chair, a smile playing around his mouth.

Dexter added, "We just want to hear a good story. You must be pretty damn resourceful to keep these little ones not just alive but in good health." He gave Cassie a warm smile.

"I wish I had a good story to tell you, but that's really all there is to it. I'm afraid I'm a bit boring." She opened her arms for a second before resting them back on the children's warm hair. "There was no reason to turn on the radio or television. The kids watched TV, but they watch children's shows on

Netflix or even the occasional DVD. I'm like a dinosaur and had a DVD player."

"I'd kill to watch a DVD right now." Jalen poked at the fire with a stick, his words hanging in the air. She had a feeling the teen wasn't referring to just a DVD but to everything they had lost.

"Yeah. Me too." Tears welled in her eyes. She'd not had time to mourn. She'd had to stay strong for the kids and pretend everything was okay. She'd been afraid that if she stopped to think about the utter and complete desolation surrounding her, despair would overwhelm her. Cassie dashed a hand across her eyes. She'd had to stay strong for the kids. But now, she wasn't alone anymore.

2

Noah took a break from unloading boxes of Leona's supplies into the freshly cleaned storage shed. The supplies were now neatly stored in cabinets, and the stainless steel counters and cabinets, scrounged from the animal hospital, stood ready and stocked for a minor emergency.

He stood in the doorway and swiped his arm across his forehead, the scent of earth, hay, and bleach mixing into an unusual combination. Underneath the scent of the bleach used to clean every nook and cranny, he could even detect the faint odor of motor oil. It was likely that the shed had been used to store the garden tractor in the winter, but when they had found the farm, the tractor had already been used to turn over the large garden.

Not for the first time, Noah wondered where the owners of the farm had gone. Why had they abandoned this place? Had they died while away, or had they fled on purpose? He thought it was the first one because the house had too much stuff that someone would have taken with them if they were going to leave for any length of time.

He heard laughter and turned to see the boys weeding. The garden was looking good. Dexter approached with yet another box, and Noah groaned. "I thought we had it all unpacked?"

"Nope. The good doctor found another box in with her household items. That woman sure did come with a lot of stuff."

At another burst of laughter from the boys, Noah nodded to them and said to Dexter, "They seem to be getting along okay."

Dexter paused to look. "They do, so far."

"So far?"

"Well, I don't want to get my hopes up. I know I was uneasy about you leaving, and Vivian was, too, but last night we talked about how good it was for Jalen to have a boy his own age around. So I guess I'm thanking you for bringing him back here. He seems like a good kid."

"Cassie seemed to think so too."

Dexter passed Noah and returned a few seconds later, minus the box. "I'm ready for something to drink. How about you?"

"It's still early."

Throwing his head back, Dexter laughed. "You know the saying. It's five o'clock somewhere. But anyway, I meant a cold glass of iced tea—minus the ice and probably not all that cold either." He laughed again and slapped Noah on the back. "Come on. Vivian told me she'd make a pitcher of it. We can always add a little somethin' to it, though."

"Okay. You twisted my arm." Noah grinned.

Ten minutes later, they sat beneath the big oak flanking the cooking fire. It had come to be one of Noah's favorite spots. From it, he could see the road on one side, and he always looked for movement on it. He'd seen none so far. Noah wasn't sure if that was a good sign or bad, though. If he looked in the other direction, there was the clinic, the chicken coop, a small pole barn for the goats, and the big old barn where Daisy, the cow, lived. Half of the floor was taken up by a large combine. Getting that going for the harvest was going to take some doing. He hoped Dexter had a clue.

No animals seemed to have been in the barn in years before they had arrived and cleaned one of the stalls for Daisy. It had junk piled nearly to the rafters on the second floor. Noah had only gone up there once but had been overwhelmed with the random parts to cars, tractors, trucks that didn't have their original bodies anymore, old chairs, a few bed frames, tables, trunks, and God only knew what other junk. Well, it probably wasn't junk, Noah thought, as he sipped his tea, dosed with a little bourbon. They couldn't afford to assume anything was junk these days.

"I still can't believe that sweet little Leona shot you." Dexter chuckled.

"Don't let her size or age fool you." Noah rubbed his side. "It was a lucky shot."

Dexter snorted then started coughing before he managed, "Yeah, lucky for you that you didn't die."

Noah couldn't help laughing as Dexter coughed a few more times and wiped his nose. "Are you dying here or what?"

"No, just snorted tea up my nose. The bourbon burns!"

Their laughter died as they sipped in a comfortable silence. Noah smelled bread baking and marveled at Cassie's makeshift ovens. She'd heaped coals over clay garden planters upside down on clay tiles. After letting the coals burn down all morning, she'd raked them away from the pots and put two pans of bread dough beneath each super-heated planter. With three planters, she'd been able to bake six loaves. Noah wasn't sure it would work, but his sense of smell told him he was wrong. He had never been so happy to be wrong in his life.

As if he was thinking about the same thing, Dexter sniffed. "Damn, smell that bread! That was one smart move on your part to bring your sister-in-law back with you too. Why didn't you tell us she was a baker?"

"I didn't even know she was alive. She or the kids."

Dexter's gaze flicked to his. "Yeah. I'm sorry about your brother. I never got a chance to tell you."

Noah nodded and swallowed. "Thanks. It sounds like he didn't suffer."

"Not sure any of them suffered. That's the only good thing in all of this. Those who died didn't seem to be afraid."

"True. I'm glad I went, and not just to find my brother and his family, but because I finally saw what you guys saw at the beginning. Even though I knew you were right about all of this, seeing what happened with my own eyes was... sobering."

Noah peered into the bottom of his glass, contemplating a refill with a larger dose of bourbon to combat the depression from remembering what he'd seen.

"I know we have to get supplies, but if I never see another corpse, I'll die a happy man."

"Let's not talk about dying." Noah tried to make his voice light, but it came out flat. He cleared his throat and changed the subject. "I was thinking that the clinic needs a lot more equipment. If we're going to have one, we might as well do what we can to have something that will be more than a first aid station."

Dexter set his glass on the small table between their chairs. "What do you have in mind?"

"I looked on a map, and there's a hospital about fifteen miles west of here. I thought I could take Leona and maybe one or both boys to see if there's anything we can get."

"What about taking me? I'm starting to get a complex about being left behind." Dexter's chuckle sounded forced, and he didn't meet Noah's eyes. Noah hoped he didn't feel slighted or that he wasn't useful.

"I would love to take you, but I feel like one of us should always be here to protect the place. Either me or you. I mean, if you want to take Leona and the boys, you could go."

Dexter shrugged. "I guess you're right. And no, you go ahead since you know where you're going."

"You're not mad?"

"Aw, hell no. You'll know when I'm angry." Dexter tipped his chin at Noah. "You'll definitely know." He smiled, but Noah took a second before returning it. He felt like he'd just been warned.

"ARE YOU GETTING FOOD TOO?" Cassie stood near the truck as Noah approached.

"If I find something I think we might need, yes. I'd never leave anything behind as long as there's room. Why? Do you have a particular request?"

"See if you can find more yeast. I've started a sourdough,

but yeast is always good to have for making other kinds of bread."

"Are you almost out? I thought we had quite a bit."

"I brought a lot with me, but some of it will be expiring soon." She shoved her hands into her front jeans pockets, dipping her head as if reluctant to look at him. Noah didn't know if she saw his brother when she looked at him, or if she was naturally shy. He'd barely known her before, and in the days since he'd found her at her house alone with the children and Ethan, they hadn't really touched on the subject of his brother. All he knew was they had been divorced while his brother had been in prison.

"Sure, if I see some, I'll take it. Anything else?" He opened the door and waited, one foot on the running board.

She shook her head. "No. I don't think so." Cassie backed away as he stepped into the truck.

"See ya later, Cassie," Ethan called as he hopped in the passenger seat.

Cassie smiled and waved at Ethan and shot Noah a tight-lipped smile when he gave her a wave.

Noah wondered if he'd done something to anger her but couldn't recall anything. Maybe Cassie was feeling weird being left with a bunch of strangers. He knew everyone, so it was hard to remember that Cassie had only just met Dexter and Vivian.

Craning his head, Noah tried to see into the truck Leona was driving, but the angle was wrong. "Is Jalen with Leona?"

Ethan nodded and grinned. "Yeah. He's hoping she'll let him drive some of the way."

"Well, it's not that far. He may not get a chance. If the roads are passable, we could be there in less than an hour."

"What are the chances of that?" Ethan rolled the window down and slanted Noah a look of doubt.

Noah thought about it. They hadn't encountered a completely cleared highway all the way from Cassie's house. Sometimes the back roads weren't too bad, but it depended on how close they were to the main highways. If they had a ramp onto the highway, they tended to be full of crashed and abandoned vehicles for up to a mile on either side of the entrance and exit ramps. The route he'd traced on the map wasn't direct but might be faster if they got lucky.

Just in case they had to detour, he'd filled both of their vehicles with gasoline and had loaded several five-gallon containers of gasoline in the back of his truck. It had put a dent in their reserves, but it couldn't be helped.

Once they made sure Leona was right behind them, Noah settled back. Ethan thumbed through cases of CDs Noah had wedged into a cubby on the passenger-side door.

"CDs? I didn't think anyone listened to them anymore. Except, like, old people."

Noah didn't spoil Ethan's teasing by pointing out that nobody listened to streaming music anymore either. Because there was nobody. Instead, he pretended to be offended. "Are you calling me old?"

"Nope, but if the shoe fits..." Ethan grinned, then he raised his eyebrows. "Barenaked Ladies?"

"That's a classic." Noah reached to snatch the CD from the kid's hand, but Ethan evaded him and leaned back against the door, laughing.

"'If I Had a...'" Ethan paused and appeared to be counting something on the cover. "A hundred thousand dollars?"

"That's 'a Million Dollars,' genius." Noah grabbed the CD

and flipped it out of the case with one hand, bracing the case against his thigh. He popped it into the CD player slot. "I love this song."

"Hey, the truck hit a bump, and I must have missed a zero."

Noah shot him a smirk. "Sure."

Singing the familiar song took him back to a wedding he'd attended with an old girlfriend. Everyone had sung along when the DJ had played the tune, shouting the lyrics like a drunken, well-dressed chorus. That had been a fun night. He couldn't have been more than twenty years old, and it seemed a lifetime ago.

"Funny song," Ethan commented, pulling Noah back to the present.

"Yeah. They were a fun band to watch in concert."

As the song ended and the next began, Noah started to tell Ethan about how the band got its weird name when Ethan gasped, stiffening and staring at the CD slot. Noah followed his gaze, expecting a spider or something to crawl out. "What? What's wrong?"

"I know this song."

Noah listened for a second. "'Call and Answer?' It's a good song, but I don't recall it being all that popular."

"My mom would play it. Like, all the time. It was on her playlist. Every time she took me to baseball practice, the same songs would play. I got so sick of them." His voice broke.

"Oh." Noah didn't know what else to say.

"The last time that I remember hearing it, I cut it off in the middle of it to put *my* list on." Ethan stared out of the passenger-side window, his elbow resting on the door handle as he chewed on his thumb.

Noah didn't know if he should change the song or not, so he let it play, waiting for some hint.

There came a strangled sound from Ethan, and then, his voice muffled, he said, "I told my mom her music was stupid."

Noah drew in a deep breath and blew it out, his eyes fixed on the road as he heard Ethan sniff. "I think every kid tells their parents that. I never once heard of a parent being angry about it."

Ethan didn't respond, and Noah turned the music off. They rode in silence for miles with Noah occasionally swerving to avoid the numerous car crashes, barely glancing at them anymore. They were part of the scenery. At least on the back roads, he was able to drive off the road, sometimes into fields for a hundred feet or more before turning back onto the road.

Ethan finally stirred from where he had slumped against the passenger door and pointed. "There's a sign for a hospital. Is that one we're going to?"

Noah glanced at the blue sign. "Yep."

3

Ethan followed Noah, Leona, and Jalen up the stairs of the hospital. The stench threatened to make him vomit, but Leona had given him a mask to wear and had smeared mint leaves along the inside of it. It helped a little. The oppressive heat and odor almost took his mind off the CD and song that had been on repeat in his head ever since he'd heard it in Noah's truck. He'd never paid much attention to the song when his mom had listened to it. Most of the time, he'd had his face buried in his phone, watching stupid videos, but somehow it had imprinted in his memory. The instant he recognized it, images of his mom driving him to practice or singing along to it while cooking in the kitchen had flashed through his mind.

Even as his eyes had burned and he'd blinked hard to hold back tears, he'd basked in the memories. Her face was still clear in his mind, especially her smile when she thought he'd said something funny. Today, while he'd closed his eyes and leaned against the door, he'd pretended his mom was the one driving and that it was just a regular day. The hum of the wheels gliding over the road, little bumps from irregularities in the pavement, and the coolness of the AC chilling his skin added details to his fantasy. He'd imagined they were going to the dentist or maybe to get a new pair of sneakers at the mall. For a few minutes, he'd almost believed it, and a feeling of peace had washed over him.

Then he'd opened his eyes when the truck slowed. They were beside a pile-up of cars, trucks, and contents from an overturned semitruck, and he'd caught glimpses of bodies, nearly unrecognizable as such after several months of exposure. The cozy dream had popped like a soap bubble hitting a sharp piece of grass.

"You doing okay, Ethan?"

Ethan looked up from the stairs, where he'd focused on each plodding step upwards. He didn't even know how many floors they'd gone. "I'm fine, Noah. Where are we going?"

Leona answered, "Just one more floor. There's a lab I want to check out before we get other items on my list."

Ethan shrugged and followed Noah's back, with Leona leading the way and Jalen right behind Ethan.

"Yo, Ethan. You realize whatever they want, we have to bring down all of these flights?"

He looked over his shoulder. He couldn't see Jalen's mouth, but his eyes danced. Ethan shook his head with a tired smile. "It's better than having to carry it all up here."

"That is true! Still, this place creeps me out. I just want to get what she wants and get the hell out of here." Jalen gave an exaggerated shudder. "I wonder how many people died in here?"

"I don't even want to know."

Finally, they paused outside of a door marked No Admittance. A keypad on the wall was faded on certain numbers, and Ethan figured that given enough time, he could figure out the code just by looking at which numbers were most faded. But with no power to the hospital, the door opened freely, and they didn't need to crack the code.

A rank odor cut through the mint, making Ethan try to breathe only through his mouth, but it was different from what they'd encountered upon entering. It smelled like someone had left a lot of rotten fruit in the fridge. Leona explained it was probably from lab cultures gone crazy and had them use hand sanitizer still in the wall-mounted dispensers. They also grabbed blue gloves from boxes on the wall.

"Whatever you do, don't touch your eyes or your mouth while in here," Leona warned.

Immediately, Ethan felt an itch in corner of his eye and a hair or something tickling his nose inside the mask. He wiggled his nose in an attempt dislodge it with little success.

"Wonderful. I was hoping we'd find one of these." Leona had her hand on a piece of equipment that didn't look much bigger than a handheld video game.

Doing his best to ignore the itch and tickle, Ethan asked, "What is it?"

"This analyzes blood for oxygen levels, pH, CO_2 levels, and a bunch of other tests. Now, we have to find the cartridges that go with them." Leona looked around the lab and spotted a cabinet labeled with the same name as on the piece of equipment. She opened it. "Yes!" She pulled boxes out and stacked them on the counter then moved to another cabinet, pulling some items from that one as well.

Ethan didn't know what they wanted, and afraid to touch

anything, he crossed his arms and waited for instructions. He didn't wait long.

Noah had a bank of what looked like rechargeable batteries and put it beside the boxes. "We should have grabbed some empty boxes to cart what we find out of here. Ethan, can you look around and see if you can find anything we can use?"

"Uh... sure." Ethan turned and didn't see any cardboard, but he spotted several blue plastic bins tucked under desks. They had the recycle symbol and paper in them. He dumped the paper from three of them and brought them to Noah. "How about these?"

He nodded. "Perfect."

It didn't take them long to fill the bins with the items Leona pointed out to them. They had a few more devices that looked similar to the blood gas one as far as Ethan could tell and a couple of microscopes, which he thought looked pretty cool. Those filled one bin, and the other two were full of supplies needed for the devices to be useful.

Leona carried a third microscope while the rest of them carried the bins out to the vehicles. They returned for more supplies, cleaning out a whole storeroom of things called reagents, culture mediums, and items even Ethan recognized from science class, things like beakers and pipettes.

Next, they found the hospital stockroom. It had been hit hard by either other scavengers or vandals. Many of the boxes were torn open and supplies dumped on the floor, or the boxes were empty. Still, they were able to find syringes and supplies Leona said would let her start IVs. Ethan knew what those were but had no clue what was necessary, not that he needed to know. He knew he and Jalen were along to be the muscle.

The smell here wasn't as bad as the rest of the hospital, but even here, he'd seen at least one, but usually several, bodies decomposing in hallways and in the stairwells. From the increased stench near the bathrooms, he imagined they were full. He didn't even want to think about what it was like in the hospital wards. Noah had said they weren't going to those areas. They were staying in the parts of the hospital where patients wouldn't have been.

Jalen groaned as he lifted a bin filled with small bags for IVs and cartons with various inhalers in them. Ethan's best friend, Kelvin, had had asthma, and he recognized the same inhalers his friend used to carry. He remembered the time in gym when Kelvin had an attack and Ethan had been sent to get the nurse. It had been the scariest day in his life until the virus hit. Kelvin had gone to the ER, but he'd survived. Ethan wondered if he'd survived the virus, too, but guessed he hadn't. Not many had. The familiar weight of loss settled on him like an invisible weighted blanket.

Jalen nudged Ethan with his elbow, pulling him from his memories. "We shoulda stayed back at the farm. I'd rather be weeding the garden about now." He laughed even as he took the heaviest bin.

Ethan nodded. "Right?" He waited while the smaller boy balanced the bin then said, "Maybe I should take that one."

"No, man. I got it." Jalen hiked the bin up higher against his chest. "Yeah, I'm shorter than you, but we both know I'm stronger."

Ethan grinned. "Yep. You're right."

He grabbed the bin Leona had filled with bags of what

looked like water. There weren't more than a dozen of them in the bin, with a lot of room left over. "Hey, Leona, is there something else you have that will fit in here? There's lots of room still."

"Those are bags of saline. They're a lot heavier than they look. Have you tried lifting it yet?"

Ethan grabbed the handles of the bin and grunted. "Damn. I should have let Jalen take this one."

Noah heard him and laughed. "I can take that one. Here's one full of bottles of pills."

Gritting his teeth, Ethan shook his head. "Nope. I got it." No way was he going to let Jalen carry out the heaviest bin. And no way was he going to let Jalen know it had been the heaviest bin.

They broke for lunch in a patch of shade beneath oak trees on the overgrown front lawn of the hospital grounds. It was clear of human remains, and they sprawled on the grass, eating a meal of protein bars they kept aside for scavenging excursions and drinking cans of dietary supplement shakes they'd found in the pharmacy. Ethan chose chocolate while Jalen picked strawberry. Noah and Leona each had vanilla.

"These are pretty good." Ethan took the last swig from his, wishing for more even though he was full. He followed the shake with a gulp of water from his water bottle.

"I used to sneak one from time to time when I was with a mom who was having a long, difficult labor. I'd forgotten how much I liked them." Leona grinned. "As much as we all like them, we'll have to keep the rest for emergencies."

Ethan sighed. So much for a second can. He burped then grinned when Jalen swatted a hand in front of his own face, his nose wrinkled in distaste. "*Dude!*"

"Okay, guys, let's get back to work. Is there anything else you want from here, Leona?" Noah stood, picking up his empty can. Ethan didn't know why he bothered. Every trash can he'd seen overflowed with garbage, and it wasn't like anyone was going to come along and empty them. Even so, he did the same. He'd noticed how clean the farm was and didn't want Noah to think he was a slob.

"I think we got all of the equipment, supplies, and medications we can use. Although, I would like to get oxygen tanks if we can. We never know when we'll need it."

Noah made a face. "Hmmm... I'm kind of leery of transporting tanks, but I suppose we can get a few."

"The hospital's main supply would be liquid oxygen, so we can't get that, but there are bound to be tanks in storerooms."

They couldn't find the storage rooms for the oxygen tanks, but they did find eight cylinders and little wheeled carts of small tanks. Then Leona had to find the right tubings and masks to use them. It took them another hour to get all of that back in Noah's truck and carefully tied down so they wouldn't move.

Next, they hit the hospital kitchen. Rats scurried in all directions when they opened the door. Cringing, Noah closed the doors, pushing Ethan, who had been to the side but slightly behind him, out of the way. "I don't care what we need. We're not going in there."

Ethan backed away. "I've seen rats in kitchens before." He had seen plenty of rats while on his own. They were in every town he'd gone through. He'd wondered if they had always been there, hiding, but only now felt like it was safe to come out during the day when most people were dead.

"I don't doubt it, but from the droppings and urine stench, I think we'd be hard-pressed to find anything that wasn't ruined."

They headed back to the vehicles, and Ethan grabbed his water bottle from the truck. The water was still cold, just like the commercials for the brand had always promised. He leaned back against the truck, and Jalen leaned beside him.

"Think we're going back to the farm now?"

Ethan shrugged. "You know Noah better than I do."

"It seems like a long time ago that we met him on the road, but I think it's only been about three months. This summer has been crazy! School seems like a lifetime ago." Jalen tilted his head back, guzzling his water too.

Ethan thought back to spring. Everything had been so normal then. There had been no hint of what was about to happen. He wondered if he would have done anything differently if he'd have known. "Hey, Jalen, if you had known about the virus and"—he motioned with his arm, indicating the dead city—"what was about to happen, would you have done anything differently?"

"Hmmm... I don't know. I probably wouldn't have bothered writing that essay on states' rights in my history class."

Ethan laughed. "Yeah, I think there are a lot of assignments I would have skipped, but seriously, what would you have done if you knew?"

"I don't know. I'd have warned my friends. I know that much. And maybe even some of my teachers."

"Same. But I'd have tried to get my family out of town. I don't know where we'd have gone, but somewhere far away from people." Ethan imagined a place similar to the farm where they lived now, but there was no way they could have headed to one before the virus. They only had their home. There had been no place for them to run to.

"It's terrible about your family. Sorry, man." Jalen kicked at the dirt with the toe of his sneaker, his head bent.

"Thanks." Ethan let the subject drop as he saw Noah nod to something Leona had said and head back toward the truck. "It looks like we're about to find out what's next."

"Okay, here's the plan. We're going to see if there's a bakery nearby. We're hoping some of the things Cassie needs will be available."

It turned out that the first bakery they found had been completely destroyed by someone. The front window had been broken and all of the glass pastry cabinets left in ruins with broken glass everywhere. The kitchen had been stripped of all food except what had been torn open and flung around. Ethan couldn't figure out why anyone would have wasted flour and sugar like that, but he figured it had been virus victims in the middle of their crazy stage just before they died. Several bodies, now just lumps of rotting flesh in the back parking lot, were probably the ones guilty of destroying the place.

The second bakery was untouched. It was possible the owner and workers had never made it back to work. Whatever the reason, the door was still locked and the windows intact. Noah handed Ethan a crowbar he'd pulled from behind the driver's seat. "Here, you go ahead and get the door open. I'm going to hop in back and make room for what we find."

Leona sat inside her truck, writing something down. Maybe she was making lists of the supplies they'd just gathered.

The bakery was in a building that had to have been at least a hundred years old. Other businesses were on either side, one a clothing store and the other a hair salon. The little strip of shops in the weathered red-brick building looked untouched, as if it was a holiday and the next day they would reopen for business.

Ethan stood in front of the door, hesitating. The door was thick wood with glass in the middle, and he could have broken the glass and cleared the edges of shards. He or Jalen could easily fit inside and open the door from there or a back door, but he hated the thought of breaking the glass. A pink-and-teal picture of a doughnut had been painted on the glass below the arched name of the bakery. The pink part was the icing, the teal the outline of the doughnut. Just the image made his mouth water at the thought of fresh doughnuts.

He set the crowbar down and felt in his pocket for something to pick the lock. He wasn't an expert at breaking and entering, but he'd jimmied a few locks since he'd been on his own. Sometimes there wasn't a window to break, or he didn't have anything handy to break one with. But he'd taken to carrying a small screwdriver, and it was still in the side pocket of the cargo pants he wore.

Jalen went into the recessed entryway, pressed his hands against the glass, and peered inside. "Why don't you just bash the window? I'll do it if you don't want to."

"Let me try the lock first. Then we won't have to worry about broken glass getting into anything." It was a weak excuse, but Jalen seemed to buy it. He shrugged and stepped back.

"Man, I wish there were real doughnuts in there. Think Cassie can make doughnuts?"

"Probably. I think she'd need oil to fry them in."

"I'm gonna look for oil."

Ethan waved a hand at Jalen as he used the screwdriver. "Shhh... let me listen."

Jalen laughed. "What are you, a safe cracker now?"

Rolling his eyes but unable to hide the grin, Ethan shook his head. "No. I just like to try to hear if it clicks." He twisted the screwdriver several times. It was a tiny screwdriver, meant for miniscule screws, and fit inside the keyhole with no problem, but it might have been too small. He couldn't get the door unlocked. Sighing, he picked up the crowbar and jammed it between the door and the frame. Pushing hard, he nearly fell forward when the wood gave way.

"Good job, man." Jalen clapped him on the shoulder before pushing inside. "Wow! This place still smells like a bakery!"

Ethan took a whiff. It did smell faintly of good things. Bread, doughnuts, cakes, and underlying it all, coffee. He closed his eyes, soaking it in. It smelled like Saturday mornings before baseball practice or Sunday after church.

For once, they had found a place that didn't reek of death. He opened his eyes when he heard a whoop of delight from Jalen. "Found the oil!"

Rushing past the empty display cases, Ethan found Jalen standing next to a shelving unit with four huge jugs of oil. He grinned from ear to ear.

"Nice!" Ethan had no trouble finding a fifty-pound bag of flour on a shelving unit across from the oil. Picking it up was more of a challenge. It wasn't because of the weight but rather that there was nowhere to grip it. He ended up driving his shoulder into it and letting it fall onto his back. With a grunt, he straightened. "I'm taking this out. Be right back."

He delivered the bag to Noah then returned for more, hearing Noah tell him to be on the lookout for yeast. On the way in, he picked up shards of wood from the door and set them on the counter. A couple of iced sugar cookies with smiley faces were the only items left in the bakery case. He was surprised they weren't eaten by rats or mice, or even ants, but the bakery was spotless. With so many other places to find food, he supposed the rodents and insects had ignored the bakery.

A case of twenty-four bars of yeast was on the second shelf from the top of the shelving unit. Ethan grabbed it, thinking about how happy Cassie would be. He almost ran into Jalen as the other boy returned from hauling out the oil.

"Yeast!" Ethan lifted the box in triumph.

Jalen gave him a look like Ethan was crazy. "Okay."

"Cassie asked for yeast."

"Oh. Okay." Apparently not impressed, Jalen sorted through other supplies on the shelf. "Baking powder. Baking soda... why do they need both?"

Ethan shrugged as best he could while holding the yeast. "I don't know, but better get them both. And that huge bag of sugar." He started walking out and saw a giant can of shortening. "Oh, and we can't forget that either."

"You better come back and help me with all of this stuff!"

Laughing at the whine in Jalen's voice, Ethan pretended not to hear him.

It didn't take them long to clear out everything they thought they would need, plus a few extras like jars of cinnamon, nutmeg, cloves, and allspice.

Ethan sniffed his sleeve after he sat in the truck, waiting for Noah to get in. He smelled good, even though he was sweaty.

"What are you smiling at?" Noah settled into the driver's seat and raised an eyebrow at Ethan. His tone was teasing. Light.

"I smell amazing."

Noah burst into laughter. "Oh, you think so, do you?"

4

Ethan entered the kitchen, unsure what he should do.
While this was his home now, it didn't feel like home. It
felt weird, like he was a guest and staying with a bunch of
strangers. Which, actually, he was, when he stopped to think
about it. Even Cassie was basically a stranger. He'd only
known her for maybe a week. Time had ceased to have any
meaning, so he couldn't be sure of how many days he'd
known her, but it wasn't long. Anything beyond three or four
days ago just blurred into the past month.

He yawned and scratched his head, unaccustomed to
waking up without the immediate need to assess his chances
of eating and surviving another day. For now, food seemed to
be plentiful if in strange combinations. Nobody here was sick,
and they were isolated on a farm. Hopefully, that meant no
chance of the virus, if it was still even around, getting them.

Ethan glanced at a clock on the wall above the sink,
surprised to see the second hand moving. It must have a
battery. He chuckled. What was the point of knowing the
exact hour? It wasn't like they had any place to go.

Stretching, he ambled to a pitcher of water on the counter and helped himself to a glass, keeping half of the water to use to brush his teeth. He'd slept later than he had in ages, probably since before the virus hit and he'd still been a normal teenage boy. He always wanted to stay up late but would have a hard time waking up for school. His mom would get so frustrated with him, but she'd never stayed mad. Now, there was no more school, but he'd give anything to have to get up early to go.

After yesterday's arrival, he'd been busy nonstop between unloading the vehicles and stashing the supplies wherever he'd been told they'd needed to go. He and Jalen had taken care of the goats, and Dino had seemed to fit in like he'd always belonged. Maybe he had been a farm dog before.

Sitting around the bonfire after dinner had felt so normal. He could have almost closed his eyes and pictured his parents on the other side of the fire, like they used to do on the few camping trips they'd taken when he was younger. It was probably the smell. Someone had pulled out a bag of marshmallows, and they'd had fun roasting them. It was the most normal night since the whole thing began. Except his family wasn't across the fire, and nothing was really normal anymore.

As he stood, wondering where everyone else was, Vivian entered the room. Ethan had only spoken a few words to her so far. She'd seemed nice, but she was definitely a mom. When she told Jalen to do something, there was that tone. While Cassie was also a mom, her kids were little, and she must not have acquired the tone yet. But Vivian needed to only say Jalen's name to get him to agree, reluctantly, to do what she'd requested. Other kids' moms usually liked him, but Vivian intimidated him.

"Good morning, Ethan." She gave him a brilliant smile. "I hope you slept okay. It can get kind of hot in the bedrooms at night."

Ethan shrugged. "I didn't notice. The windows were open." Even if the room had been stifling, he'd wouldn't have complained. No way did he want to give anyone a reason to make him leave. Already, he felt like a slacker for sleeping so late. "Where is everyone?" Then it dawned on him that he hadn't seen Dino. "And have you seen my dog?" He prayed he hadn't run away. When he'd gone to sleep, the dog had been in the room with him, but there'd been no sign of him this morning.

"Oh, everyone is outside doing this and that. I think Noah wanted to see if he could find any more livestock loose in the area, so he took the truck with the horse trailer attached. I'm pretty sure he took Dino with him to help. He noticed how the dog had rounded up the goats like he was born to do it, so he was thinking he might help gather any animals he might find."

"Oh, okay. That's cool."

"My husband is working on a project, and I think Jalen was going to help Cassie weed the garden."

She walked behind him and reached into a cupboard. She looked over her shoulder. "Are you hungry? We have oatmeal."

Ethan's stomach growled. "Yeah. Sure. Thank you."

"Here you go." She handed him a couple of packs of instant oatmeal. Both were strawberries and cream. He'd never had that flavor, but it sounded good.

He took them and looked around the kitchen. The pitcher of water was room temperature, but he made a move toward it anyway. Eventually the oatmeal would soften, he supposed.

"Oh, hon, that's too cool. There's a pot of water we keep warm on the edge of the fire outside. It's the best we can do until we get the cook stove working."

"Cook stove?"

"A few days ago, Dexter found one in a neighboring farmhouse. It was in the cellar and all rusted up, but Dexter's been scrubbing it, and we're hoping to connect it so that it can exhaust outside. That's his project. Won't that be great?"

Ethan nodded, although he hadn't done much cooking in his life. He supposed it was a lot harder on an open fire than over a stove. He glanced around for a bowl, and Vivian nodded to another cupboard. "Right up there, and silverware is in the drawer beneath."

As he gathered the items, it struck him again how homey it all was. "Thank you."

"You're welcome. We just ask that you drop it in the bin of water out there beside the stove so it can be washed later. We do them all at once to save on soap."

He nodded and went out to fill his bowl. Someone had moved most of the chairs away from the fire, probably so it was easier to cook around, but the bench was still there, so he sat on it and ate his oatmeal. It tasted overly sweet to him, which was odd because he used to love sweetened cereals. Still, it filled him up, and he wasn't about to throw good food away.

As he ate, he looked around. Milo and Bella were following Ava around the chicken pen like they were on a mission. Ava carried a basket, and when he saw her reach into a pile of leaves that had blown into a corner and pull out an egg, he figured out what they were doing. They were too far away for him to hear, but it seemed as if Ava was giving them a lesson of some sort. He grinned around a mouthful of oatmeal.

As he finished, he looked for the others, especially Jalen, then spotted him in the garden wielding a hoe. Feeling guilty that he had overslept while everyone, even the kids, were working, he gulped the rest of his meal, added his bowl to the pan of water, and went in search of a garden tool to help his new friend.

"Hey, Jalen."

"Hey, sleepyhead." Jalen threw him a grin.

Ethan bit his lip and toed a clod of dirt. "Sorry. I don't normally sleep late. Not anymore, anyway."

"Nah, I'm just giving you a hard time. You want to help?"

"Yeah, that's why I came out here. Where's a hoe?"

Jalen gave him a sly look like he was about to crack a joke, but then Cassie came around the end of the row. "Good morning, Ethan!"

"Hi, Cassie. Sorry I slept late. You should have woken me up."

She waved a hand. "It's fine. You were exhausted. I was, too, but I can never sleep late. With two kids, I learned I needed to wake up at the crack of dawn to stay ahead of them."

Ethan smiled. "I'll help with the garden, but you might have to show me what to do. I've not done much more than dig a few rows for my mom in her flower bed."

The memory of doing that early last summer came to him with a hazy vision of his mom smiling as she knelt on a foam cushion to plant some little blue flowers in front of the house. He'd pretended he was going to spray her with the hose while she gave him a stern warning not to, but her eyes had danced, and he'd known she wasn't angry. A warmth filled him even as he blinked hard.

"I didn't see any more hoes in the shed, Cassie." He had to hold in the laughter at the sentence. Hoes.

Jalen held his like he was going to offer it to Ethan, but before Ethan could take it, Cassie thrust hers at him. "I need to get some bread started if we're going to have some fresh for dinner. If you could finish the last two rows, that would be great. Jalen can show you what to do." She slanted Jalen a smile.

As she walked away, Jalen pouted for a few seconds but then laughed. "I guess it'll be worth it just to smell the bread baking. Those biscuits last night were the bomb."

Over the next hour, Ethan worked his way through two rows of whatever it was that was planted. Jalen had to show him what was a weed and what was the actual plant. Apparently, they were green beans. Jalen worked at the weeds around the tomatoes, but even Ethan could identify them because small green fruits were already apparent on the plants.

When they finished the weeding, they hauled water from the creek to pour into a trough that he imagined had been a horse trough at one time. Holes had been punched into the metal and stuffed with hoses. The hoses had tiny holes up and down the length of them, and they laid them between the rows. He wondered how the plants at the very end would get water, but that was when he noticed the trough was slightly higher on one side and the holes punched lower there. He guessed it would keep the water flowing better than the higher hoses.

"Nice irrigation system. Did your dad make it?" Ethan watched as water sprinkled from the hoses and doused their end of the rows. "When it's empty, do we move the trough and then fill it again?"

"You got it."

Ethan made what felt like a dozen treks to the creek and reserved the last half of the bucket to dump over his head. Shaking his hair like a wet dog, he laughed when Jalen tossed the remnants of his water at him. Ethan danced away, pointing at the other boy. "Better watch your back!"

Jalen laughed. "I'm so afraid!" With that, they raced back to the house and met the others for lunch.

They sat in the shade of a cottonwood tree and ate grilled cheese made with packaged and processed cheese. It wasn't what Ethan would have eaten before because his parents loved cheese, and since they lived in Wisconsin, every local store had a huge selection.

When he paused before taking a bite, Cassie looked at him and shrugged. "It's shelf-stable. Noah found a box of it in a house."

"Oh no. It's fine. I'm just not used to it."

Noah sat next to him, two sandwiches and a salad of greens on the plate beside them.

"Did you find any more livestock, Noah?" Dexter sat on a lawn chair, his plate balanced on his lap and a tall glass of what looked like fruit punch sitting on a brick next to his chair.

"Nope. But I saw signs that some had survived and broke loose at a farm about five miles down the road. Of course, the animals could be anywhere now, but if they got loose, others must have too. If we keep looking, we'll find some."

"How was Dino?"

Noah smiled and shook his head. "What a great dog. He sat in the back in the seat like he was searching too. Didn't give me a minute of trouble."

Ethan beamed. "Yeah. He's great. Too bad about not finding any animals, though."

Noah speared a forkful of salad and took a bite, only nodding his head in reply, but he held a finger up. When he was done chewing, he said, "I didn't find any livestock, but I might have found something better. Or at least, better than this cheese." He grinned as he took a bite of his sandwich. Ethan did the same and wondered what Noah could have found. He waited patiently, devouring his sandwiches as he waited. His mom would have cringed at the cheese, but Ethan thought it tasted great. It could have just been that all the work he'd put in this morning had really amped up his appetite, but he thought he probably liked the cheese anyway. It was really gooey.

Noah finally spoke again. "I found a pick-your-own-berry farm a few miles from here. I think tomorrow we should all go and pick as many as we can. Cassie knows how to can them so we can have blueberries through the winter."

Everyone turned to Cassie who held up a hand. "I know how, but keep in mind, I've done it with modern appliances. It might be trickier working over an open fire."

"I'll help," Ethan volunteered. He shrugged when everyone looked at him. "I used to help my grandma before she died. Only it was strawberries, not blueberries."

Noah put a hand on Ethan's shoulder. "Great. You're hired."

The others laughed, and Ethan grinned and took a drink of water from his cup. Everyone was so nice. It was strange. While he had been on the road and it was just him and Dino, he had thought about his family, but he missed them differently. He wanted to be with them and wanted them alive, of course, but he knew they weren't, and he had felt a black emptiness. Now the blackness was easing, a little, and he didn't feel so empty. But it made him forget for moments that his family was gone, and he'd have a fleeting thought of what his mom or dad would say when he told them something funny Jalen said or a cute thing one of the little ones said. And then he'd remember that his parents were gone, and he could never tell them anything again.

Dexter set his glass on the brick and raised a hand. "Hold up. I might be able to help with the cooking issue. I think I have the woodstove ready for use. I'm going to test it today to make sure it vents right then put it in the kitchen. I have to measure for the exhaust pipe, insert it, and seal around it, but we could have it ready in a few days."

"That would be perfect. Do we have many jars? I brought some, but we'll need some for the vegetables too."

Vivian, who had been quietly chatting with Leona at the other end of the table, spoke up. "There's a big case in the basement here, and I'm sure we can probably comb some of these farmhouses on this road for more."

"So I guess that's the plan for tomorrow? We can get an early start before it gets too hot." Noah looked around the group. Everyone nodded or agreed.

"I can make extra bread and sandwiches for us to take."
Cassie stood and took her plate to the dishpan.

"What should I do now?" Ethan put his plate in the
bucket as well and turned to Noah.

"Right now, I think we're good. You can nap, or if you
want to explore the woodshop, be my guest. The people who
lived here had a nice setup in that building over there." He
pointed to an outbuilding Ethan hadn't really noticed. It was
only a little larger than a shed. "Come on. I'll show you."

Ethan studied the building as they headed toward it. It
didn't look so small once he drew closer, but a pile of wood
along one side had seemed to crowd the building.

"There's no electricity for the sander or other equipment,
but there are saws, chisels, awls, and other tools that use old-
fashioned elbow grease."

Ethan had no idea what elbow grease was but felt too
timid to ask. Hadn't he heard his dad use that same expression a few times? He should have paid more attention.

"Here we are. Maybe you'll like working with your hands.
I'm encouraging everyone to branch out and find a skill that
will help all of us. Jalen's been working with the goats, Ava
the chickens, Vivian fishing, and Dexter has been working on
getting antique stoves and such into working order. I'm
brushing up on my farming and exploring the area for
edibles in the woods."

Ethan thought back to when he was on the road and
eating yet another canned meal. It would have been nice to
have something fresh. "How do you know what you can eat
and what you can't?"

"Some I learned in the Army, and some I learned as a
chef. You wouldn't believe how much someone would pay at

a fine restaurant for a salad that was made out of the same weeds they'd spray in their backyards." Noah chuckled and shook his head. "Dandelion greens, mustard greens, clovers, and even thistle, washed, dressed with a little vinegar and oil, and put in fine china, commanded top dollar. I started letting my backyard go wild and would eat a lot of the weeds."

Ethan glanced at a dandelion growing from the foundation of the shed. "So I could eat that flower right there?"

"You sure could. As long as it wasn't sprayed with chemicals in the last year or so. That's the hard part now. We see all these weeds in yards but have no idea if the homeowners had sprayed them this spring or last fall or even last spring. So, we've been sticking to those we see out in meadows or in clearly overgrown fields."

"Cool! Can you show me more sometime?"

"I'd love to. Let's get these blueberries picked tomorrow and then see about all of us going out on a foraging hike."

NOAH HAD EVERY EMPTY BASKET, bucket, and pan they could find gathered up and put in the back of his truck. Everyone piled into two vehicles and followed him to the farm.

Ethan, Jalen, and Cassie rode with him while Dexter and Vivian had Leona and the three little ones, who had become inseparable in just three days. They'd left Dino in the barn with a big bowl of water and a chew toy Ethan had taken from a store at some point. They'd worried the dog would run off while they were busy picking.

The boys were in the back seat of the cab, and Cassie rode in the passenger seat. Between them was a large insulated cooler packed with sandwiches and jars of water kept in the creek all night. They weren't exactly ice packs, but they helped a bit. The sandwiches were a selection of peanut butter and jelly or egg salad. It was the egg salad that worried Noah a bit, but they'd just have to take an early lunch and meanwhile keep the cooler in a shaded area. They were lucky the day was cooler than it had been. His truck said it was only seventy-three degrees outside, but it was still early, and he knew the temperature would climb with the sun.

5

Noah turned in to the blueberry farm, his truck bouncing over the uneven ground. "Hang on to your hats!" He thought he heard Cassie's teeth snap together and threw her an apologetic look. "Sorry."

"It sounded worse than it was." She grinned as if to prove it, and he was relieved to see all of her pearly whites intact.

There was no actual parking lot, but a sign beside the turnoff directed vehicles to park in rows. He supposed that the number of vehicles navigating the field, plus regular mowing, would have kept the weeds down normally, but now, it was overgrown. He pulled as close to the blueberry patch as he could. "We won't have to haul them too far. I just hope the birds haven't gotten them all yet."

As they'd parked, a flock of birds had taken flight, but already, they were settling again. Noah jumped out of the truck and waved the other vehicle in beside him.

The fields lay before him in neat rows in spite of the recent neglect. Between the rows was where most of the weeds had sprouted, but Noah didn't worry about that. He rounded to the back of the truck and took out baskets and pails, distributing the largest ones to Dexter, Vivian, the teens, and himself. The three little kids had smaller baskets about the size of Easter baskets.

"Okay, well, I guess everyone grab a bush and start picking."

The birds took flight again, circling and squawking at them, but eventually, they settled in another section of the field.

"These are good!" Ava picked beside Noah, eating as many as she put in the basket.

Noah laughed as he popped several into his mouth. The berries burst in his mouth with a sweet tang. He was hard-pressed not to stuff his own face, but after an hour, the little ones had moved to the shade of the truck and were quietly playing on a blanket Vivian had spread for them.

At first, everyone joked and chatted, but soon the monotony of picking and wandering away from each other precluded chitchat, and Noah was lost in his thoughts. He wondered how to get fresh water to the farm without hauling it and ran over in his mind different ways. The farm had a well, but it relied on a pump to get the water into the house. He wondered if there was a way around that. Or if they could affix a hand pump somewhere along the line so they could at least pump it closer to the house. He missed running water a lot more than he did electricity, but ironically, it was the electricity he needed to get the water he craved.

Noah lugged a full bucket to the truck. They had brought a large cooler to empty buckets into, and when he added his, the cooler was half full with what others must have already emptied. He found his water and took a long drink, sparing a little to splash on his face and neck.

"Hey, Bella, did you manage to get any blueberries in your basket?"

The little girl looked at him, wide-eyed. "Uh-huh." Her lips were stained blue. Noah wasn't sure he believed her. "You guys did a great job."

Milo had a Hot Wheels car in one hand, racing it over the folds of the blanket. He leaned back and looked up at Noah. "How much longer?"

"Maybe another hour."

"Ugh. I'm bored." He drew the last word out and flopped back.

"You can keep picking if you want."

"No. I'm tired of picking blueberries. I don't even like them very much."

His lips weren't stained, proving his claim.

"You might like them in oatmeal though or in muffins or whatever else your mom comes up with."

Milo sighed. "I guess."

Noah grinned. "Hang in there, tough guy. We'll be done before you know it." He reached down and ruffled the boy's hair, noting that the girls had brought dolls and looked to be engaged in some kind of tea party with them. No wonder the little boy was bored.

Noah glanced around. The rest of the group were lugging their pails. Then he squinted. One of the buildings on the other side of the parking area had a pump of some kind in front of it. Was it just for show or had it been a working hand pump? He pointed to it. "Look there, Milo. Maybe you can help me get some fresh water."

At first, the little boy didn't seem very interested. He sighed and stood, his expression becoming puzzled. He probably hadn't ever seen a hand pump before.

"It'll be fun. Come on. Oh, and grab your bucket."

Milo scampered to the other side of the blanket and grabbed his red plastic sand bucket.

"Why do you have to pump it, Noah?" Milo asked between skips and hops.

Noah hid a smile at the boy's newfound energy. "It's how you get the water up through the pipes. It's great because all you need are strong arms." He paused and rubbed his chin, pretending to assess Milo's strength.

"I'm strong!" Milo made a muscle with his arm.

"I don't know..." Noah reached out, and with two fingers, gently squeezed the tiny bicep. It was surprisingly firm for such a little kid, but Noah didn't know enough about kids to decide if the kid was abnormally strong or he himself was just an idiot when it came to kids. Probably the latter. After careful consideration, he said, "I think you might... maybe be able to pump it." Of course, Noah would help as unobtrusively as he could. Now he really hoped the pump was in working order.

A minute later, they stood beside it, sweating as they strained. The pump was stiff, resisting their efforts until Milo pointed to a blue-and-yellow can perched on the railing of the building nearby. "My mom uses that stuff to help her oil it up good."

Noah gave the kid an appraising look. "I think your mom is one smart lady." He jogged the few steps and grabbed the can of lubricant. It was good for a lot of things, and he was glad to feel that it was nearly full. He gave the pump handle a quick squirt around the base of the handle, and they waited a minute or so before trying again.

"It's moving!" Milo turned huge eyes to Noah, a grin splitting his face.

Noah grinned back. "It is!" After several painfully slow pumps, the handle moved easily, and at first a trickle then a gush of water rushed from the spigot. Milo held his bucket under it, peering inside, then frowned. "It's yucky."

Noah looked in the bucket and grimaced at the orange-tinted water. "It's just rust. It should go away after a few more pumps."

He was happy to see he hadn't lied when the water ran clear a few pumps later. Milo filled his bucket then Noah's. Then the boy upended his own bucket on his head. "Ah..."

"Milo..." Noah didn't have the heart to chastise him. There was plenty of water, after all. Instead, he laughed and tossed his own bucket of water at Milo at the little boy's dare.

Before long the girls joined Milo, and Noah went back to picking.

"You really got them started."

Noah turned to find Cassie at the bushes behind him. "Sorry about that." He wasn't the least bit sorry, though. Their laughter was the sweetest music to his ears, and judging from the smile Cassie gave him in return, she must have thought the same.

"It's great to see them behaving like normal kids." Her tone turned wistful. "What I wouldn't give to keep them this happy and safe forever."

Noah watched the two girls and boy chasing each other with their brightly colored buckets, the water flying through the air and catching the sunlight like precious jewels. He swallowed the lump in his throat and managed a "Yeah. Me too."

Soon, all the buckets were full, and they couldn't fit another blueberry in the vehicles. The teens ran to join the little kids around the pump while the adults loaded the blueberry haul and packed up their picnic.

Vivian raised an eyebrow. "I don't know about you all, but I'm not letting those kids have all the fun!" She laughed and jogged across the field toward them.

Dexter mopped his brow with a rag then shrugged. "They need an adult to watch over them." As he sauntered after his wife, a shot rang out, and Vivian screamed and went down.

Noah blinked, not comprehending for a second, until a second shot blew the leaves off a bush just behind Dexter.

Cupping his hands around his mouth, Noah shouted, "Get down! Shots fired! Get down!" He ran to the truck for a rifle. He'd brought it thinking maybe they'd need it if a bear showed up. Or maybe they'd get lucky and spot a deer. But in the back of his mind, he always thought of the men who'd been in the Northwoods. There were other survivors, and they weren't all friendly.

6

Cassie instinctively ducked at the shots but immediately lifted her head to find Bella and Milo. Noah's instructions to get down registered but barely. She had to make sure the kids were safe.

Vivian writhed on the ground with Dexter lying half over her, his arms protectively wrapped around Vivian's head. Jalen yelled something as he raced toward his parents, but he dropped like a rock when his dad yelled at him to get down.

The pump was still at least a hundred feet away, and Milo stood frozen with fear, his hands on the pump handle while Bella's were cupped under what was now a trickle of water. Ava crouched, her hands covering her ears.

In her peripheral vision, she saw Noah sprint in the other direction to the truck. She heard the door open and remembered the rifle he always took with him.

She turned and started racing toward the kids, passing Vivian and Dexter and waving acknowledgment when Vivian screamed at her to keep her baby safe. Cassie intended to keep all the babies safe. How she'd do that, she didn't know.

She didn't even hear the bang before something plucked at the back of the bandana she had wrapped around her head to stop the sweat. She dove into the blueberries, panting for a second before bolting forward again, keeping her head low and staying near the bushes for cover.

Branches tore at her shirt, but she scarcely noticed the scratches as she strove to reach the kids. Her right foot hit an old tire rut and twisted as pain shot up her leg. She stumbled on.

Another few shots sounded like they shattered glass somewhere, but her eyes were glued to the children. Bella now clutched Milo and screamed, "*Mommy!*"

Unable to pinpoint who was shooting, Cassie didn't know where to tell them to run. A small building, probably a store from when the farm had been open, stood behind them. A rusted metal drum of a trash can was beside it. She pointed. "*Milo! Bella! Ava! Hide there!*"

Cassie had closed the distance to only a few dozen feet, but she tripped on another rut, cursing as she went down. Her ankle throbbed, but she paid it little heed. She lifted her head. "*Hurry! Use the barrel!*"

Ava didn't hear her, but Bella did and reacted. She grabbed Ava's arm with one hand and Milo's shirt with the other, dragging both kids with her initially until they realized where she was headed—then Ava raced ahead. A few years older than the other two, she figured out the objective and grabbed the edge of the barrel, managing to tip it, and rolled it just far enough from the building for all three of them to crouch behind. They were protected on three sides, at least.

A deeper boom made Cassie flinch until she realized it was Noah firing the rifle toward the woods on the other side of the blueberry field. She tried to stand, but more shots rang out, this time from the woods as leaves on a bush to her left flew into the air like so much green confetti.

They were targeting her, she realized, which at least was better than the children. Anger broke the grip fear had on her, and she pushed to her feet, facing the source of the gunfire.

"Why are you shooting at us, you assholes!"

She was beyond angry. They had done nothing wrong and had harmed nobody. If someone else wanted blueberries, for God's sake, there were plenty of them. They'd have to pick for days before they were all gone.

Nobody replied, but they didn't shoot either.

Ethan hopped in Dexter's van and started it. The van burst forward, and for a horrible instant, Cassie thought Ethan was abandoning them, but he circled the van and pulled up beside Vivian, Dexter, and Jalen, shielding them. The driver's-side window rolled down, and the barrel of a rifle emerged.

Had he brought his rifle too? He might have. The kid was a pretty decent hunter. A few rows to Cassie's left, Leona peered over a bush, gripping a small handgun. She should have known the older woman would be prepared. Cassie cursed her own lack of foresight. She had a weapon, but it did her no good sitting on the top shelf of the kitchen cupboard back at the farm. Dammit. She'd become complacent. Thank God Noah, Ethan, and Leona hadn't.

A flash of movement on the far side of the berry field caught Cassie's eye a second before a shot pinged off the side of the van.

After that, it sounded like an all-out war. Leona stood and

fired, Noah's rifle boomed, and it sounded like Ethan was returning fire as well. Cassie took the distraction and cover to hobble the last feet to the children.

She ran a hand over each of their faces, plucking a cobweb from Ava's hair and then wrapping her arm around the little girl for a quick hug. "Thank you, sweetie." She crouched beside them with Milo and Bella clinging to her sides and Ava between her and the barrel. Now that Cassie knew where the gunfire was coming from, she decided to bring the children around to the other side of the building, dragging the barrel with them as cover. They were already almost out of the line of fire, but she wanted walls around them.

She told them her intentions, and all three kids complied without question, shuffling backwards as Cassie tugged the barrel.

On the other side of the building was a door and a broad window with a rolling metal door covering it. A two-foot ledge jutted out from it, forming a counter of sorts. A sign above the window listed prices per pound of berries or per basket. Another sign had a menu of delicious berry treats.

The door was locked, but Milo pointed to the window. "Look, Mom."

There was a half-inch gap between the edge of the rolling door and the ledge.

Cassie tried to raise the metal door, but while she felt it move slightly, she couldn't quite get her fingers beneath it to get the right leverage. Cassie cast about for something to use as a lever and spotted a branch near the door. She wedged it in the gap, but it broke when she applied pressure. Ava handed her a rock that was mostly flat and about three inches long. Cassie took it, not sure if it would fit either, but it did, and it was just long enough to wedge the window open. It rolled a few feet up then stopped. No amount of pushing would make it budge.

Cassie pulled all three kids in close when a flurry of gunfire sounded from the other side of the building again.

"I can fit in there, Cassie." Ava tried to lift herself up to the ledge but couldn't quite make it, but Cassie saw what she was trying to do and put her hands around Ava's waist and lifted the little girl all the way up. Ava lay on her belly and slid through.

"Be careful!" Cassie worried about what was on the other side. Dead bodies? There had been no stench, so that was a good sign, but not knowing what was inside made her jump when she heard a loud crash.

"Are you okay? Ava?"

"I'm fine. I tripped on a bucket. It's dark in here!"

A few seconds later, the doorknob on the door rattled, and the door opened. Ava was covered in dust and cobwebs, but she was all in one piece.

Cassie ushered the other two inside and shut the door, turning the dead bolt. The light from the window gave her enough light to see the dim interior. Empty coolers lined one wall. An ancient cash register sat on the other side of the ledge. It was a good thing it was on the far side of the window, or else Ava would have been partially blocked.

Wooden tables filled the mostly empty building, but faded signs above the tables showed it had been where various produce had been available for sale in season. Her gaze skimmed them. She needed a weapon or at least a light of some sort. She'd locked the door, but there was no reason the shooters couldn't get in the same way Ava had. But if they rolled the window down, they'd be in pitch blackness. Cassie had the kids crouch beneath the interior's matching ledge. Someone would have to come all the way inside to actually shoot them, as the ledge protected them from someone sticking a gun in and shooting randomly. It wasn't much, but it was better than nothing.

A light flashed beside her, and she whirled, ready to fight. Ava flinched away from her, a tiny flashlight in her hand. It wasn't much bigger than a laser pointer and had a small clip on one end. "Oh, God, Ava. I almost decked you." She pulled the little girl in for a one-armed hug as she pressed her other hand to her own forehead.

Shaking, she reached for the light. "Where did you get this?" Not that it mattered.

"I keep it on a chain around my neck. When we lived in the woods, I always had it if I had to use the outhouse."

"Smart girl!" She gave the light back. "Hang onto it for now. I'm going to roll the window down and hope we can secure it somehow."

Ava nodded and aimed the light at the metal gate.

Cassie found a handle in the middle of the gate and rolled it down, searching for a latch or somehow to secure it.

"I think that's how you lock it." She aimed the light at a padlock dangling from a metal ring. There was a key still inserted in it. "Brilliant!"

Cassie wrestled the lock into a matching loop. It wasn't easy, and she saw why whoever had left it unlocked had done so. The loops were misaligned slightly, but she pulled and tugged until it fell into place then turned the key and let out a breath. "There! I think we're safe, but let me go look around to make sure there isn't a back door someone can get in. Can you stay here with the twins, Ava?"

Ava nodded and sat on the floor beneath the ledge, where Milo and Bella huddled, arms around each other.

Cassie had been so focused on the window, she hadn't paid attention to what was going on outside. As she made a quick circuit of the small building, she was relieved to find that a back door did exist, but that it was locked securely. A small square window gave her a partial view of the blueberry field, but she couldn't discern what was going on. She pressed her cheek to the door and tried to see back toward their vehicles.

Dexter's minivan had moved from where it had been beside the fallen Vivian. She prayed that meant they all were able to board and get to safety. They'd come back for her and the kids.

Suddenly she heard voices, and they seemed to be approaching the building. She scurried back to the children, realizing the voices were louder on that side of the building.

She pressed a finger to her lips and turned the flashlight off just in case it showed through a crack or something.

"Come out of there! This is our patch! You can't play your zombie tricks on us. We saw you go in!"

Cassie pulled the children close. *Zombie tricks?* What did that even mean?

Something banged on the rolling window, making all of them jump and clutch each other. Bella whimpered before Milo clamped a hand over her mouth.

"*Zombies gotta die!* We can't let you live, or you'll take over the world. Besides, you're dead already!"

They banged on the window again, and Cassie watched

the bottom of the window start to buckle. Anger and fear blazed through her as she shouted, "Go away! You're crazy! Don't you realize you're scaring these children! Keep all the damn blueberries. Just get the hell away from us!"

"Zombies gotta die!"

Cassie pounded back on the metal. "Stop with the zombie crap already! We're not zombies!"

"We saw you dancing and laughing, just like the people did before they died. They became zombies! That's what everyone was saying. And zombies give everyone the virus so they can eat them!"

Confused, Cassie shook her head. "What are you talking about?" Before the other person could answer, Cassie shook her head. It was no use reasoning with them. She just wanted them gone. "You know what, I don't care. *Just go away!*"

The voices became lower, and she couldn't understand what they were saying, but a loud splash and broken glass sounded right outside. With it came the stench of gasoline. Another crash of glass followed.

"Burn, zombies, burn!"

Several shots rang out, and a piercing scream not far from the building made Cassie attempt to cover the ears of all three children. With only two hands, she couldn't, but they all clung to her, pressing hard against her, their own hands clapped over their ears.

Seconds later, tendrils of smoke slithered under the door and around the metal window cover.

Horrified, Cassie gathered the kids, pulling them away from the wall. She reached for the handle of the door but pulled her hand back with a yelp of pain. Cassie ignored the pain and pushed the children toward the back door. She hadn't seen the group approaching from that side. She hoped they didn't know about the back door.

She peered outside. There was nobody in sight. Where was Noah and the others? She knew Vivian had been shot, but no way would they leave the kids behind. She was certain of it.

Voices still came from the front of the building, still chanting. She heard a faint breaking of glass again. If they were going to make a break for it, which was their only chance with the building on fire, they'd have to do it now.

Crouching, Cassie gathered them close. "We have to make a run for it. I'll go first. Just to that little shed. Then I'll motion for you guys if the coast is clear."

"What if it's not?" Ava held each of the smaller children's hands, her eyes huge but her expression determined. Cassie wanted to hug her for her bravery, but there was no time.

"I'll try to draw them away, and you wait as long as you can, but the building is on fire. You'll have to run out as soon as you can." She thought dying by gunfire preferable to burning to death, but she wasn't about to rationalize that with an eight-year-old and two kindergarteners.

Taking a deep breath, she turned, took another peek through the window, opened the door, and dashed out, certain that any second she'd feel the impact of a bullet, but she made it to the shed unscathed. She turned. Nobody had seen her. Cassie caught Ava's eye and motioned her to come. Ava pulled Cassie's kids with her, and Cassie wasn't even sure their feet hit the ground more than a couple of times, so great was Ava's grip.

"You're amazing," Cassie whispered to Ava, pulling them all close as she swept the surroundings. The sound of glass crashing was louder. They must be making their way to the back of the building.

Cassie peeked around to the other side of the shed. The coast was clear, but there was a huge open area between them and to where they had all relaxed after eating lunch not long ago. Panic grabbed her by the throat, stealing her breath. Noah's truck and Dexter's van were both gone. She couldn't—wouldn't—believe that the others had left them. They must be here somewhere. Pulling back, she gave all the kids a reassuring squeeze. "The others are trying to get to us." She knew it had to be true.

Gunfire erupted from what sounded like the front of the building. Someone started wailing. It sounded like a child, and if she hadn't already had her arms securely wrapped around all three of their little ones, she'd have sworn it was one of them. As she stole another look, she thought she heard Noah's voice. There! She was certain of it. She couldn't make out what he was saying, but it was definitely him.

Cassie sagged against the wall. She'd never doubted that they would come back for them, but relief almost buckled her knees. She straightened quickly. They still weren't safe as far as she knew.

When she'd looked around the corner, she noticed a broken latch on the shed doors. The children could hide in there while she investigated what was happening on the other side of the building, which now had flames shooting from the roof. Thank God they'd escaped that inferno.

"Here's what we're gonna do. There's a door to the shed right around this corner. I'm going to make sure you can get in there, then have you all hide out in there until I come back for you. Understand?"

Ava and Milo nodded. Bella whispered, "Okay, Mommy."

A lump came to Cassie's throat, and she prayed she was doing the right thing. They couldn't hide back here forever. She had to find out what was happening so she could plan accordingly. If she had to, she would take the kids into the woods, follow the road out, and hope they came to an abandoned vehicle she could start.

After another glance and seeing nobody, Cassie rushed the kids around the corner and pulled open the shed. A small tractor filled most of it, but the children were little and had no trouble squeezing in. Cassie pointed to rake and said, "Put the handle between these so nobody can open the doors from the outside." She motioned to the two handles on the interior of the shed doors.

Ava nodded, her eyes huge as a tear slipped from one. "I want my momma."

Cassie pulled her in for a brief hug. "Oh, I know you do, sweetheart." She dropped a kiss on Ava's head and then one on each of her own children's heads.

Bella wrapped her arms around Ava as Milo patted Ava's shoulder. Cassie backed out. "I love you guys."

She made sure she heard the rake handle rattle on the other side before she dashed for the side of the burning building. Creeping around the corner, she nearly bumped into the back of a young girl. Her height and build put her around age ten or eleven. A boy who looked a few years older stood a few feet in front of her, but Cassie didn't take time to process his age or intentions before recoiling, noticing at the last second that Noah's truck was parked less than a hundred feet away.

Cassie pressed back against the wall. Heat from the fire

warmed her back. She couldn't stay here much longer. She wasn't afraid of the children, but where was the person who had been shooting?

"We had to!"

Jumping at the shouted declaration that sounded like it was right next to her, Cassie scrambled back a few steps.

"No, you didn't! They never hurt anyone! What's wrong with you?" It was Noah's voice, but it sounded strangled and angry at the same time.

Crouching, Cassie pressed close to the corner and peered around it. The boy and girl had moved away a few feet and blocked some of her view, but Noah stood, his hands clasped behind his head. He wasn't even looking at the kids. His face was twisted with anguish as he stared at the burning front of the building.

"They were just little kids!" Noah turned in the direction of the boy. He strode toward him, his face twisted. Cassie flinched.

"Get back, or I'll shoot you too!" The boy raised his rifle, aiming it at Noah.

Noah halted, but his hands clenched at his sides. "Why? Why are you shooting at any of us? We never hurt you."

"You just killed my dad!"

"He's not dead, Luke!" The girl tugged at the boy's shirt. "He was moaning. He might still be alive."

"He's *gonna* die. Might as well be dead."

Noah lifted a hand. "I was trying to stop him from murdering my family." He flung a hand at the flaming building. "And you let them burn to death!" A cloud of black smoke billowed from the fire, engulfing him, and he coughed. "Why would you *burn* them?"

Cassie had never heard Noah's voice so choked with emotion. He must think they were all dead. She had to let him know she and the kids were fine. She didn't want anyone else to get hurt. If she called to him, it might distract him, and the boy with the rifle could shoot him. But she had to something. They were at a standoff.

Screwing up her courage and praying she was doing the right thing, she moved away from the building, backing up and using an ancient tractor that looked like it hadn't moved in a decade as cover. She darted from it to a tree that brought her parallel with Noah. She called out to him, "Noah! Noah!" Keeping half of her body behind the tree in case the boy decided to shoot, she waved an arm.

Noah started... then began trotting to her until the boy screamed, "Stop!"

Stopping, Noah glowered at the boy. "Put the damn gun down."

Luke wavered, glancing back at the young girl, then over to Cassie. "You're not zombies?"

Cassie shook her head and left the safety of the tree. This was a scared boy. She didn't think he really wanted to kill anyone. "No. There are no zombies. Even the sick people who died were just normal people who caught a virus."

"They didn't eat people and turn them into zombies too? Why would my dad lie?" His voice hardened. "My dad wouldn't lie. If he said they were zombies, then that's what they were."

"I don't think he lied. He might have honestly believed that. I'm sure everything was very confusing." Cassie had been busy baking in her house when the virus had first hit, so she didn't know what rumors had been flying around, but

Vivian had told her how crazy it had been, and that people concocted wild stories that the virus. Cassie could understand how, for people in a state of panic and fear, zombies had seemed as plausible as any other source of the scourge.

Noah's voice softened. "Luke, listen. Maybe your dad isn't dead, and we can help him still. We have a doctor with us."

"Why would you want to help him? He tried to kill all of you."

"Because there aren't many of us left."

Luke's shoulders sagged, and the rifle lowered.

Noah raced to Cassie, wrapping her in a tight hug. "Jeez, I thought you were dead." He stepped back. "Where are the kids? They weren't in..." He glanced at the building.

"We were, but we got out. They're in the shed back there." Cassie pointed. "I'll get them." She started but turned back. "Where's everyone else?"

"I sent them back to the farm. Vivian was shot."

"I know. I saw that. Is she bad?"

Noah shrugged helplessly. "I wish I knew. I didn't get a good look, but Leona is helping her, so she's in good hands."

Cassie nodded. "That's true, but I'm so worried about Vivian, and poor Ava knows something is going on. I don't know what to tell her."

"Tell her the truth, I guess. I don't think it would be good to make light of it, but then again, what do I know? I don't have kids." Noah made a noise that sounded like a cross between a sob and a chuckle.

"Vivian is strong. If anyone has a chance, it's her." In the short time they'd known each other, Cassie had grown close to the other woman.

"Ethan picked them up and waved toward the main road,

so I hope they're already back there and Vivian's getting help." He looked grim. "Right now, I'm going to find out where their father is. You should probably wait here with the kids. I'm not sure what we'll find."

Cassie nodded.

7

Noah approached Luke and the girl, his hands up to show he meant no harm. "Let's help your father. I swear I never wanted to shoot anyone. I did enough of that in Afghanistan."

"You served?"

Noah gave him a curt nod. "Army. Two tours."

"So did my dad."

Dropping his head, Noah drew a ragged breath and blinked hard. He prayed the other man was still alive, and that they could save him somehow. If not, at least they could give him a proper burial. "Where was he when he was shot?"

Luke pointed back toward the woods. "He's at the edge of the woods. There was so much blood, I thought he was dead. I was so mad, I just..." His voice broke, and he raised his hands to his face, covering it as he let out a sob.

Noah motioned toward his truck. "If you guys want to hop in, we can go find him."

Luke glanced at the girl and then nodded, his shoulders stiff as they headed to the truck.

Noah climbed in but pointed at the rifle Luke still held, the barrel upright and angled out of the window. "That has to go in the back." He slid the window open between the cab and the back of the truck.

Luke hesitated, but the girl elbowed him in the ribs. "Do it, Luke. We gotta help your dad."

The boy glared at her then scowled at Noah. He grumbled but did as Noah instructed and put the rifle in the back. Noah nodded then drove across the fields toward the woods.

"How deep in here is he?" Noah slowed as they approached the first scrub trees.

The girl pointed. "He's right over there by that white tree."

"The birch?" Noah drove another hundred feet then parked. He almost left the truck running but thought better of it. He reached behind his seat and grabbed his first aid kit. Stocking the kit hadn't been difficult, and he'd kept it well stocked. Leona had further added to it.

Luke cupped his hands around his mouth as he moved ahead of Noah. "Dad!"

The girl trotted after him. "Daniel!"

Noah raised an eyebrow. So the girl wasn't Luke's sister. Or maybe she was a stepsister. The woods thickened, but the undergrowth was dense. He pushed away tall weeds, cursed as he brushed up against a plant with burrs, and slid down a slight embankment to a narrow stream. This was farther into the woods than the girl had led him to believe. Wary of a trick, Noah slowed, his hand tightening on the barrel of his own rifle.

"I thought you said he was on the edge of the woods?" Noah doubted he'd have hit the man if he had been this deep in. For one thing, he never would have been able to see him.

When he'd been shooting, he'd seen a man for only a brief moment after the shooting had begun. His training was to only shoot what he could see. He wasn't going to take potshots into the forest.

"He was shot on the edge, but he headed back into the woods toward our camp but didn't make it all the way. I'm not sure how far we walked."

The explanation made sense, but Noah remained tense until the girl darted ahead. "I see him!"

Luke raced after her while Noah approached with caution, pausing to see if it was a trap. When the girl dropped to her knees and Luke fell beside her, he strode to their sides. A man who looked to be around fifty lay sprawled beside a tree. Blood soaked his shirt, and his skin was pale, with a sheen of sweat. When Noah bent on one knee to feel for a pulse in the man's neck, he breathed a sigh of relief. It was there but not very strong. His skin was cold and clammy. A sure sign of shock. Noah's jaw tightened. It might already be too late.

He opened the kit and sorted through it, pulling on a pair of nitrile gloves and setting aside a bottle of sterile water. "I'm going to try to help him. See if he'll respond to you." Noah didn't want the man to open his eyes and see a stranger and possibly become violent. Before he began, he took a handgun from the man's waist holster, ignoring the protest from Luke. "I'm sorry, but I can't risk him shooting me if he thinks I'm trying to hurt him."

A hunting knife was strapped to his thigh as well, and Noah removed it but kept it nearby in case he needed to cut through anything. His own knife was back in the truck.

Gently, he raised the man's T-shirt on the side that

seemed to be the nearest the source of the bleeding. The shirt was already tattered, and so he couldn't tell a tatter from a bullet hole.

He spotted the wound high on the man's left chest. The bullet could have gone anywhere once inside of the chest, or even into the abdomen if it hit a bone and ricocheted, so Noah didn't assume it had stayed in the shoulder area.

There was no telltale froth of blood on the man's lips or in his nose, so he took that as a sign that his lungs were okay, for now. He created a thick pad from gauze squares and then grabbed a roll of bandages, layering them around the man's torso. He secured another layer as vertically as he could around the man's shoulder and collarbone, attempting to create some pressure to help stanch the blood flow.

Noah rested on his haunches, swiping his arm across his forehead. "Okay. That's all I can do for now."

He stood and looked around. About twenty yards away was a campsite, of sorts. A tent listed to one side, and a couple of lawn chairs bordered a blackened spot with a pile of ashes in the middle. Garbage was strewn everywhere— empty potato chip bags, packages of cookies, soda cans, water bottles—and Noah became aware of a thick stench. In his concentration, he hadn't noticed it before, but he'd bet that they were close to the latrine area—if they even had one designated. Maybe this whole area was used for waste.

"What should we do for him?" Luke asked, kneeling beside his father. All the bravado he'd displayed before was completely gone.

The girl squatted nearby, her arms wrapped around her knees. Noah sighed. He couldn't leave them like this, but how would the others react if he brought them back to the farm?

Vivian was probably already there, and Noah didn't know how serious her wound was. If she died, it wouldn't be right to bring her murderer back for treatment. Not only wasn't it fair, but valuable supplies would be used. But if this man died, the kids were alone. Even if they were living off of junk, at least they were alive.

"I don't know what you should do for him. I'm not a doctor. I just have a little medic field training, and I've reached about the extent of it with this bandage." Noah motioned toward the man's arm. "The only thing I can suggest is we try moving him to the farm."

"The farm?" The girl lifted her head from where she'd rested it on her knees. Her dark hair was a mass of tangles with bits of grass dangling from what he thought must have been braids at one point.

"It's where we all live. We have a building we outfitted as a clinic, and we have a doctor. I don't know what, if anything, she can do for him, though, and I can't guarantee that he'll even survive the drive back to it."

Luke bit his lip as his gaze moved from his father to the girl. After a moment, something must have been communicated, because she nodded.

"How do we move him?" Luke rested a hand on his dad's uninjured shoulder. For a brief second, he looked like he was about to cry, but then his face became a stoic mask as he met Noah's eyes.

"We can try to carry him between us, or I can put him over my shoulder. I don't know how he'll tolerate either, though. Do you have any long boards or even a couple of long rods? We can make a stretcher or travois out of them."

"Um..." Luke scratched his cheek, but the girl jumped up.

"I know something that might work." She raced off then returned dragging the frame for a canopy with the canopy trailing behind.

"The wind tore it down and broke off the other two legs, but if we put the canopy between these with some of the rope from the tent, we might be able to make a stretcher. Sort of."

Noah formed a picture in his mind of what she was describing and nodded. "Get the ropes, and I'll see about getting the canopy stretched between the legs."

Noah turned the canopy and, using the knife, poked holes along the edges. His plan was to thread the rope through the holes and then bind the ropes to the legs.

By the time he had enough holes in the thick material, the girl was back with the rope. "Here you go."

"Thank you…" Noah hesitated as he accepted the rope. "What's your name?"

"Ruby."

Noah nodded. "Thank you, Ruby. I'm Noah."

She only shrugged and drew the toe of her scuffed-up sneaker through the dust, nudging a candy bar wrapper to the side.

He wound the rope through the holes and around the poles, and after watching for a few moments, Ruby started on the other side. Luke crouched near his father's head, his expression stoic. Noah gestured to the bandage, noting the amount of blood that had already seeped through. "Put some pressure on that, Luke."

Luke hesitated. "I don't want to hurt him."

Noah shook his head. "It's going to hurt, and there's nothing we can do about that. But we need to slow the bleeding, or he might not make it back to the farm."

Nodding, Luke put his hand down, flinching when his father moaned, but he didn't let up.

"Good job, Luke."

Noah tied his side fast then moved to help Ruby. She struggled with a few of the holes that were too small, but she'd done pretty well at matching Noah's job.

At first, they tried lifting it like a stretcher, with the kids each taking an end on the same side and Noah on the other side, but even with the two of them, the stretcher listed dangerously to their side, and the man gave a strangled moan.

"This isn't working." Noah set his side down, and the kids followed his lead.

"Now what?" Luke rubbed his hands on his thighs, leaving bloody streaks.

"Ruby, move up behind Luke, and each of you grab onto the top end of the pole. I'll do the same, and we'll leave the back of the poles to drag. It should be a lot easier."

The move wasn't easy, but they didn't drop the makeshift travois, so Noah counted it as successful. When they reached the truck, Noah had them set it down while he hopped in the bed and rearranged the baskets of blueberries. Some would probably spill, but there was nothing he could do about that.

Afterward, he took the back end and had each of the kids take the front poles. With him pushing and them leaning on the poles to keep them level, he was able to slide the stretcher into the bed of the truck.

"Can I sit back there with him? I won't hop out and leave him or anything. I swear." Luke swiped a stray blueberry from where it had rolled up against the stretcher then looked at Noah like he feared a rejection, or worse, anger.

"You guys aren't prisoners, you know. I'm just trying to help your dad."

"He's not my dad." Ruby crossed her arms.

"Oh. Well, whatever." Noah didn't care about the relationships. "We can sort all of this out later. Right now, we have to go back and get Cassie and the other kids, so you both are going to have to ride in the bed so there's room."

By the time they got back, Cassie and the kids were stretched out on the grass near the water pump. Cassie lay on her side on one of the blankets left behind in the rush to evacuate. Her children had curled in beside her, and Ava lay on the other side of them, on her side facing Cassie. Noah thought they were all asleep until Cassie waved at him.

He stopped the truck and rolled down the window. "We found him. He's alive but just barely."

"Is he in there with you?" Her expression was unreadable as her face was shadowed, but she sat up, craning her head to see.

"He's in the back with the kids he was with."

Cassie nodded and stood. "What are you going to do with him?"

"Well, I can't just let him die there and leave the kids, so..."

"We're taking him back to the farm?" She braced a hand on each hip.

"What else can I do?"

"I don't know. It's just... Ava's right here. And he's the one who..." She tipped her head and raised an eyebrow.

"I know, but it's not like I can call 911 for him now. So what the hell should I have done?"

She sighed and shook her head. "Yeah, I guess. I'll wake the kids."

Noah nodded and looked straight ahead until the sleepy kids shuffled up to the truck and settled in the back seat of the cab. The twins fell back to sleep, but Ava sat quietly between Noah and Cassie, her hands folded in her lap.

Noah put an arm around her and gave her shoulders a gentle squeeze. Ava glanced up at him, her eyes wide, and he wished he could erase the stark fear he saw in them. He wanted to reassure her, but he couldn't. He wouldn't lie, and he refused to offer empty promises. All he could do was offer comfort and support. After a moment, she leaned against him, and he could feel her small body shaking. The best thing he could do was to get her back to the farm and her father and, God willing, her mother, as quickly as possible.

8

"I need to go find my baby." Dexter paced outside of what they'd dubbed "The Clinic." "But what if something happens while I'm gone?"

So far, they'd only used the clinic to treat minor wounds. Ethan had cut his knee on a piece of equipment, and Leona had stitched it up and treated it with antibiotic ointment. She'd said it was a good thing he remembered getting a tetanus shot in the spring as part of his yearly physical. His arm had been sore for the next couple of days and had affected his pitching.

"I can go, Dexter." Ethan thought he could remember the way.

Dexter paused in his pacing. "I would love to send you, but if something happened to you too... we don't know if there are more of those people out there. I sure do appreciate the offer, though."

Jalen sat with his back against the wall, his arms draped over his bent knees, staring at the dirt in front of him. Ethan went over and sat beside him. Jalen didn't acknowledge his presence. Ethan pulled his knees up and draped his arms around them, and he searched the road. Noah would find them and bring them back. He said he would, and Noah never made promises he didn't keep. At least, he hadn't yet, but his promises had been minor, like finding gasoline or saying Ethan could do some new skill that Noah had shown him when Ethan doubted his ability. Ethan sighed. This was so much bigger.

Jalen's shoulders suddenly shook, as if he'd had a chill. Ethan glanced at him to find tears rolling down his cheeks as the boy silently cried, his gaze still fixed on the ground.

Ethan reached out, tentatively, and put his hand on Jalen's shoulder. "Leona's really good. Remember when she stitched up my knee?" He pointed to the dark-pink scar. "Look, it's completely healed, and it didn't even get infected."

Jalen swiped a hand against his face and muttered, "This ain't no stupid cut. She got shot."

"I know." Ethan let his hand drop and faced the road again. Why had he said something so lame? It wasn't as if getting a tiny cut on his knee in any way compared to being shot. "Sorry."

There was silence except for the crunch of Dexter's feet on the ground and birds chirping and cawing in the background.

"You don't have to be sorry. Not your fault." Jalen's voice was so quiet, Ethan almost missed the comment.

"Yeah, but..." Ethan didn't know what to say and let the sentence trail off.

They sat without speaking until Ethan's butt started falling asleep, and he shifted. As if his movement had broken a spell, Jalen cleared his throat. "Man, I don't know what I'm gonna do without my mom and Ava. She's a pain in the ass most of the time, but what if... what if she doesn't come back? What if something happened to her? What are me and my dad gonna do?"

Ethan knew the answer to that. There were only two choices. He could have given up or pushed on, but giving up was never really a choice. Not for him, anyway. His parents would have wanted him to live on, and so he had. So he knew what Jalen faced. He'd faced the same, only worse. He didn't have a dad anymore to help him bear the loss, but he wasn't about to say any of that to Jalen. Not only wouldn't it help, but he wasn't certain he could speak about his family. The few times the subject had been brought up, his throat had twisted into a tight knot, and no words had come out.

He did the only thing he could think of and scooted closer, draping his arm across his friend's shoulders. Jalen dropped his head onto his knees, and his shoulders shook as Ethan rubbed a hand up and down the other boy's back a few times. Then he stood, rubbing his backside to get the feeling back.

He felt useless, so he asked Dexter, "You want me to fix you something to eat?"

Ethan wasn't great at cooking, but he could open a can of beans, and Cassie had baked extra bread yesterday since she knew they'd be gone today. He could toast it over the fire. Ethan glanced at the firepit. He'd stirred it up not long after they had arrived and boiled water for Leona. The fire was a hot bed of coals now.

Dexter gave him a blank look. "Huh?"

"I can make some food. Beans or something."

Dexter scrubbed a hand down his face. "I'm not hungry,

but go ahead and make some for yourself and Jalen. The others should be back soon too." He turned to look over his shoulder toward the road as he said it.

"Okay."

Glad for something to do, Ethan raced into the house and grabbed a can of beans and the can opener. They had been eating fresh as much as possible and saving the canned food for the winter, but Ethan figured this would count as an exception to the rule. Not that it was a real rule anyway. He dumped the can into a pot and set it aside. It wouldn't take long to heat up on the coals, so he decided to make peanut butter and jelly sandwiches to go with the beans. Vivian had made awesome strawberry jam from berries they'd found in the overgrown and mostly unplanted remnants of a garden. Noah had said strawberries came back every year, and they had taken some of the plants for their own garden. He'd said it would help the original strawberries if they thinned it out, and they would have their own too.

He spread the peanut butter on slices of bread and then jam on the matching slices, mashing them together. In all, he made eight sandwiches, using the whole loaf of bread. After he stacked the sandwiches on a tray, he threw a dish towel over the stack to keep the flies away and to keep it from getting stale too fast. He wondered if he should have left some of the loaf to eat plain or to dip in the beans.

Glancing at the other two loaves encased in plastic wrap from a huge roll snagged from a restaurant, he shrugged. He could always come back and cut more.

Next, he took three plastic cups from the cupboard and set them on the tray, then snagged a large wooden spoon from a jar of utensils and set it in the pan of beans. With the pan in one hand and balancing the sandwiches on the other hand, he headed to the fire. He put the pan on a rack he'd already set up when he'd boiled the water and put the tray on the stump they used as a table. Noah called it his prep table.

The smell of the beans made Ethan's stomach rumble, and he gave a guilty look back at Jalen. It didn't seem right to be hungry when his friend's mom might die. He wasn't worried about Ava, though. No way would Noah and Cassie let anything happen to Jalen's little sister or the others, Milo and Bella. They'd die protecting them. He was certain of it.

When the beans began to bubble, he used his T-shirt to protect his hand and move the pan to a corner of the rack that was near the edge of the coals to keep warm and not burn. It was then he realized he'd forgotten plates and utensils, so he dashed back to the house to get them. As he bounded down the steps to return to the fire, he spotted Noah's truck approaching. He pointed with a fistful of spoons. "Look! They're coming!"

Ethan ran back to the fire and dumped the utensils and plates then raced down the driveway to where Noah usually parked. He could see Cassie in the front seat and, thank God, Ava between her and Noah.

Jalen ran up beside Ethan, with Dexter close on his heels. "Ava looks okay!" Ethan grinned and turned to Jalen and Dexter. When tears started trickling down Dexter face, Ethan shifted his focus and didn't look at Jalen either, concentrating on the truck as it rolled to a stop.

Noah opened the door and grimaced after he stepped out.

"Are you okay, Noah?" Ethan asked, although he stayed back to make room for Dexter and Jalen to reach Ava.

"Yeah. I'm fine. Just a stiff back. I'm getting old." He

looked like he was trying to joke, but his tired smile faded almost immediately. "I'm going to need your help with something, Ethan. Could you come around to the back of the truck with me?"

Cassie was still on the other side of the truck, leaning into the back seat.

"Sure, Noah." He rounded the truck to the passenger side on his way to the back. He needed to know the kids were okay. They were almost like siblings to him already, even if they did annoy him sometimes. "Hey, Cassie, are you and the kids all right?"

She glanced up at him and nodded, but her expression was also grim. "We're fine. The twins were sleeping, but now they're awake." Cassie bit her lip and shot a look at the clinic. "Is Vivian...?" Her voice was low as her gaze darted to Ava, Dexter, and Jalen, who stood in a group hug on the other side of the truck.

"Leona is still with her."

"So, she's alive?"

"As far as I know, yes."

Cassie nodded. "Thank God. Poor Ava has been asking about her, and I didn't know what to say." She reached in the back of the truck and helped Milo out then did the same for Bella.

Milo yawned then leaned against his mom's hip. "I'm hungry, Mommy."

"Me too." Bella wrapped her arms around Cassie's waist.

"I'll get you something as soon as I can. I need to check on something first."

"I made sandwiches and beans. They're down at the fire."

"You did?" Cassie turned to him. "Fantastic. Thank you so much, Ethan."

He ducked his head. "It was no big deal."

"Ethan! You coming?"

Ethan started and hurried to the back of the truck. "Sorry, Noah. I was just telling Cassie that I made sandwiches." He glanced into the bed of the truck as Noah lowered the gate.

A girl huddled in one corner, hugging her knees to her chest while a boy about his own age, maybe a little younger, sat beside a man sprawled on a floor of the truck. The man's skin looked dead white. Ethan recoiled. While he'd seen plenty of dead people over the last several months, he still didn't want to get too close.

"Who's he?" Ethan ignored his revulsion and moved forward to take the end of a pole when he saw Noah taking the other one.

Noah motioned instead for Ethan to jump into the back of the truck. "I think Luke will need help on that end. I can handle this one."

"Uh... okay." So the boy was Luke. He had so many questions, but he'd save them until the man was out of the truck.

Luke barely acknowledged Ethan. Instead, the boy focused solely on the injured man. Luke held a blood-soaked wad of cloth pressed against the man's shoulder but nodded when Noah said that on the count of three they'd slide the man toward the gate.

The sudden movement caused the man to moan, so at least Ethan knew he was alive. Before that, he'd wondered if they were moving a body. The girl scooted past Ethan and scrambled from the truck. He lost sight of her when Noah did another three-count. This time, they moved him so only his head and shoulders remained in the truck.

Noah grunted as he shifted. "You guys will need to come out and get a firm grip on your ends of the poles. We'll lower him to the ground, then I can drag him to the clinic."

Ethan understood Noah's plan as far as the actions he had to carry out but was confused. Why were they taking a stranger there? Vivian was already being treated. "Uh, Noah... Leona has Vivian there."

"That's okay. We have a couple of beds. I can do a few things for him until she has time to treat him."

Ethan shrugged. That was true. They'd snagged gurneys from a few empty ambulances. "Why don't I run and get one of the gurneys? Instead of dragging him, I mean." He jumped from the back of the truck and turned to grab the pole as Luke did the same on his side.

Noah nodded. "One... two... *three!*"

It wasn't as gentle as Ethan had hoped, as Luke's side slipped from his grip and dropped the last six inches with a thud.

"Sorry, Dad." Luke dropped to his knees and resumed pressing his hand against the wound.

"Okay, run and grab the gurney, Ethan." Noah snagged Ethan's arm as he passed, holding up his hand. "Hold on... how is Vivian?"

Ethan shook his head. "I'm not sure. Leona's been in there a long time. We got the generator going so she can use her equipment. Also, I boiled water and brought her a few other things, but we haven't seen her for about an hour now."

Noah's mouth set in a grim line as he looked toward the clinic. "Okay. Hurry."

Nodding, Ethan spun and raced to the clinic, passing Dexter, who held Ava against his side like he'd never let go, and Jalen, who leaned his back against the building only a few feet from his dad and sister. Ethan hesitated at the door before he gave it a tentative knock. "Leona?"

"Just a second!"

He waited, shifting from one foot to the other. It seemed like forever, but finally, the door opened, and Leona slipped outside. She wore a white lab coat, but it was now stained with blood. Ethan winced, his mission forgotten momentarily, as he asked, "Is Vivian going to be okay?"

Leona glanced at him but turned her attention to Dexter and Jalen. "I've stopped the bleeding and did what I could to save the baby."

Ethan's mouth dropped open. *Baby?*

Jalen stared at his dad then glanced at Ethan, his expression as shocked as Ethan imagined his own to be.

"What about my wife? Is she going to be okay?"

Leona drew a deep breath. "I've done what I can. The bullet nicked her liver. I was able to stop the bleeding there, but I had to take out her gallbladder. She was lucky, as the bullet seemed to have angled down and lodged against her pelvis. I was able to get it out. It missed her uterus, but one ovary was obliterated."

"Will she be able to give birth okay?"

Leona shrugged. "I'm hopeful. The bullet missed the uterus, and the pregnancy is still early enough that there's time for her to heal, but I'm afraid I can't give you an answer yet. It's too soon. At this point, I'll be happy that she holds on to the pregnancy. The next few days will be important."

"Can I see her?"

Dexter looked as if he was ready to bolt inside whether Leona gave him the approval or not, but luckily, she nodded. "Yes, of course. In fact, I'm going to need some help getting her into a more comfortable bed." She looked at Ethan. "You and Dexter can help me."

"What about me?" Jalen stepped forward.

"I know you're anxious to help, but your mom probably won't want you to see her until we get her all cleaned up, okay?"

"And I need you to watch your sister. I'll come and get you in just a little bit."

"Um, Leona, I'd love to help, but I came to get one of the stretchers. Noah needs it."

"Oh, dear. Who's hurt? Is it Cassie?" She pressed a hand to her forehead. "In all the confusion and taking care of Vivian, I forgot about Cassie and the kids. Are they okay?"

"Yeah, they're okay, but Noah brought back a man who's also shot. He's in the back of Noah's truck. He looks really bad."

Leona took in the news, straightened her shoulders, and nodded. "I'll get ready for him. Come on, Dexter, and Jalen, you're going to have to help now."

Dexter glanced from Leona to Ethan, his expression dark. "Wait... is this the man who was shooting at us?"

Ethan shrugged. "I'm not sure. You'd have to ask Noah."

Dexter looked to where Noah's truck would be parked and seemed undecided as he glanced back at the clinic door.

"Come in and see your wife, Dexter." Leona gave Dexter's arm a gentle tug, and Ethan was glad to see him agree, although he was clearly torn between confronting a man who may have shot Vivian and seeing with his own eyes that his wife was okay.

"Ethan, the gurney is pushed back against the wall on the left." Leona pointed toward the far corner.

Nodding, Ethan slid past Dexter and entered the clinic. He couldn't help but notice Vivian lying still in the middle of the room. A bright light shined on her, and a white sheet covered her up to her chin. Blood-soaked towels were tossed on the floor, and one sheet held various bloody lumps of bandages and wads of gauze. Two IV poles flanked the bed, and one held a clear solution, the other a pale, yellowish liquid.

Ethan averted his gaze, secretly glad he had another mission. Seeing Vivian like this was hard enough. He didn't want to have to get even closer. As he unlocked the gurney and pushed it through the doors, he caught a glimpse of Jalen's face and immediately felt guilty for his thoughts. His friend looked as if he was about to cry, and Ethan wished he could be the one to help move Vivian so Jalen wouldn't have to.

He pushed the stretcher over bumps and ruts, out of breath by the time he reached the truck.

"What took so long?" Noah pulled the gurney alongside the injured man and sent Ethan a look of irritation.

"I had to wait because Leona was taking care of Vivian."

Noah's expression softened. "Is she okay?"

"For now, I guess."

"Sorry I snapped at you."

Ethan nodded. "I'll help get him on the gurney."

"Okay. You and Luke can get that side, and, Cassie, you hold his head. I'll get this side." They all took a corner of the makeshift stretcher and, on the count of three, lifted him onto the gurney. Bella and Milo trailed behind.

The trip back to the clinic was much slower as they guided the gurney around many of the bumps and potholes, and even though Ethan knew this was the guy who had probably shot Vivian, he still winced when they rolled over even small bumps and the man moaned.

By the time they were back at the clinic door, Leona had changed her soiled clothes, and Vivian had been moved off to a corner of the clinic. A folding screen blocked off her corner from the surgical area, where they rolled the injured man's gurney.

Ethan backed away, rubbing his hands on his thighs. He turned and caught a glimpse of Dexter's head over the top of the screen and guessed that was where Jalen and Dexter were. Should he peek in and see how Vivian was? Ethan decided to wait, even as Cassie headed that way.

"Hey, Ethan?" Cassie turned before she entered the screened area.

"Yeah?"

"Do you think you could keep an eye on the kids? And give them some of those beans and sandwiches you made?"

"Of course." Relieved to have a task that took him away from the clinic, Ethan started to turn away but stopped when Ava appeared around the end of the screen, holding Jalen's hand. Jalen gestured to Ethan. "Can you take Ava too? She's hungry."

Ethan held out his hand. "Come on, Ava. Let's go eat."

9

Cassie dipped a washcloth in a basin of warm water and bathed Vivian's face. She'd already cleaned Vivian from the toes up and had just changed the water. It worried her that Vivian had only awakened briefly a few times during the bath, moaning when Cassie had partially turned her to wash a hard-to-reach spot.

Finished, Cassie returned the cloth to the basin and set it aside. She pulled the sheet and blanket up to Vivian's chin when the woman murmured that she was cold. Then, with nothing left to do, she peered around the screen to find Dexter, Jalen, and Ava all patiently waiting on the folding chairs Noah had found in the basement of the farmhouse.

"I'm done."

"Did she wake up at all?" Dexter stood and was heading around the screen even as he asked the question.

"Only for a moment here or there."

When they all went behind the screen, Cassie saw the empty chairs and decided to move them beside Vivian's bed so the family could sit together. The second Dexter saw what she was doing, he told Jalen to get the other two chairs, but Cassie waved him off. "I got it, Dexter. Did you all get something to eat?"

Jalen and Ava nodded, but Dexter was already focused on his wife. Cassie left them to see if Leona needed any help. She had the other man on the table Vivian had vacated only an hour or so before.

"Is there anything I can do for you, Leona?"

"I don't suppose you have a few units of packed cells stashed away somewhere, do you?" Leona bent over the table as she pulled a suture and deftly tied it off. She snipped the thread and started dressing the wound.

Cassie gave her a wan smile but kept her distance, as Leona was masked, and Cassie didn't want to pass on an infection or anything. "I wish I did." She gestured to the man. "Is he going to live?"

Leona taped the dressing down then stood back with a sigh. "I have no idea. He needs to be in a trauma unit at a big hospital being treated by trauma surgeons, not one old ob-gyn who's working in a farm shed."

"I'd say he's lucky he's not in a patch of weeds in the forest." Cassie crossed her arms. It wasn't right that Leona should feel she wasn't enough. She was more than this man deserved.

"Oh, I know. He could have it worse, but I still wish I had more. Not just for him but especially for Vivian."

"She's resting comfortably for now. I just finished bathing her, and now Dexter and the kids are with her."

"Good." Leona stripped off her gloves and gown, tossing

the gloves in a bucket of soapy water and the gown in a larger bucket of soapy water.

Even though the gloves were normally disposable, none were thrown out unless they were torn. They were washed and then dried on a couple of mannequin hands Leona had taken from a clothing store before Cassie had met her. It made for a creepy display when she had the hands standing in a row on the back shelf with various colored gloves drying. When they were dry, she'd put them in a separate box. While they were "clean," they weren't hospital-grade clean, and Leona used them when she tended to the animals, as she was the closest they had to a veterinarian.

Cassie looked at the pale man on the table. "Is he going to stay here?"

Leona tilted her head and lifted a shoulder. "Well, not here on this table, but yes, he'll have to stay here in the clinic until he's well enough to leave. In fact, if you could get Noah and Ethan, I think between the four of us, we can get him moved to the other bed."

That would officially fill all of the beds in the clinic. "What if one of us needs that bed?"

Cassie heard the resentment in her own voice but couldn't help it.

Leona raised an eyebrow. "If that becomes the case, we'll deal with it then. I'm sure we can figure out something." She crossed her arms and leveled her gaze at Cassie for a long moment.

Cassie shifted her feet and felt compelled to explain. "I mean, this guy shot at us, and now we're going to take care of him? Feed him? Go to all of this trouble to save a bad man?"

"We don't know what he was like before. The virus brought out the best in some men, probably men like Noah, and perhaps brought out the worst in others, like this man. In these times, with so few of us left, I'd like to give him the benefit of the doubt. In his mind, maybe he was protecting his family."

Cassie didn't totally buy the argument, but she kept her thoughts to herself for the moment. Leona was always kind, but Cassie couldn't help feeling like she was a teenager again, and Leona was her mom scolding her. She conceded that Leona was much less severe, but the feeling was still there. So instead of arguing back, Cassie nodded and said, "I'll go find the other two."

"Thank you."

She found Noah scrubbing out the back of the truck. The water ran pink from the bed as he sluiced more from the tailgate with a fat sponge. "Yikes. What a mess."

Noah glanced at her and nodded. "Yep, but I can't let it sit. Already, flies were all over the blood when I came back."

Cassie shuddered at the image that put in her mind. She'd seen too many flies on too many bodies. "Do you think when you're finished, you could help me, Leona, and probably Ethan move the injured man to the other bed in the clinic?"

Noah grimaced. "Yeah, of course."

She noticed the grimace and a set to his jaw. "What's wrong?"

He tossed the sponge into a bucket behind him and picked up a towel scrap to dry the bed. She spotted another scrap and grabbed it to give him a hand.

"I guess I'm having second thoughts about bringing him back here."

"You and me both." Cassie blotted a pinkish puddle near the edge of the bed. Already, her scrap was almost soaked.

"But what was I supposed to do? Those kids weren't going to leave him... at least not the boy. I haven't figured out the girl yet. And I couldn't leave the kids there, could I?"

He was looking for reassurance that he'd done the right thing, and Cassie nodded. "Of course not."

And as soon as the words were out of her mouth, she knew it was true and admitted it to Noah. "I'd have done the same thing. However, that's not going to make it any easier on Dexter and Vivian's kids to accept him. I hate to be the one to explain it all to Dexter."

Noah rested his hands on his waist and scuffed a toe through the gravel, avoiding Cassie's gaze. "Yeah, I'm not looking forward to that conversation." He sighed. "I plan to talk to him after I'm done cleaning the truck. He has enough to worry about, so I didn't want to tell him when we first arrived. He has to know now, though, what with the guy right there in the clinic." Noah sucked in the corner of his lip, biting it for a second, his brow furrowed. "I hope he doesn't hate me for it, but just between you and me, I didn't think the man would survive." He shook his head and gave a wry chuckle. "Leona is damn good at her job. Maybe too good."

"I know. I'm not exactly thrilled that we have to care for him now. We have to feed him and his kids. That's going to be a strain."

"I'll make another supply run tomorrow."

"Another run would be good. If you can find some more cooking oil, or shortening, that would be great."

"I'll put them both on the shopping list." He sent Cassie a quick smile. Then his smile faded. "The last thing I want to do is cause anyone else hardship because of what I did."

She threw up her hand, palm out. "Whoa, stop right there. You didn't do anything wrong. You couldn't leave that man there. We can't ignore those who need help—as long as it's reasonably safe to do so. To do otherwise could launch us down a slippery slope where we stay too insular. I don't know about you, but I hope there are other survivors. We'll just have to be careful, obviously. What was the point of surviving the virus if we lose our humanity?"

Cassie knew they needed supplies but hated when anyone went on a supply expedition, so she could scarcely believe what she was thinking of doing. After her scare when she and the kids had their terrifying encounter with the man who had shot at them before she'd met Ethan or Noah, she volunteered to stay back with all of the young children and cook a big meal for their return. Now she realized she hadn't been fair to the others. They shouldn't have had to take all the chances. Vivian hadn't ever acted afraid. She'd laugh her big laugh and give Cassie a wink as she gave the men a hard time when they got clothes that fit only them and forgot to get dish soap. Tears welled in Cassie's eyes. She'd better hear that laugh again, or that injured man would wish Leona wasn't so damn good at her job. Cassie blinked hard and pretended she got water in her eye from the truck bed.

A few times, Leona had gone along on the excursions, too, and she never seemed to be afraid. Her knowledge was invaluable in building up the clinic's resources, and she was the only one qualified to know the most important medical supplies that they could feasibly work with. She never failed to come back with something.

Cassie felt proud of how professional the former shed looked, even though it seemed silly to be proud of it. But they had all worked hard, and just knowing that they had health care available brought a little peace of mind. It was a far cry from the filthy building they'd discovered when they had first arrived. Now, it was her time to contribute.

"I'll go with you tomorrow."

"What about the kids?"

"I'm sure Ethan will keep an eye on them. They know where they can go and where they can't, but most of the time, they follow Ethan around anyway. Especially Milo."

"I thought you preferred to stay here?"

"I do, but I can't stay here forever, and it would be better to have Ethan here watching the farm. Dexter is going to be distracted. Jalen too."

"The kid is developing into a crack shot." Pride ebbed in Noah's voice.

"He's way better than I am."

"Besides, with Vivian injured and Leona busy, you'll need a woman to help. I want to find some baking items, and the kids could use some winter clothes, if we can find them."

"I can do all of that." Noah crossed his arms. "I'm not a baker, but I'm a pretty good chef. I think I can manage to find some spices or baking powder."

"Come on, Noah. You know that isn't what I meant." He was an excellent chef, even in these rustic conditions. He could make even beef jerky into a gourmet meal or, at least, a tasty meal.

He tilted his head, conceding her point. "Yeah, I do. And

you'll probably go faster than Ethan. He's a great kid, but he does tend to linger over items that aren't quite necessary." Noah looked to be stifling a laugh, and Cassie decided she was better off not knowing what he was talking about.

She noted the sun dipping farther in the west, pink streaks hitting the easternmost clouds. Soon the streaks would slide west. "I think we better get back to the clinic and help Leona move that man. She needs to get some food and rest."

Noah nodded. "Yeah. I'll be there in a minute."

"I'm going to go find Ethan and send him to the clinic. Then, I'll round up the little ones to head up to the house and get ready for bed before it gets too dark."

Just a few months ago, she'd have had to supervise their bedtime routine, but things were different now. Bella and Milo still acted like the young children they were, of course, but they followed directions better and seemed more self-sufficient. She guessed it was the complete change in lifestyle, and they'd had a lot more freedom on the farm. Before, they were never out of her sight, but after the virus, she'd had to leave them alone to get food. Now, they ran around the farm while she did chores. She couldn't watch them every second, and not surprisingly, they had become more independent.

Cassie found the kids and Ethan rounding up the goats to put in their pen and sent Ethan to the clinic.

With a hand on each of her children's heads, she gently nudged them toward the house. "Wash up and get ready for bed. I'll be up shortly. I have to help Leona in the clinic for a minute. No candles! If you hurry, there will be plenty of light to change by."

Milo's shoulders sagged. He'd been caught with matches once already.

"What about me? Can I see my mom now?" Ava held Cassie's hand.

"I'm sure you can, for a minute. Your mom will want you to get a good night's sleep, though. Then I'll take you up to the house with me."

10

Noah trudged up the drive and around back to the clinic. He paused outside. It was strange to see the bright glow of electric lights inside. While they had some bright battery-powered LEDs in the house, it wasn't the same warm glow as the incandescent bulb that shined above the door of the shed. It was actually not very bright, but the soft yellow light felt welcoming and familiar. The generator was behind the building, and he made a mental note to check to see if it needed to be topped up. Now that surgery was finished, it looked like Leona had turned off everything that wasn't necessary. His hand was on the knob to turn it when the door opened, and he found himself face-to-face with Dexter.

"Oh, Noah. I was just coming to find you." Dexter's voice sounded tired, but Noah didn't detect any anger.

"I was doing the same—but for you, of course."

Dexter made a come-with-me motion.

Noah looked beyond Dexter inside to the clinic. Leona still needed his help, but the last thing he wanted to do was put off Dexter so he could help move the man who had shot Dexter's wife.

"Uh... I'll be with you in a minute. I have to see Leona about something."

"If it's to help move that man, we already did it. Me, Jalen, and Ethan."

"Oh. Ethan was here already?" He didn't think he'd taken that long finishing cleaning the back of the truck, but his feet had felt leaden on his way up the drive. Embarrassed, he coughed and rubbed the back of his neck. "Sorry, I was supposed to do that. I was cleaning the truck." He didn't go into details.

"Come on, man. I'm hungry." Hands shoved in his front pockets, Dexter headed toward the still smoldering fire. "Ethan said he left me some soup keeping warm on the back of the rack."

Noah's stomach growled, and he realized how hungry he was.

Dexter slanted him a glance. "Hopefully there's enough for both of us."

Too weary to make small talk, Noah ambled alongside Dexter, but when they got to the fire, he motioned for the other man to sit while Noah dished up the soup. A loaf of bread wrapped in a damp cloth sat on a second tier above the fire. Too far from the heat to bake but still close enough to stay warm and, with the damp towel, moist, he knew it would be delicious.

He carved off a couple of thick slices and handed one, along with a generously filled bowl of soup, to Dexter, wondering about the variety of soup they were going to be eating. He sniffed it and swirled it but wasn't able to discern the flavor. He glanced at the discarded pile of empty cans set away from the fire. Beans, beef vegetable soup, and chicken noodle. It looked like Ethan had mixed the soups. The kid wasn't a picky eater, that was for sure.

Noah lifted the lid of the bean pot, but it had only a few beans stuck to the side. The rest must have been given to the kids. He didn't mind, and he wasn't sure Dexter would even notice. The soup and bread would be good enough tonight. He wondered if Cassie had eaten and decided he'd throw on a few more cans to heat up for her and Leona before he ate his own. He reached into the box of canned goods they'd taken to leaving at the fire. It was easier than dragging them out every meal. He found a can of chicken and rice and another of cream of chicken and shrugged. One was clear and one was creamy, but they should still be tasty.

Noah almost laughed as he thought about the meals he'd created not more than six months ago. After leaving the military, he'd vowed he'd never eat food out of a can again or, even worse, an MRE, but here he was, not only eating it but looking forward to it and serving it to someone else.

Settling into a chair, Noah dipped the bread into the soup and took a bite. Ethan's combo was damn good. Or maybe he was just hungrier than he thought. He took a second bite then broached the subject he'd been avoiding before Dexter brought it up.

"I'm sorry I brought that man here, Dexter. I didn't know what to do. Those kids were there, and the boy was almost crying..."

Dexter didn't reply for a long time, and the bread in Noah's mouth seemed to turn to sawdust as he waited.

"I'm tired, Noah. I'm too damned tired to be angry. I hate

that man and will always hate him, but Vivian would be the first to tell me that hatred is wasted energy. I just don't have any energy to waste right now." Dexter dunked his bread and let his drip into the bowl, staring at it for the space of several breaths before he finally took the bite.

"How's she doing?" Noah gave himself a mental kick for not asking sooner.

Dexter shrugged. "Leona says the next twenty-four hours will be the most important. She's worried about her kidneys being damaged from shock and loss of blood. And it's not like we have a blood bank available, so that's a big worry too." He ate the last bite of his bread and tilted the bowl, downing the rest of the contents. "And she may lose the baby."

Hot soup sloshed over Noah's hand as he almost dropped his bowl, and his bread fell on the ground. "Ow! Dammit." He set the soup on the upended log beside him that served as a table. After wiping his hand on his jeans, he turned to Dexter. "Baby?"

Dexter nodded. "Only Leona knew. We were going to announce it in a few days but wanted to make sure first."

Noah nodded. At a loss for words, he picked his bowl up again but didn't make a move to eat. Congratulations were on the tip of his tongue, but if the pregnancy was now in jeopardy, it was hardly the sentiment Dexter would probably want to hear right now. He shifted the soup to his left hand, reached out, and gave Dexter's shoulder a light squeeze.

Sighing, Dexter set his empty bowl on the seat beside him and leaned forward, his hands clasped. "I don't even know what we were thinking, bringing a new baby into this crazy world. But it probably happened before the virus hit or maybe the week we were holed up in our house. After that, we used protection. When she missed her first... period... we just assumed it was all the stress, you know?" He glanced at Noah and didn't seem to expect an answer, but Noah gave him a nod anyway.

Spoon in hand, Noah dipped into the soup again, blew on it out of habit, and ate it. Dexter's words about bringing a baby into this world pinged around in his mind. He understood where the other man was coming from. It was bad enough that the little ones would hardly remember what the world was like before. What kind of existence would a new baby have? There were no schools, no hospitals, no society to speak of. Just a handful of survivors living in someone else's house, hoping to make it through the winter.

Dexter leaned back, his voice weary. "What am I gonna do without Vivian, Noah?" He had a hand shielding his eyes, rubbing them with his thumb and fingers.

Noah wished he had a ton of experience to call upon, but he hadn't lost anyone close to him. There was his brother, but they hadn't been close in years. It hurt to lose him, but it wasn't the same thing. He thought back to his days in Afghanistan. He'd lost someone there, and it had been his fault. He should have suspected the broken-down truck in the middle of nowhere was a trap, but he'd been so exhausted then. All he'd seen was the woman pleading with them to help. It wasn't until after the truck exploded that he'd realized the "woman" had actually been a man. There was just enough left of him to identify his gender. Adam hadn't been so lucky. The truck he'd been driving was behind Noah's and took the brunt of the explosion. Noah had led him to his death.

They'd gone through basic training together, shipped out

together, and Noah had gone to Adam's family's house during more military leaves than he could count. He'd had no real family to go back to, and Adam had known that. He, Miguel, and Adam had been dubbed The Three Musketeers by others at the base. As his throat squeezed tight, Noah remembered Adam's young son and recalled what Adam's wife had said to him at the funeral. That Adam's life hadn't been in vain. He had left a son to carry on. That son would be around ten now, if he had survived the virus. Maybe it was all pointless. If the son was dead, which he probably was, then Adam's death had been in vain. Maybe all of their lives were meaningless.

Ethan, head down, walked toward the clinic from the goat shed, and Noah was ashamed of his negative thoughts. That kid had endured more than all of them but still found a way to smile and help everyone. "If you have to, you'll go on because you have to. You have to think about Ava and Jalen. They'll need you more than ever. And the baby... not much we can do except pray. I've only known you and Vivian for a few months now, but I never met a stronger woman. If anyone will survive, it'll be her."

They fell into silence, watching the last embers pop and spark. Noah finally stood and scattered the embers so they'd burn out more quickly. It hadn't rained in a week or more, and the ground was getting dry.

"I expected Leona to be out to get a bite, but she must not have had a chance yet. So what do you say we take the soup and bread to her?" Noah found a pot holder on the cooking table behind the fire and grabbed the pot. "Want to get a few bowls? I don't know where Cassie went. Maybe she sneaked in when we weren't looking. She was going to meet me there."

Dexter didn't reply, but he stood and found several clean

bowls stacked on the table and propped the end of the bread in the top one. "I got the knife."

Noah shot him a look. While it was a sharp knife, it was a bread knife with a blunt end. If Dexter had ideas of killing the man in the clinic, he'd have to do it by sawing him to death. The picture in his mind forced an involuntary snort of laughter.

"What's so funny?"

Noah explained what had popped into his head.

Dexter shook his head, but a slow smile spread across his face. "You're sick, man. Damn..."

Noah dropped off the soup but stayed only long enough to make sure everyone got something to eat. Cassie and Ethan were there, too, with Cassie caring for Vivian while Leona and Jalen ate. Cassie insisted the slice of bread she'd had was plenty.

He left the clinic, topped up the generator, and checked their fuel stores. Fuel was one of his biggest worries. For now, there were plenty of vehicles to get gasoline from, and they'd even figured out how to use the emergency pump at the nearest gas station, but he knew gasoline degraded over time. He didn't know what they'd do when they ran out of usable gasoline.

He walked around the farmyard, aided by the floodlight, which only operated when the generator was running. Noah wasn't sure how much he liked having the light. While it certainly aided in seeing things, it felt harsh and unnatural. They had all been getting used to softer light, using a camping lantern or, some nights, finding their way by moonlight. In the mostly open countryside, moonlight was often all that was needed. They didn't walk around much at night anyway, but a few nights had been too hot to sleep inside the old farmhouse, and they'd slept in the side yard. A few other times, they'd had to investigate a disturbance in the henhouse or with the goats.

Worse than the light, though, was the constant noise of the generator. It wasn't so bad inside the clinic, but out here, its constant drone grated on Noah's nerves. While exhausted, he was still too keyed up to think about sleeping and moved to sit on the back stoop of the farmhouse.

This had to be one of the longest days he'd ever experienced. It was hard to believe that only twelve hours ago, they'd all headed out to pick berries on what began as one of their most carefree days since... well, since the whole apocalypse had begun.

The door behind him opened, and before he could stand, there came a small screech.

Noah didn't know who was more startled, him or Ruby. She almost fell back into the house, and he caught the screen door just before it closed on her shins.

"Hey... hey, it's just me." Noah put out a hand, which the girl hesitantly took. As soon as she regained her balance, she pulled her hand from his as if his palm had scalded her.

"Thanks... mister." Ruby scooted to the far corner of the small covered stoop, hemmed in by a railing around three sides.

"I'm Noah." He thought he'd told her his name already,

but in all the confusion, he couldn't blame her for forgetting it. "Where are you going?"

"Nowhere! I wasn't sleepy." She crossed her thin arms over her chest. "I thought I'd walk around."

Noah hadn't meant to sound like he was implying she was doing anything nefarious, but her tone in reply had sounded defensive. He glanced up to see only a sliver of moon in the sky. "If you go beyond the floodlight, it'll be pitch-black in an area you're not familiar with."

Her gaze darted beyond him, scanning the fields cloaked in darkness. She shrugged.

"Why don't you have a seat and talk with me?" Noah indicated a spot beside him on the wide stoop.

Her eyes widened as she shook her head. "Uh no, I'll just go back inside."

Noah swore to himself. Obviously, she was terrified of him. He nodded. "That's fine. I only thought we could get to know each other. I don't even know how old you are." He was sitting on the stoop sideways with his back against a porch column.

She straightened. "I'm thirteen."

Noah tried not to let his doubt show. She was either a very late bloomer or wasn't a day over eleven. "That's great. Ethan is about fourteen, and Jalen is twelve, I think." He wasn't positive of the boys' ages, as he didn't know their birthdays, and they might have had one since he'd met them. He was pretty sure Vivian would have let everyone know when Jalen's birthday was, as she kept track of the days, for the most part, and had a calendar. He should suggest they all write in their birthdays on it so they'd know.

He became lost in his thoughts and almost forgot about Ruby until she muttered, "Luke's fourteen too."

She'd moved forward on the porch and stood leaning against the column opposite Noah's, still with her arms crossed but not as tightly.

"That's great. We need strong, young men to help with all the work to prepare for the winter." Noah smiled up at her.

Her arms tightened even as she lifted her chin. "I'm strong."

"I'm sure you are." She looked like a toothpick, but she'd survived somehow, so he knew she wasn't weak. He wasn't sure why she still sounded defensive, only now there was a hint of fear in her voice.

"I can haul water, and I don't mind butchering animals. I'm not much of a cook yet, but I'm learning. And I don't eat much, and I can sleep anywhere—"

"Hey, slow down." Noah stood and reached for her shoulder to reassure her, but she flinched. He immediately pulled back his hand, letting it fall to his side. She was probably afraid to get too close in case he had the virus. He'd learned those who were in the thick of the disaster had developed an aversion to close contact.

"I'm sure you can do all of those things, and while we have enough food, everyone gets a fair share. Beds aren't an issue either. When we need one, we just go find one in an empty house, but I'm not sure why you're telling me all of this."

She shrugged, her mouth set in a thin line.

Noah sighed. "I'd assumed you ate with the others before I did, but I need to ask, did you get any soup and bread? If not, we can find something else for you. I'm sure we have something we can make that doesn't need cooking. I know we have peanut butter."

"I ate with Ethan and the little kids. Thank you."

"Good. Let me show you where you can sleep. There's a pull-out sofa bed in the den downstairs. Luke might have to bunk on the floor until we can get another bed in the next few days, though."

"What about...?" She tipped her chin toward the clinic.

"He'll stay in the clinic for now."

"What about when he gets better?"

Noah wasn't sure the man would recover from his wound, but he tried to stay positive. "We'll deal with it in the next few days. Right now, we're all exhausted." He walked past her, careful not to come into contact, and waved for her to follow him.

A few LED lights stuck to the wall lit the way downstairs, and he tapped one on the wall inside the den. "It's a little dusty down here, but it should do for tonight. There's another light right there." He pointed to one on the end table beside the sofa then moved to pull the bed out. They had only used the bed a few times. The girls had slept down here one night. Noah smiled as he recalled the night. Ava and Bella had treated it like a little girls' sleepover, complete with shrieks and laughter well into the night.

The blankets they'd used were still bunched in the bed, and he shook them out. They looked clean. Glancing at the girl beside him, he was more worried about her getting the blankets dirty than the other way around.

Noah showed her the bathrooms. "We keep a few buckets of water in here to flush the toilets, but use only what you need. To save on hauling water, we generally don't flush pee, just... just the other."

"Ethan told me already. And said not to use the green bucket for flushing."

"That's right. We have clean, boiled water for washing. You use the ladle and pour a little in the sink with the stopper in then wash, a little more for rinsing. Once a week, we try to get in a bath. However, we have a rainwater shower rigged up on the other side of the house. It's cold but great for getting clean between hot baths."

She nodded, her gaze sliding away from him. Noah realized how awkward all of this must be for her. He should have asked Cassie to explain all of this, but Cassie had been in the clinic. While he'd heard her come in while he was giving his little tour, he'd also heard her talking to the kids upstairs. He couldn't catch what she was saying, but from her tone, it sounded as if she was comforting them.

"Anyway, that should do it for now," he said as he showed her back to the den. "I should probably go find Luke and give him the tour too."

Noah headed for the stairs but turned back to see Ruby standing hesitantly in the doorway. *Poor kid.* He wondered what horrors she'd been through.

11

E than scattered feed for the chickens and gathered eggs. He left the eggs near the firepit and then headed to the goat pen, searching for Dino as he went. Last night, all the commotion had unsettled the animal, and he'd refused to come in the house to sleep but had curled up on the porch. When Ethan had first awakened, the dog had been there, but while Ethan did his chores, the dog was gone. He must have smelled a rabbit or something.

"Dino!" He put his fingers in his mouth and gave a shrill whistle. It was a good thing they'd left the dog at the farm yesterday. He could have been shot. Ethan couldn't imagine what he'd do without the dog. He laughed as Dino raced from the woods, ears flopping, tongue lolling. Ethan bent a knee and put his arms around the dog, burying his nose in the soft, if somewhat stinky, fur. "Whew! You need a bath!"

Dino panted, his tail thumping. The sound of the back-door screen slamming made the dog start, and he looked back at the house. "It's okay, boy. I know these new people are kind of scary, but the kids seem okay. I don't know about the man, but I'll protect you. Don't worry." He dropped a kiss on top of Dino's head. "Let's get the goats out."

After filling the water trough for the goats and cleaning the pens, Ethan had Dino stay with the livestock, promising to bring him his breakfast soon, then headed back to the house. His stomach rumbled, and he glanced at the cookfire. They'd rounded up a nice smoker from a nearby home, and already, smoke was escaping around the edges. He wondered what was inside. The cookfire was cold, though, so he guessed breakfast was going to be simple.

As he opened the door to enter the farmhouse, he nearly crashed into Leona as she came out with a tray. Leona had a pillow clenched between her elbow and her side, and she almost lost it when the tray teetered.

"Oh, excuse me!" Ethan reached to steady the tray in the doctor's hands, noting the pitcher of water and a sleeve of crackers. "Here, let me carry this for you."

"Thank you. In fact, since you're here, I think I'll head in and grab a few more items."

Ethan tipped his head toward the clinic. "You want me to take this on over?"

"Yes, please. And if you could give each of them a glass of water and a few crackers, that would be wonderful."

"Sure." Ethan made his way, also noting two small bowls of blueberries, each covered by a napkin. He opened the door and caught it on his hip as he made sure the door didn't hit the tray as he entered. He set the tray on a table beside an empty tray already there. He divided the crackers and poured two glasses of water. Adding a bowl of blueberries to the second tray, he took the first to Vivian.

She lay still, and he paused a few feet away and bit his lip.

He didn't want to wake her, but Leona had asked him to give her the tray. He cleared his throat. "Uh, Vivian?"

Her eyelids fluttered, and she turned her head, squinting at him. A skylight and two windows let in natural light, but it was still fairly dim inside. "Hey, Ethan. Is that for me?"

"Yeah. Leona asked me to give it to you."

She started to sit up then grimaced and lay back. Ethan set the tray on a rolling table beside the bed. The table had been one of Leona's acquisitions from the hospital. "Here, let me help you."

"There's a crank on the end of the bed. If you turn it, it'll bring the head up a bit."

Ethan found the crank and gave it a few turns until Vivian waved her hand. "That's good, hon."

He put the table in front of her and made sure she could reach everything. She still had an IV in one hand, and her skin had a slight gray cast. Her lips looked pale.

"How are you feeling?"

"Like I got run through a meat grinder and then put together again at the other side." She chuckled but then groaned.

Ethan looked for something he could do to help her, but there was nothing. He pointed to the blueberries. "There's a bowl of the berries we picked yesterday." Then it was his turn to groan but only inwardly. What a stupid thing to say, as if she was blind, not injured.

"So there is." She tugged the napkin off the bowl. "They better be the best damned blueberries I ever ate. I sure did pay a lot for them."

Ethan smiled as she ate one but then frowned when she

only took a nibble on one cracker and sipped the water before lying back, apparently exhausted.

A deeper groan filled the clinic then a loud grunt and swearing. Ethan turned. There was a divider between the beds, so he had to back up and look around to spot the other man. He'd heard his name was Daniel.

Vivian turned toward the divider, but he couldn't read her expression.

"I gotta give him his breakfast too. Do you need anything else?"

With a shake of her head, Vivian closed her eyes. "No. I'm just going to rest a bit."

"Okay. Leona should be here in second. She just went back in the house to get some things."

"I'm fine. That Leona, she needs to get some sleep. She was here all night long and..." Her voice trailed off, alarming Ethan, until he saw her breathing deepen into sleep.

Reluctantly, he took the second tray around the divider. He dropped it on Daniel's table, not really meaning for it to sound as loud as it did.

"What the hell?" Daniel's eyes flew open and found Ethan. "Who are you? Where am I?" He rose up on one elbow. "Where's my son? And the girl? What have you done with them?"

"You mean Luke and Ruby?"

He nodded, his jaw flexing, but Ethan couldn't tell if it was from pain or anger. He backed away from the table. "They're probably up at the house. I get up early and let the goats out. I didn't see anyone else except Leona so far this morning."

"Leona? That the lady who's been poking and prodding

me all night long?"

Ethan stood tall, shoulders back. "She's Dr. Leona, and she saved your life."

"Humph." He glanced at the tray. "What's that?"

"Food. Crackers, berries, and water."

"It ain't much, is it? You guys don't have food here?"

"We got—have—food. But this is what the doctor asked me to give you."

In spite of his grumbling about the lack of food, Daniel only picked at the tray before he, too, fell back in exhaustion. "I don't feel so good."

Ethan darted an eye toward the door, hoping Leona would appear at any second. When Daniel started retching, Ethan grabbed a gray plastic bucket thing from the end of the bed and handed it to the man. "Here." Cringing as Daniel vomited in the bucket, Ethan scurried backward, almost tripping on a folding chair in his haste. Puking always grossed him out, but at least his prior encounters with it had been family. His little sister had once vomited all over him while he'd been playing a video game. At the time, he'd thought it was the worst thing in the world to ever happen to him. While he'd hollered about how disgusting it had been, his mom had cleaned Amber and scolded him for being so harsh with her. After she had been bathed and dressed in fuzzy pajamas with feet in them, she had toddled to him, her eyes large. He'd melted and even risked getting puked on again as he'd cuddled her. Ethan blinked the memory away. This guy wasn't his adorable little sister. He was a coward who shot innocent people from a distance. He didn't deserve to even get handed a bucket, but it was either that or clean the mess from the floor, and Ethan didn't want to risk it.

The door opened, and Leona entered, her arms full of towels, blankets, sheets, and a few other items. "Oh good. You're here. He's getting sick." Ethan nodded to Daniel.

"I was afraid of that." Leona could barely see over the items, and Ethan moved to take the stack from her, glad for something to do. He set the stack on the table where he'd divided the breakfasts.

She squirted a pump of sanitizing foam on her hand from a jug on the table. Ethan gave a guilty look to his own hands. He hadn't seen the jug when he'd entered. He plunged his hands into his pockets.

"Could you wet a washcloth, Ethan? There's a clean one in that pile."

Ethan nodded and sneaked a pump from the jug, rubbing it in as best he could so he wouldn't soil the cloth with his hands. Not that he cared about Daniel, but Leona would see the dirt, and he didn't want to receive one of her looks. He took a pitcher of water and filled a bowl beside it, dipping the cloth into the lukewarm contents. Stepping back, he watched as she helped Daniel clean his face and hands, wondering how she could be so kind to him after what he'd done.

Leona glanced his way and must have sensed his revulsion, because she shrugged. "I don't judge. Not here. Not when I'm working."

Ethan buried his hands in his pockets again and shrugged. "I can't help it. I was just talking to Vivian, and she... she's not—" He wanted to say she wasn't the same bubbly woman he'd come to know, and that he was worried about her, but his words failed him. He didn't normally talk about other kids' moms. He'd never worried about one before, but she and Cassie had come to mean a lot to him. If anything happened to either one, he didn't know what he'd do.

"I know. She's running a fever."

Ethan threw a look toward Vivian's bed, even though it was hidden behind the divider. "A fever? That's bad, right?"

"It's not good, but it's to be expected after being shot. I have given her some antibiotics, and hopefully, she'll be able to fight off it off." Leona wrung the washcloth out and gave it to Daniel. "Here. Next time you can clean yourself up. You look to be doing better today. A little later, we might even get you up to sit in a chair for a while."

"Oh no... I'm in too much pain to get up. I need something."

"I'll see what I can give you. It'll be a few minutes."

Daniel nodded and closed his eyes, but his mouth remained set in a hard line, his jaw clenched. Ethan felt the tiniest prick of sympathy.

Leona dumped the water and rinsed the bowl, leaving it upside down in a dish rack on the counter. "Do you think you can help me with Vivian, Ethan?"

"Sure. I guess. I'm not sure how much help I can be, but I'll try."

"Let's get some of these clean towels, and I heated some water. I want to bathe her."

Ethan gulped. "Bathe her?"

Cracking a smile, Leona said, "It's okay. I'll keep her covered. I just need you to help me turn her and hold her on her side. You can look away while I wash her back. It's no big deal. Consider yourself a nurse's aide now."

"Great." Ethan groaned but squared his shoulders. Here was another opportunity to earn his keep.

After he'd helped Leona, and it hadn't been as gross as he'd expected, Ethan headed to the house. The smell of baking bread drew him like an ant to a picnic. He bounded up the steps, and just as he'd hoped, he found racks with naan bread cooling in the kitchen. His favorite. It had become a staple because it was easier to make than a whole loaf, according to Cassie. He washed his hands in a basin and dried them on a towel. "Cassie?"

His stomach rumbled, and he spotted a pot of what looked like jam on the counter. Blueberry jam. "Cassie?"

"Is everything okay?" Cassie came from the back hallway, wiping her hands on a towel. She wore her usual green apron. Splotches of flour speckled the front with a few darker stains scattered about.

"Yeah. I just wondered if I could have a few pieces of bread?"

"Of course. It's still warm, and I cooked down a batch of blueberries to spread on it like jam. It's still warm too."

Ethan sat at the table and practically inhaled his first piece then slowed down to savor the second. Cassie was mixing another batch of dough, but he wasn't certain if it was more naan or regular bread.

Swallowing a bite, Ethan cocked his head. It was so quiet. "Where is everyone?"

"Well, Milo and Bella are around here somewhere. They may have gone to collect the eggs."

"I already did."

"Oh. Well, I guess they're playing down by the creek."

The creek was a thin trickle of water that ran across a corner of the property. Sometimes the kids would catch frogs or even the occasional crawfish. Bella probably had a few interesting bugs in a jar. She had no fear of them, which seemed weird to Ethan. Girls usually hated bugs.

"Jalen, Ava, and Dexter are still sleeping. They were up late last night, worrying about Vivian." Cassie frowned, a faint crease in her brow. "I'm worried about her too."

Ethan nodded. "She's getting antibiotics for a fever."

Turning to look at him, Cassie paused kneading the dough. "She is? How do you know?"

"I was helping Leona in the clinic for a little bit. She said I was her nurse's aide now." Ethan pretended nonchalance, but Cassie tilted her head, a smile tilting her lips.

"Really? Nice work, Ethan."

Ethan shrugged and took a large bite of the naan, chewing for several moments before managing to ask, "What about the new kids? And Noah?"

It struck him that he hadn't seen Noah anywhere.

"Noah took them back to their old camp to get their belongings. They didn't have time yesterday to get them."

"They're staying here for good?" Ethan downed the last bite of naan and looked longingly at another piece but turned his head away. He couldn't be a pig. Everyone needed to eat.

Cassie laughed and snatched a piece from the cooling rack. "Here. It's best while still warm. Don't worry. I'm making a lot of them today. Enough to last for a few days, at least."

"Do we still have peanut butter?"

"Sure. Quite a bit, actually. It seems every house has peanut butter in their pantry, and it has a long shelf life. Not sure what we'll do when it finally runs out. Grow peanuts?"

"That would be cool." Ethan went to the pantry and took

a jar, wondering how hard it would be to grow them. He'd never thought about it before.

"I want to get this naan made as fast as I can so I can help Leona more. She's exhausted."

"Is that why you're making so much?"

"Yep. I can do a bunch today, and we'll be set for a bit."

"What can I do to help?"

Cassie wiped her hands on her apron and looked around. "I'm going to need a lot of wood or charcoal to get these blueberries made into jam and canned. Do you think you could make sure there's plenty of both down at the cookfire?"

"Absolutely." Ethan hopped up and paused before leaving the kitchen. "Thanks for making the naan. It's my favorite."

Cassie's eyebrows rose in a look of surprise, then she smiled. "Oh... well, you're welcome, Ethan."

Ducking out of the door, Ethan raced across the yard to the woodpile. Charcoal was great, when they could find it, and propane was also good, because it was easy to use only what they needed. Over the last month, they had found a couple of propane grills, but getting the propane was harder. Noah was sure it was out there, but it was no longer at the gas stations. Instead, tanks were scattered in individual homes. Propane must have been one of the dozens of things people had stripped from the stores.

Ethan hadn't paid too much attention, but he remembered his parents fighting about trying to get more flour, yeast, and even toilet paper. The fight stuck in his mind because he was still haunted by the expression on his father's face that day. It had been a mix of fear, panic, and worst of all, resignation.

Grabbing a wheelbarrow, he filled it first with wood from

the woodpile and took it to the cookfire, arranging it so it would burn evenly. Noah had taught him how. Then he looked in the shed for charcoal. They had a dozen bags, which seemed like a lot, but at the rate they went through it, it would be gone in a week at most. Ethan made a note to chop wood this afternoon. It was a never-ending chore, but he was getting pretty good at it now.

As he brought the charcoal back, he spotted Noah's truck rumbling up the drive. He suppressed the urge to run to meet it. He was curious about the other kids, especially now that the shock of yesterday had worn off, but he wanted to play it cool.

Pretending he hadn't noticed them, he emptied half a bag of charcoal in one of the grills then arranged the pieces evenly. He heard someone approaching but continued arranging until he had a good distribution. Finished, he brushed his hands together before turning to see the boy, Luke, standing a little way back.

"Hi. Uh, Noah sent me to help you."

"Help me do what?"

Luke shrugged.

Ethan wiped his palms on his thighs, thinking. Noah was leaving it up to him. Straightening, Ethan nodded. "Yeah. Okay, let's check out the vegetable garden, gather what's ripened, and make sure it's watered and weeded."

Just a few days ago, Vivian had set he and Jalen to the task. They'd groaned but only for a few seconds because Vivian had pointed her finger at them, shaking it with that look in her eye that meant she wasn't going to hear it.

"What about me?" Ruby had approached while Ethan had been thinking.

"I guess you can help too. How old are you?"

"Eleven. Almost twelve... I think."

"You think?"

"I... my birthday is in September. Is it September?"

Ethan wasn't sure, so he shrugged. "Close enough. You can help us. It's hard work, though. You'll have to keep up."

She nodded. "I can work as hard as Luke."

"No, you can't." Luke shook his head and rolled his eyes. "She's a pain in the ass. That's what my dad says."

Ethan looked at the boy. He was probably only a little younger than Ethan's fourteen, but Ethan felt a lot older. He wasn't sure why. "Whatever. I don't really care what your dad says. If she wants to help, that's great. Come on, Ruby."

An hour or so into their task, Jalen joined them. He was there in body, but his mind was clearly on his mom or maybe what happened yesterday. Ethan noticed him stopping several times, lost in thought, his hands gripping the shovel or hoe, whatever he happened to be working with, but he'd stare at the ground.

"Hey, are you doing all right?" Ethan asked in a low voice as he worked beside him.

Jalen shook his head. "I guess. Kind of."

"You don't have to do this, you know. Me, Luke, and Ruby can handle it today."

"Nah, I need something to do. Sorry I'm so useless today."

"No, you're doing great. In fact, why don't you take five? Then I think we're ready to run the water in here."

Jalen nodded. "Okay." Jalen sprawled under the oak tree on the north side of the garden.

"Hey, why is he resting? I want to rest too!" Luke threw his hoe down.

"Pick that back up. The row isn't finished." Ethan took a step toward Luke.

"I'm hot. I want a break."

"You'll get a break when I take one—at the end of this row." Ethan felt his jaw tighten. He'd never been one to confront anyone, but he couldn't back down. Noah put him in charge. Sort of.

Luke glared at him, but when Ethan stared back, Luke's gaze flickered to the clinic. "I want to go see my dad. I'm worried about him."

Ethan wavered.

"My dad's in worse shape than his mom. He almost died!"

Squaring his shoulders, Ethan stepped closer to Luke. "Pick up the hoe and get back to work. If you're going to eat our food, you're going to have to work for it the same as the rest of us."

Luke crossed his arms, his mouth tight but then, with a last hateful look at Ethan, picked up his rake. "Fine. But it's still not fair."

Ethan threw his shovel down, his fists clenched. "*Fair?* Nothing is fair anymore. Not Milo and Bella's dad dying on their front lawn, not Ruby losing her parents. Not me losing my mom, my dad, and even my baby sister. Not Jalen's mom getting shot by your dad for no reason. And none of them shot anybody!"

Luke threw his hands up as if to ward off an attack, his eyes wide as he reeled away from Ethan. "Sorry!"

Ethan took a deep breath and stepped back. He wasn't sure who was more surprised, Luke or himself, that he'd flown into a rage.

"But my dad did have a reason to shoot Jalen's mom."

12

"Cassie... you should have seen it. They were living in complete filth." Noah sipped his coffee as he leaned back against the kitchen counter. Yesterday, he'd noted the squalor, but he'd been concentrating on saving Daniel. Today was an eye-opener. Ruby had only the bare minimum of clothes, and what there was probably hadn't been washed since the virus had decimated the world. The poor girl had only a thin blanket and not even a pillow to sleep on. The only shoes she had were the flip-flops she'd been wearing. Luke hadn't fared much better, but at least he had sturdier clothes and a couple of pairs of shoes.

Daniel had more, but like the kids, everything was caked with dirt and grime. Noah had been tempted to leave it all there. There was no point in bringing it back. It needed to be burned.

"Why were they living like that? There are plenty of empty homes or stores where they could have gathered what they needed." Cassie wrapped the last of the naan in plastic wrap. He counted twelve stacks of ten, which was how she sealed them, but he and the new kids had already eaten several, and the others had probably eaten breakfast this morning too. That was a lot of bread, but he stopped to calculate. Their group had grown by three. They were up to thirteen people now. That meant the bread wouldn't even last three days if they each had a piece with every meal. He made a mental note to check their flour stores. It was probably time to scour some more stores and homes in the area.

"Damn, Cassie. You work too hard. What time did you get up this morning?"

"I don't know. It was still dark for a while, so maybe four —or four thirty?" She wiped the back of her hand across her brow, leaving a faint, floury streak.

"Why don't you go take a nap, and I'll see to the other meals today."

"I thought you were going to be making jerky or something today?" Cassie wiped the counter with a damp cloth and nudged Noah out of the way when she needed to get behind him. He moved but not before giving her a playful nudge back. She blew a strand of hair out of her face and rolled her eyes, but he wasn't fooled. He saw the smile threatening to crack through.

"I am. I can do both, though. Making jerky, after cutting the strips, is mostly a matter of just letting it dry. While it's doing that, I can make a nice stew out of the venison I won't be turning into jerky."

"That sounds delicious." She stilled for a few seconds and glanced around the kitchen. Apparently satisfied that it was clean, she took off her apron and hung it on the back of the door. "I love the idea of a nap, but Leona needs a break in the clinic, and clothes need washing. I have to make jam, vegetables need to be picked—"

"The clothes can wait, and the kids can get the vegetables. I sent Luke and Ruby to help Ethan already. I think I saw Jalen heading that way too."

"But Leona—"

"I agree, Leona needs a break, but why don't you get a quick nap and then spell her? It does no good to anyone if you're exhausted too. And I can spell you both later tonight."

"Really?"

"Really." Noah grabbed a handful of blueberries from one of the bowls on the table. "And tomorrow, we can tackle making jam as a group. It'll be good to teach the kids how it's made."

"That's true." Shoulders sagging, Cassie gave him a wan smile. "Okay. I'm going to rest but no more than thirty minutes. If you don't see me before then, come and get me up."

Noah saluted. "Yes, ma'am."

Cassie started to walk past him but hesitated at his side. "Is this what life it going to be like from now on?"

Noah sighed. "I don't know. I guess we'll get better at all of it as we go along. Humans survived without electricity forever until recently. We can do this."

"But can we do it well?" She leaned against him, and he wrapped an arm around her, pulling her close.

"We're already doing it well. Especially when I compare our setup with what Daniel and those kids had. Shooting him might have been the best thing that happened to him since this all began."

Cassie pulled away. "You can't mean that!"

Noah shrugged. "Well, it would have been better if we could have met under friendly terms, but I don't know how they would have survived the winter."

"I worry about us surviving the winter."

"We will. We're storing away lots of food, and we haven't even begun doing our serious preserving yet. I'm waiting for it to get a little cooler. Provided we get enough game, which I think we will because it seems deer have come out of the woodwork now, we'll have enough set aside to get us through. Add to that the vegetables from the garden and all of the canned and packaged foods we've scavenged. This year will be both the hardest and the easiest. After this, much of the food, except for the canned stuff, that we find in houses will be no good."

"Yeah. Rodents are getting into everything." Cassie shook her head.

"Yep. Which reminds me. I want to find a few kittens to raise to help out with that problem. There are feral cats everywhere, so we just have to keep an eye out and get a few before they are beyond taming."

"Oh, a kitten!"

Her eyes lit up. It had been a long time since Noah had seen that spark. If only he'd have known her love of kittens, he'd have suggested it weeks ago. "Several. While I hope to make them into pets so they'll stick around, I don't think they'll be the pampered house cat you seem to want."

"Not even one of them?" Cassie grinned.

"Well, maybe one. After all, we need to keep the mice from the larder." Noah loved that the old farmhouse had a true larder. He had only heard about them in culinary school, but he'd found that the pantry in the house still had the vents to create the airflow necessary for a true larder like people used over a hundred years ago. It was just one of the features that made this farm so perfect for them.

"Thanks, Noah." Cassie patted his arm as she left.

He wasn't sure if she was thanking him for the future kitten or for suggesting the nap, but her touch seemed to linger long after she had gone upstairs.

"Hey, Noah, we have a basket of new little potatoes, carrots, onions, and even a few turnips."

Noah turned from where he'd been hanging strips of venison to dry in the hot sun. Ethan carried a box his way. Dirt streaked his face, and his hair was matted. He made a mental note to make sure the kid also took a break.

"Turnips? That's fantastic!" He'd noticed turnips in the garden and worried it would be too hot for them, but they were lucky the farmer had planted them at all. While they hadn't had a huge harvest of them then, it had given him the idea to plant more. They were hardy vegetables, and so he had headed to the nearest town and sifted through the remains of a garden shop. Like he'd suspected, there were plenty of packages of turnip seeds. They'd planted some right away.

Ethan plopped the box onto the picnic table and lifted one of the vegetables. "There should be a few more in the next couple of days."

"I'm making a big stew for dinner. I have the venison

already simmering, so if you could do one more thing for me, that would be great."

Ethan shrugged. "Sure. What?"

"Just rinse those in the bowl of water I have over there." Noah tilted his head toward the stump they used as a washstand.

"No problem." Ethan lifted the box once more, and Noah noted how the kid had filled out. He had probably grown an inch or two over the summer, and the physical work had given him muscles that even a football player would envy.

Noah finished hanging the strips of venison and started a thin line of fire below the lines of drying meat. It would not only help them to dry faster, but the smoke would help keep away flies, with the benefit of adding flavor.

Ethan was washing the last carrot when Noah joined him at the washtub. "I lied. I need one more favor." He almost laughed when Ethan's shoulders slumped.

"Okay. What do you need?"

Noah had to give the boy credit. He didn't complain or whine. He just asked what needed to be done. "I think your dog is getting lonely, and I bet both of you could use a good dip in the swimming hole."

Ethan grinned, his slump gone. "Really?"

"Really."

"Should I take the little ones up there too?"

Noah searched Ethan's face. It would probably help if the kids bathed, too, but this was supposed to be fun for him, not another chore. As great as Milo and Bella were, they needed a lot of watching around the pond. "No. You can go on your own and take a break. I don't want to see you back here until dinnertime."

"Yes, sir!" Ethan took off at a run up to the pasture where Dino usually hung out during the daytime.

"Where's he going?"

Noah turned to find Luke watching Ethan, his expression sullen.

"He's going to clean the goat pens. Want to help him?" Noah watched to see Luke's reaction.

"Uh... not really."

Noah tried not to compare Luke's attitude with Ethan's, but it was difficult. He had to remind himself that Luke was still young and had survived horrible conditions. It wasn't fair for Noah to expect him to be eager to help the people who had shot his father.

"Let's see... what can you do instead?" Noah rubbed his chin and looked around. "I got it. You can be my sous-chef."

"Your sue chef? My name's not Sue." His nose wrinkled in distaste.

"No, not Sue but sous." Noah spelled each word aloud. "You can chop all of these vegetables into about one-inch chunks." He slid the carrots, potatoes, and turnips over to one side of the table. He kept the onions and said, "I'll cut the onions."

Noah got Luke a knife and watched as the boy awkwardly attacked the carrots with it. He took it back and showed him how to hold it properly.

Luke resumed chopping, only marginally better.

Noah pulled one of the carrots toward himself and demonstrated how he wanted it cut. "See? Like this." He rapidly reduced the root veggie into neat, even pieces, the knife flashing in the sun.

"Damn. You're good at that!"

It was the first spark of life that Noah had seen in the boy. "Practice like I showed you, and you'll be doing that, too, very soon."

"Who said I wanted to be good at it?"

But Noah felt Luke's eyes on him as Noah cut the onions into uniform pieces, sweeping them into a large bowl. "Add everything you cut to this. I'm going to check the pot to see if it's time to add these to the venison."

When Noah returned from the pot, Luke was still laboring over the turnips. They were harder than the other vegetables, but Luke had managed to get most of them into fairly uniform-sized chunks that would cook evenly. He helped finish the last turnip and swept it all into the bowl. "Good job, Luke."

Luke shrugged, but he watched as Noah added the vegetables to the venison in the water.

"What else is in here?" Luke peered into the large pot simmering on a grate over coals.

"I added a few bay leaves, rosemary, and thyme. Plus salt and pepper."

Luke nodded. "It smells great."

"Thank you."

"How'd you know how to make it? My dad just gave us beef sticks, cheese, and chips, mostly."

"I'm a chef. Or I was, before." Noah gathered scraps to feed to the chickens. They couldn't afford to waste anything.

"A chef? That's a wuss job." Luke smirked.

Noah bit back a retort. He didn't need to justify his career to a pimply-faced teen. "I don't think there are any 'wuss' jobs, but regardless, everyone has to eat, and it's better and safer to eat properly cooked food." He couldn't help adding, "And it certainly beats eating MREs while on deployment."

"What was it like in the Army when the virus started killing everyone?"

"I don't know. I got out eight years go. I became a chef."

"That's cool. I guess."

"Glad it meets your approval." Noah didn't try to keep the sarcasm from his voice, but it must have gone over Luke's head. The boy simply nodded. Noah couldn't help chuckling.

LATER THAT NIGHT, he spelled Cassie, who had, in turn, spelled Leona, in caring for the two patients. Leona had finally had a chance to wash, then eat, and was asleep before the sun went down. She would return around midnight to take care of Vivian and Daniel.

Noah yawned as he tried to read *The Martian*. He loved the book but had read it before, and as good as it was, he could barely keep his eyes open. He'd been up since dawn and hadn't taken a break. With the generator running and electric lights on, he had thought to take advantage of them to read, but he needed to get up and move around or Leona would find him slumped in his chair sound asleep.

He rose and checked on Vivian, who was sleeping comfortably, or so it appeared to Noah. Leona had said she was doing better, with her fever subsiding, so he assumed she was sleeping soundly. He eyed the IV bag. It was about a third full. Leona said she'd be back before it needed changing, according to Cassie. He sure hoped so, but he decided he'd stick around to watch her change it when she got back. It couldn't hurt for more of them to know how to do it.

After carefully tucking a blanket around one of Vivian's feet that had escaped, he moved her cup of water to a place where she could reach it more easily if she woke up thirsty.

Satisfied she was doing as well as possible on his watch, he moved around the divider to check on Daniel. The man had one arm flung over his eyes and his knee bent.

Noah cleared his throat. "Do you need anything, Daniel?"

The arm came down. "Hey, it's Noah, right?"

"Yes." Noah crossed his arms. The light was dim on this side as Noah had turned off the overhead lights over the patients and left the lights on where he was sitting on the other side of the shed they'd converted to the clinic.

"I'm okay. I guess. Getting a little hungry."

"I made stew earlier. Did you get some?"

Daniel sighed. "I had a little, but that witch wouldn't let me eat too much."

Noah's jaw clenched. "Witch?"

Daniel chuckled then winced. "Just my nickname for her. I know she saved my life, but that's her job, right? As a doctor?"

"Her job is whatever she decides it is. She has chosen to treat you. I know you realize things are much different now. Yes, she used to be a doctor before the pandemic, but I think she was retired. She's helping us now because she wants to."

"And so you'll let her live here with you all."

"Whoa... where'd you get that idea?"

"My kid, Luke, says everyone has to earn their keep. That's why he couldn't come and see me earlier today. He was forced to work out in the hot sun. And then he had to cook dinner too."

Noah drew a deep breath, forcing himself to keep calm before he answered. "Luke did the same chores as the other boys his age. Also, Ruby was working too. I didn't hear her complain once."

Daniel's lip curled. "Ruby? She's worthless. I don't know why I let her hang around with Luke. Do you think she steals?"

Surprised, Noah shook his head. "I haven't noticed anything missing."

"Yeah, well, you don't know her well enough yet. I caught her stealing food from us several times, and I'm pretty sure she got away with it other times."

Noah thought of how scrawny the girl was. "Maybe she was hungry. Did you all have a hard time finding food?"

"Well, the meat ran out pretty quick, but that was before Ruby was with us. We've been making do with what we found at a gas station down the road from that blueberry farm."

Noah tried to recall seeing a gas station but couldn't. Of course, it may have been in the opposite direction from where they'd come from. "I see. Well, gas stations have quite a bit of canned goods, I guess."

"Canned goods? And what were we gonna open them with? Our teeth?" Daniel sneered.

"Uh, a can opener?"

"I guess I forgot to pack one when we fled for our lives."

Noah gave his head a little shake and decided to change the subject. "How did Ruby find you?"

"Oh, well, we found her, actually. She had that tent in the woods, and we decided to stay with her and share her food."

"Hold on a minute. Did she invite you to share her food?"

Daniel's eyes narrowed. "I gave her protection. That was the deal. I took a risk to protect her. I could have just left her out there alone, but no, Luke said we should help her. So I did, out of the goodness of my heart."

"I'll bet you did." Noah vowed to get Ruby's version of the story from her before passing judgment, but Daniel sounded like a piece of work.

"I did! I took a risk even though she could have turned into one of the zombies."

Noah took a step back in shock. "Zombies? What the hell are you talking about?"

Grimacing, Daniel tried to hitch himself higher in the bed. "People turned into zombies. I saw it with my own eyes. They'd be laughing and partying, and then they'd bite someone and start eating them."

"You saw people *eating* each other?" Noah raised an eyebrow in disbelief.

"Hell yeah, I did. More than once too. They usually died near their victims, so it was hard to tell, but the zombies had blood around their mouths."

"Look, I'm pretty sure as horrible as the virus is, it didn't turn anyone into zombies." Noah shook his head and stretched, about ready to walk away from this lunatic.

"Are you calling me a liar?" Daniel's tone dropped low as he glared at Noah.

Noah dropped his arms from the stretch and sighed. "I'm saying you're mistaken, but look, I'll let the doctor explain it all to you." He didn't add that he, personally, had no experience with those infected with the virus. He only knew what he'd read in the paper Dexter had given him and from what the others had shared of their experiences. It had been tragic and gruesome, but there had been no hint of zombies.

"The government did this to us, you know. They wanted to control us, but the experiment got out of hand."

Noah waved his hand dismissively. "Yeah. Sure."

"You don't believe me, do you?"

"Look, I was fishing in the woods when the whole thing went down. I can't say what did or didn't happen, but what I can say is that none of the others reported seeing or hearing anything about zombies or that the government infected everyone with the virus."

"They was zombies, and the only thing that would stop them was shooting them dead before they could try to eat me and Luke."

"You shot people?"

"Goddamn right, I did." Daniel crossed his arms.

Noah couldn't believe what he was hearing. The man was certifiable. The next thing, he'd probably tell Noah that gremlins and demons were real too. A horrible thought entered his mind. He forced the question between clenched teeth. "Why did you shoot at us? Why did you shoot Vivian?"

"You all was acting like them. Laughing and shit. I had to protect me and Luke. And she was laughing the loudest."

Noah clenched his fists, his body stiff. "That's crazy."

It took several more deep breaths before he was calm enough to add, "It doesn't look like you need anything, so I'm going to check on Vivian again. I think I heard her moving around." As soon as he said it, he realized he had heard a rustling from Vivian's side of the divider.

"You should thank me! I probably saved everyone's life. I shot the zombie right outta her!"

Noah had turned away and been heading toward Vivian but stopped short at Daniel's outburst. He spun back and jabbed a finger in Daniel's direction. "Let's get this straight right here. *Right now.* Vivian is not a zombie—never was— and as soon as you're on your feet, you're out of here. There's no place here for someone like you!"

13

"Noah?" Vivian struggled to sit up as Noah rounded the curtain into the sectioned-off area where Vivian lay.

"Whoa. It's okay. Lay back."

"I heard yelling..." Confusion clouded her eyes as she still struggled to sit, her neck craned as if to see around the curtain. "What's going on? Where are the kids?"

"The kids are all fine. They're up at the house sleeping."

"And Dexter? He's okay?" Her worry seemed to be easing, but her brow furrowed in concern.

"Also sleeping. He's been at your side most of the day. The kids have been off and on too. They'd stay all day if they could, but Leona urged them to go outside. She'd call them when you woke up."

"What time is it?"

Noah glanced at his watch. "It's two thirty in the morning. Do you need something for pain? Leona left some pills for you if you need them."

Vivian shook her head. "No. I'm tired of the fogginess. And the nightmares."

Noah moved to her side and reached for her hand. "Do you want me to get Dexter? Or Leona?" He was probably the last person Vivian wanted to see at her bedside. Of all the people in their group, he and she had very little in common. He was an unrelated male, and she was at her most vulnerable.

But to his surprise, she gave his hand a squeeze. "No. I'm okay. If you could scoot that glass of water closer to me, that would be wonderful. I'm so thirsty."

Noah glanced at the bedside table and slid the water glass to where Vivian could easily reach it. "Do you want fresh water? I don't know how long that's been sitting there."

She tilted the glass. "No. It's fine." Several sips later, she set it down, her eyes already closing. "Will you stay here with me?"

Noah pulled up the chair Dexter usually sat in. "Absolutely." Even if she hadn't asked, and if he hadn't already committed to staying until Leona relieved him later, he wouldn't have left her alone with Daniel.

"Who's the other guy over there? And what's he yelling about?"

"He's a very confused and angry man, but he won't be here long."

"That's good, because maybe I was still in the middle of my nightmare, but I could have sworn I heard someone talking about zombies."

Noah patted her hand and forced a teasing tone in his voice. "I promise I won't let any zombies eat you."

"You'd best not, or when I turn into a zombie myself, you'll be the first one I'm coming after." She smiled although her eyes were closed.

Noah chuckled. "Get some sleep. I'll be right here if you need anything."

CASSIE WATCHED Noah trudge back to the house from the clinic. She had a tray with breakfast for Daniel. Dexter had already brought Vivian's, and Leona had taken a plate with her when she went to relieve Noah.

"Hey, Noah."

Noah lifted his head and gave her a weary smile. "Good morning."

"How'd it go last night?"

A shadow passed across his face, and Cassie's heart almost stopped. "Is Vivian all right?"

"Oh yeah. She woke up this morning begging to get out of bed and move back up to her room up at the house."

Relieved, Cassie smiled. "That's great to hear." She tilted her head, trying to catch Noah's eye as he looked past her, as if thinking of something. "What's wrong?"

He shook his head. "I'll tell you later. I'm so beat now, I'll probably make it sound way worse than it really was."

"Okay... well, I left you a few slices of bread wrapped in a clean cloth. It was still warm. There's a jar of apricot jam too. I found it in my supplies. I'd wondered where it had gone."

"Thanks. Oh, and I know I promised I'd help make jam, but it might have to wait until later today."

"No worries, Noah. I know how to make it, and I'm sure the kids will help me. You get some sleep."

He nodded and started to the house again, only to pause. "If you could, try to show Luke how to do what you're doing. I think he might show some interest in cooking."

She shrugged. "Sure." Cassie had only had a few words with Luke so far, but she couldn't tell if he was shy or didn't like them. For now, she was giving him the benefit of the doubt. They were all in a tough situation, but at least they'd had time to adjust to each other. Being thrown into the mix under hostile circumstances couldn't be easy.

Putting him out of her mind, she opened the door to the clinic with one hand, balancing the tray against her hip. Leona sat at the table, jotting down something in a folder. "Good morning, Leona. I've brought Daniel's breakfast. Do you want me to give it to him?" She heard laughter and chatting coming from Vivian's cubicle, but the divider blocked her view. Even so, the sound of Ava's laughter soothed Cassie's worry. The poor little girl had cried herself to sleep last night.

The doctor looked up. "Oh yes. That's fine."

Cassie nodded to the folder. "What are you doing? Notes?"

Leona shrugged. "A chart. I've made one for each of them. It helps me keep track of what's going on. It's not fancy." She briefly held up a few pages, and Cassie could see a hand-drawn graph. Leona dipped her head, as if embarrassed. "I guess old habits die hard."

"Hey, we are so lucky to have you."

"I'm not so sure Noah would agree with that. Not after what I did to him."

Cassie grimaced. "True. There is that, but he doesn't hold a grudge. He thinks it's kind of funny."

Leona grinned. "Since he's okay, I can now admit it kind

of was funny. I mean, the shock on his face when he saw I was the one who had pulled the trigger..."

"I can imagine. Well, I guess I'll take this to Daniel." She straightened her shoulders and pasted on a smile as she stood outside the divider before entering his cubicle. "Good morning, Daniel. I hope you're feeling better today. I have toast with jam, and scrambled eggs."

Daniel sat propped up with at least three pillows behind him. He didn't return Cassie's smile but gestured to the table beside his bed. "Set it there and then help me turn to sit on the side of the bed."

Bristling at the tone and the commands, Cassie set the tray down just short of slamming it onto the table. "I'm happy to help you in any way I can, but a please and thank-you will go a long way around here."

Daniel grunted, but when Cassie didn't take the hand he held out for her to help him lever up to sit on the side of the bed, he grunted out a thank-you.

"You're welcome." She ignored his hand and raised an eyebrow, waiting for a request for help instead of a demand. It took Daniel a few seconds to figure it out, but he rolled his eyes and with exaggerated politeness said, "Would you please help me?"

Her mouth stretched into a thin smile as she took his hand. "Of course."

Once he was sitting, she stood back, trying to resist the urge to wipe her hand on the back of her pants. "Is there anything else you need?"

"I'll need to take a dump after I eat. Don't go far."

Cassie didn't reply but turned and left. She peeked into Vivian's cubicle. "Viv?"

Dexter and Jalen sat on chairs beside the bed while Ava sat on the end of the bed, her hand resting on Vivian's leg under the covers.

"Cassie! Look! My mom's all better!"

Vivian smiled and waved Cassie in. "Hey there, Cass. Ava's been telling me how you've been taking care of her. Thank you."

"Vivian, you know thanks aren't necessary." She reached out and smoothed a hand against Ava's cheek as she passed the little girl. She hadn't thought she could love any children as much as her own, but Ava, Jalen, and Ethan had come to occupy a special place in her heart. "It's the least I can do. How are you feeling?"

Vivian shot a look at Ava then back to Cassie. Taking the hint, Cassie held out her hand to Ava. "Hey, hon, I wonder if you could do me a favor?"

Ava nodded. "I think so."

"Could you find Bella and Milo and have them—" She struggled to find something to have them do. "Tell them to be very quiet in the house. Noah is trying to sleep."

"Okay." Ava gave her mom a kiss before racing out of the room.

Maybe there had been some silent exchange that Cassie had missed, but Jalen and Dexter both stood to leave. Dexter motioned to the chair he'd just vacated. "Have a seat, Cassie."

Giving him and Vivian a questioning glance but acquiescing, Cassie sat on the edge of the seat.

"We'll be back in a few minutes, sweetheart. I'm going to get Jalen and the other boys working on an idea I have."

"Idea?" Cassie wondered what was up. Dexter and Leona had worked together to get the clinic up and everything in place just a few days before the blueberry farm incident. Not a moment too soon either.

"Nothing too exciting. Yet." Dexter tweaked Vivian's toes over the blanket as he left.

Once he was out of the cubicle, Vivian's lip started quivering. Concern rushed through Cassie. "Oh, sweetie, what is it? What's wrong?"

"I'm scared."

Vivian's admission frightened Cassie to the core. The woman had never shown fear in the short time she'd known her. She had been a backbone of the group. At times, more so than even Noah. She'd shown Cassie how things worked at the farm and had made Cassie's children feel at home. When Cassie was busy trying to make a dozen loaves of bread, or pancakes for everyone, Vivian jumped right in and somehow managed to get the kids to help. She'd make everything into a little game, and even the older kids would get in on the act.

"What are you afraid of?"

"This baby. I don't know if it'll be okay, or even if it is, how I'm going to bring a baby into a world"—she flung her hand out, wincing at the motion even as she continued—"where everyone is dead. There are no schools. No stores. Barely any other people, and when we do find other people, they shoot us."

At first, Cassie was confused, but as Vivian rubbed a hand over her belly, she figured it out. "You're pregnant?"

Vivian nodded. "Only about eight weeks or so. Leona had brought some pregnancy tests with her, and when I missed my period, I thought for sure it was just the stress, because, damn, the last several months have redefined the meaning of the word stress. Am I right?" Vivian gave a halfhearted smile.

Cassie tipped her head, acknowledging the truth of Vivian's words. "Absolutely. But what did Leona say about the baby and how it's doing?"

"She thinks if I haven't miscarried by now, I probably won't."

"Well, that's wonderful news!" Cassie clapped her hands. "A baby! Congratulations!"

Tears welled in Vivian's eyes. "But won't this baby hate me for having him or her? They won't know about how things were before."

"Yes, I suppose so, but I think that could be a good thing. They won't miss what they never had. And look, the kids are doing the best of all of us. Why, Milo has blossomed. He was always so full of energy that he'd get in trouble at school. Now, he blows off all of his energy around here, not just in play but in actual work. He loves helping take care of the goats and chickens, or fishing. He was so proud of that little fish he caught a while back. And you made such a big deal about it, I thought his head was going to float right off his body, he was so proud."

Cassie paused, remembering the moment and so many more. Then she shook her head. "Sorry, I'm rambling. Of course, what has happened is tragic. There's no denying that, but what was the point of us surviving if we weren't going to try to keep humanity alive?"

Vivian bit her lip, then, slowly, a smile spread across her face. "Damn, girl. You're deep."

"About as deep as a thimble, but seriously, I get what you're saying. If I hadn't had the kids to look after, I'm not so sure I would have worked so hard to stay alive..."

"I think you would have. Look, we're all survivors here. We're the toughest of the lot."

"Now you're the one cheering me up." Cassie laughed, covering her mouth with her hand.

Vivian grinned. "I guess I am."

"One good thing—you have the best doctor in the world to take care of you."

Snorting but trying to stifle a laugh as she held her belly, Vivian shook her head. "Oh, damn. That hurts. But that is so true. I literally have the best doctor in the world. Maybe the only one."

"Are you two talking about me?" Leona entered the cubicle, a small packet in her hand.

"We're singing your praises."

"As you should be." Leona winked at Cassie as she addressed Vivian. "I have oral antibiotics I want to have you try. Everything is looking good. Your fever is gone. Your wound is clean and dry. I think you should be able to go back to the house tonight. Let's see how you do with your meals today. If you can eat and drink enough, I can take out the IV, and I'm sure the men can take you up to the house."

Vivian took the pill Leona gave her and swallowed it with a gulp of water. "I don't need the men to take me. I can walk by myself."

Leona glanced at Cassie then to Vivian with her eyebrows raised. "I don't want you overexerting yourself, if you know what I mean."

"Oh, I told Cassie about the baby. You can speak about it."

Leona nodded. "Very good. I want you off your feet for a week, except to use the bathroom."

"You mean I don't need to use a bedpan anymore? Thank the Lord!"

Leona and Cassie chuckled. "Not exactly. But we have a bedside commode you can use. One of the many useful things I got from the hospital."

Vivian's scowl showed her opinion of how useful it was.

Cassie clapped her hands and giggled. "I can't believe it. A baby! So exciting!"

For the first time, Cassie saw Vivian grin, her hand resting on her abdomen. "I know." Then she tilted her head and gave Cassie a sidelong glance. "Hmmm... I wonder when you'll join the club?"

"Club?"

She patted her tummy and nodded knowingly.

Cassie's cheeks heated. "Um, last knew, it took two, unless Leona has the means to whip up a baby in that little lab of hers?" She tried to take the focus off herself and throw it onto the doctor.

Leona shoved her hands in her white lab coat and laughed. "I'm afraid not. If you want a baby, you'll have to do it the old-fashioned way."

"Well, that's that. No babies for me!" Cassie stood. The conversation was getting a little too personal for her.

"I'm going to check on Daniel now." Leona's nose wrinkled as she spoke, revealing how she felt about that chore. With a little wave, she left the cubicle.

Vivian reached for Cassie's hand, catching it before Cassie could follow the doctor out. "I'm only teasing you, hon."

14

Ethan threw a ball for Dino, praising him when he brought it back. The dog never tired of the game, and Ethan, feeling guilty for not being able to play with him much with everything going on, continued to throw until Dino ran off to the stream to get a drink. Ethan followed him, although he drank from his bottle of water. He flopped down on the ground under a tree.

The garden was weeded and watered. The goats moved to a new pasture to take advantage of the long grass there, where a metal trough provided plenty of water. Ethan couldn't believe it, but he was bored and wanted something to do. He couldn't believe he actually had the luxury of being bored. Before the virus, he'd hop on the computer or play a video game when he was bored. Right now, even if he could, the idea of sitting in front of a screen didn't appeal to him. He snapped his fingers and patted the ground beside him until Dino lay next to him, panting and dripping water from his mouth. Ethan laughed and ruffled the dog's fur.

"Ethan!"

Standing, Ethan turned to see Jalen waving to him, beckoning him.

After loping across the back pasture, Dino matching his pace, Ethan reached Jalen and stopped, only slightly winded. "What's up?"

"My dad wants to show us all something."

"All?"

"Well, you, me, and I guess Ruby and the other kid."

"Luke?"

Jalen shrugged as if the kid's name didn't matter.

"What's he want to show us?" Ethan walked beside Jalen as they went to wherever his dad waited.

"I don't know. He said it's a surprise."

Once they were assembled, Dexter took them to the back of Noah's truck. "I saw these the other day on our way to the blueberry farm but only just had a chance to get a few of them." He pulled a blue tarp from the top of whatever lay in the bed of the truck.

Ethan squinted. He thought he knew what they were, but he wasn't certain. "Are these solar panels?"

"Bingo! Give the boy a prize."

"What are we gonna do with them?" Ethan leaned over the side of the truck and ran a finger down one of the panels.

"I'm thinking wouldn't it be awesome to have electricity this winter? We can get some space heaters and keep the house nice and warm. Maybe even get an electric oven and have something decent to cook on. Oh, and hot water."

The heaters and stove Ethan thought he could do without. The farmhouse had two fireplaces, and he envisioned living like they did in the olden days. But running hot water? That, he was down for.

"No way!" Jalen nudged Ethan. "Maybe we can find a game console. Oh, and a TV with a DVD player. There's gotta be thousands of DVDs around someplace."

Luke looked between Jalen and Ethan, his eyes wide with hope. Ethan looked away without giving him any and nodded to Jalen. Although he wasn't nearly as excited about those things as he would have been a few months ago, he pretended to feel excitement. He didn't really miss them, and he wasn't sure about watching a movie knowing that everyone who was in it was most likely dead. Although he'd watched old movies before and it had never bothered him, for some reason, the thought of watching a current one and knowing the actors were all dead felt almost morbid.

"I still have a bit of research to do on how to set this up, and since we can't connect to a grid, we'll need to figure out how to store some of the energy."

Ethan thought it sounded impossible, but Dexter knew about these kinds of things.

"So, what do you want us to do, Dad?" Jalen asked the question that was foremost in Ethan's mind.

"I need you guys to clean out an area on the second floor of the barn. Then take these over there, carefully. When you're finished, if there's still enough light, we can go back to where I found these and get another load."

Jalen sagged, resting his forehead against the top rim of the truck bed. "Ugh. This doesn't sound nearly as fun as you made it seem when you told me you had a big surprise, Dad."

Dexter grinned.

"THIS IS SO STUPID." Luke let his side of the panel drop to the floor.

Ethan glared at him. "Be careful!" He set his side down gently, hoping the impact on the other end hadn't damaged it. "Dexter's gonna be pissed if these are cracked."

Luke rolled his eyes. "What do you care? Dexter isn't even your dad."

Ethan brushed his hands against his backside. "So?"

"So? He's not our boss. I don't have do anything he says."

Ethan moved close to Luke. He'd had enough of the other boy's attitude. His body tense, he shook his head. "I wish Noah never brought you back here."

Ruby and Jalen brought a second panel and set it down as Ethan gave his opinion. Ruby bit her lip, her gaze shooting between Ethan and Luke.

"Uh, Ethan?"

Ethan glanced at Ruby, annoyed. "What?"

"I... I'm glad Noah brought us here."

"Oh... I wasn't talking about you." Ethan focused on the boy in front of him and poked a finger into Luke's chest. "I was talking about him."

"Don't touch me!" Luke shoved Ethan, forcing him to stumble into a bucket of metal nuts, bolts, screws, and other bits of hardware. Ethan fell backward, striking an elbow hard against the floor. A screw dug into his palm as he leaped to his feet and rushed Luke. Grabbing him around the waist, he tackled the other kid into pile of old tires. He pulled his arm back to hit him but stopped as Luke cowered beneath him, his hands up defensively.

"What's your problem, you freak?" Luke struggled as Ethan released his grasp, scrambling over a rusty bicycle with no handlebars and putting it between him and Ethan.

"My problem is you came here and act like you're too good for everyone! But you were living like filthy animals! And don't think I won't forget that your dad almost killed Jalen's mom." Ethan's body shook, and his face burned.

"We did not!" Luke charged at Ethan, and Ethan grabbed Luke's shirt and flung him aside. Months of hard work had hardened his muscles.

"Only because Vivian is way too tough to die." Ethan walked up to where Luke lay on his side and reached down and yanked him by the collar of his T-shirt to his feet. "Get your ass back to the truck for another load, and this time, you better treat it like it was made of—"

"Glass?" Jalen cut in, smirking when Ethan shot him a look.

Ethan couldn't help chuckling as he finished, "Yeah, *glass!*"

Luke stood, shaking each limb like a cat who'd just been surprised by a dunk in the water. "We're not filthy animals. At least my dad knows how to install these stupid things." He tapped the solar panel with his foot.

"Seriously?" Jalen crossed his arms, his eyebrow raised in doubt.

"Yeah. *Seriously,*" Luke sneered. "He used to work for a company that installed them, but he'd never help you guys now. Not when you're treating me like shit." Luke's voice cracked as he turned his back on Ethan and stalked back to the truck.

Ethan watched him for a second then sighed and headed

in the same direction. Ruby caught up to him halfway back and tugged on his shirt.

"Ethan? Are you mad I'm here? I could leave. I can take care of myself." Ruby's eyes welled with tears as he stopped in surprise at her question and declaration.

"No! No... Ruby. You're okay. I mean, we all like you." Nobody had actually come out and discussed it, but Ethan had already seen how Cassie's face softened when she looked at Ruby.

Her hands balled into fists as if she hadn't heard him. "I'm not like them, Ethan. I'm good."

"Yeah, of course you are. Why wouldn't you be?" Jalen stopped beside Ethan, giving him a quizzical look after asking Ruby the question. "You're cool."

Her eyes flew to Jalen's then to Ethan's, panic flitting through them. "We better get back to the truck." She practically fled from him.

As they trudged back for a second load, Jalen poked his elbow into Ethan's side. "Thanks for sticking up for my mom, but you didn't have to. I could have done it."

"I know. I wasn't doing it for you."

He wandered away from Jalen, mumbling about taking a leak, and went behind one of the big oaks that lined the long driveway. He leaned against it and put his head back.

Ethan didn't know who he'd done it for, but anger still sizzled through him. He almost wished he'd followed through and slugged Luke. He flexed his fingers. It would have felt so good to let some of the anger escape.

The instant the thought went through his mind, he saw Luke's face as he cringed in fear when he'd had him on the ground. Shame washed over him. He wasn't a bully. Or he never had been. Luke was smaller and younger than he was. Ethan picked up a stone from the base of the tree and flung it as far as he could. It landed in a ditch a few hundred feet away, flushing a flock of birds into the air.

15

"Your chariot has arrived!" Noah pushed the wheelchair into the clinic with a flourish. It was one thing they hadn't thought about when they'd scavenged at the hospital, but he'd found one in the lobby of a nursing home.

"You guys. I can walk."

"Sorry, babe. Doctor's orders."

Leona nodded. "I'm afraid so."

Dexter took the chair from Noah and pushed it up to the bed.

Vivian shook her head, rolling her eyes. "I can't believe y'all went and found this contraption." She eased to the edge of the bed and stood. Dexter gripped her elbow as she swayed slightly.

Noah shrugged. "It's a long way up to the house. We have a bed fixed up in the room off the kitchen so you won't feel stuck upstairs and alone."

The room had looked to have been used as an office, going by the desk, computer, and filing cabinet in it when they'd arrived, but they had been using it as an extra pantry.

The canned food had been moved to the basement. The filing cabinet had been emptied of files, and they still used it for storing flour. The metal drawers were good for keeping rodents out.

"Yes, and I'll be close by most of the day." Cassie handed Vivian a pillow once she was seated. "Here. Hold this tight against your stomach. We're going to hit some bumps on the way, and I'm sure it's going to hurt a bit even though I'm sure Dexter is going to be very careful." She tossed a grin to Dexter.

"I'd better, or I won't hear the end of it."

Even though Dexter affected an air of a put-upon husband, Cassie wasn't fooled. Dexter had been nearly giddy with excitement all morning as they had readied a room for his wife. Vivian played along with it, though. "Oh, you got that right, mister."

Dexter made a comical face, mouthing what Vivian had just said, and while she couldn't see him, Vivian held up a finger. "Don't you mock me!" She paused and smiled slyly when Dexter gulped. Cassie and Noah burst out laughing. Even Leona smiled. Cassie bent to adjust the footrests for Vivian.

"Just wait until you see the bed, Mommy." Ava practically danced around the wheelchair.

"Yeah? What did you do to it?" Vivian let out a sigh as she fully settled into the chair.

"It's a surprise!"

"Hey, what about me?" Daniel hollered from the other side of the curtain, making Ava jump.

Noah set his jaw. Any day, Daniel would be ready to leave. He'd pushed Leona for a time frame. As much as Leona loathed the man, she was too much of a professional to let it sway her medical judgment. Noah had to respect her on that, even if he didn't agree. As far as he was concerned, if the man was well enough to bellow for dinner, as he had the night before, he was well enough to fend for himself.

Dexter moved toward Daniel's "room," his mouth twisted into a snarl. Noah jumped to intercept him. Noah couldn't stand Daniel but wasn't certain that Dexter wouldn't kill the other man if given half a chance. The fact that he hadn't yet only illustrated the strength of Dexter's character.

"Hey, I got it, Dex. You go and take your wife back to the house. Forget about him."

Dexter's jaw clenched, and for a moment, he looked as if he was about to make an end around Daniel's bed and no doubt throttle him. His focus shifted from Noah's eyes to Daniel's bed. It was hidden by the curtain, but Dexter knew exactly where it was. "Fine. But you better get him gone before I—" He broke off when he saw Jalen watching him. "He just better be gone soon."

"He will be."

Noah stood, his back to Daniel's area, as Dexter pushed Vivian past with Ava on one side, Jalen on the other, and Leona, Cassie, Milo, and Bella trailing behind as if Dexter was the Pied Piper. Ethan stopped beside Noah.

Noah glanced at him, wondering when the kid had grown to where he was only half a head shorter than Noah's own six foot three. Ethan couldn't have been more than five foot eight, and a skinny one at that, when Noah had met him a few months before. Now, he had to be pushing six feet tall. While still skinny, Noah had no doubt he'd fill out. He wondered how tall the kid's dad had been. "Do you need something?"

"No. I thought I'd keep an eye on Daniel if you need me to. To help Leona out."

Noah considered the offer. With Vivian back at the house, Leona would be splitting her time, and nobody else would be here with Leona while she was caring for the man. The idea of the older woman being here alone with him now that he was moving around some didn't sit well with Noah. "That's a good idea. I'll spell you, and Cassie too."

"Cassie?" Doubt crept across Ethan's face. "I don't know if she should be here with him either."

Noah didn't know if Daniel could hear them, but he didn't really care. "Don't worry. She has a gun and knows how to use it."

Ethan smiled. "Oh yeah. And so does Leona."

Noah rubbed his side. "Does she ever." He turned and pushed the curtain back. There was no need for it now since Vivian was gone.

"So, what about me? When do I get to go up to the house?" Daniel sat back in the bed, the head of it elevated. Noah had turned off the generator, as there had been no need for electricity anymore. That had left the bed stuck in a semi-reclining position.

"You're not ever going up to the house. You'll be on your way to wherever when you're well enough. Leona says that will be in a few days." Noah couldn't help the smile that slid across his face.

"But... but me and Luke have nowhere to go!"

Noah shrugged. "Not our problem. Maybe you should

have come to us and talked to us before you started plugging us with lead."

Ethan chuckled at that, and Daniel sneered at him. "What about him?" He pointed at Ethan.

Noah glanced at the teen then back to Daniel. "What about him?"

"He started a fight with my boy the other day and nobody did nothin' to him."

Noah hadn't heard about a fight, but Luke looked healthy and uninjured, as did Ethan. It couldn't have been too bad. "Hmm... you shot Vivian, and nobody did anything to you either."

Daniel's mouth snapped shut, and he crossed his arms. "I told you why I did that. I thought you were all zombies."

"What?" Ethan stared at Daniel, his eyes wide. "That's crazy!"

"I'm not crazy. It was just what people were saying when everyone started dying so fast."

Ethan glanced at Noah before turning back to Daniel. "What people?"

"Folks on the internet. It was all over the place. With pictures and everything. Everyone who died from the virus turned into a zombie and ate somebody else." Daniel stated it like it was common knowledge.

"That didn't happen."

"How do you know? You said you was in the woods fishing." Daniel raised a skeptical eyebrow at Noah. "I saw some of it with my own eyes."

"You saw people eating other people?"

"Well, no. But they were acting all crazy and shit. I didn't stick around long enough to watch them have dinner. Only the evil people died. Since we're alive, we're the only good ones left in the world."

"You're a liar!" Ethan took two steps toward Daniel, his fists balled, head jutting forward. "My mom wasn't evil! Or my dad." Ethan's breath hitched, and he tilted his head, eyes narrowed. "And definitely not my baby sister. She was an angel!"

Daniel lifted a shoulder as if to say he couldn't help it. "That's what they were saying."

Noah sensed rather than saw Ethan begin to launch himself at Daniel, and Noah lunged forward, catching the teen by the back of his shirt. "Easy, there, Ethan. He's not worth it."

"Let me go!" Ethan turned, grabbing Noah's hand, pulling it from his shirt. "She wasn't evil. She was the best mom, Noah. She was..." A sob escaped him as he gave up trying to get loose. His shoulders sagged, and he turned his back to Noah and Daniel.

Not wanting Daniel to see Ethan cry, Noah moved to block his view. "I know, Ethan. She had to have been pretty great to have a son like you."

Ethan suddenly turned and pointed at Daniel. "I hate you! Why didn't you die instead of my family?" He didn't wait for a reply and bolted out of the clinic. Noah watched him go, torn. He wanted to comfort the boy but decided to give him time to collect his emotions. He knew how hard and complicated emotions were as a teen. He hated his own dad, but he still would have defended him to anyone who tried to smear him. Ethan's parents had been good people, from what Noah could tell. And a little toddler could not have been evil.

"See? He gets away with everything."

Noah spun to Daniel. "If your kid is like you, I'd say he probably deserved whatever Ethan gave him."

There was no doubt in his mind that Ethan wouldn't have fought Luke for no reason at all, but Noah had a glimmer of hope that Luke wasn't as bad as his father. Not yet, anyway. Noah jabbed a finger in Daniel's direction. "I'd advise you to keep your mouth shut. In a few hours, I'll bring you dinner."

"What? You're leaving? What if my fever comes back? Or I fall while taking a piss?"

Noah shrugged and walked away.

16

E than raced to the back of the barn and plopped down on the edge a huge half-buried tractor tire. His hands shook, but the tears had dried. His eyes still burned, though, and he scrubbed them with his fists.

Swallows dipped and soared in and out of the barn, some through the big double doors and others through spaces from missing boards. This was Ethan's favorite place to sit. With the barn on a rise, he could see down onto the fields to the west, and to the southeast was the hill to the goat shed and pasture. He circled his fingers and whistled. A few seconds later, Dino came flying down the hill to him. "Hey there." He scratched the dog behind the ears, stroking down his back. Dino's tongue lolled. "What am I gonna do, Dino? I swear to God, I could have killed that guy."

He stopped scratching, his elbows resting on his knees, hands clasped between them, until Dino dipped his head, nudging Ethan's elbow. It almost made him smile, but his mind turned to what else he'd almost done. "Dino, I remember people saying they were so angry that they saw red, but I thought it was just a saying, you know?"

Dino closed his mouth, licked his lips, and then resumed panting. Ethan drew a silky ear through his fingers. "It's not just a saying. I think I literally saw red." He stopped, replaying what he'd seen when he'd tried to attack Daniel. It was a blur, but the fleeting impression of red inside his head was there. His anger had erupted from seemingly nowhere. It was the second time in as many days. What if he was affected by the virus and it was turning him into... well, not a zombie exactly but something like one? He remembered how different his parents had acted while infected. They hadn't been angry. Instead, they had seemed crazy. Giddy with craziness. He'd spent a lot of the time in his room, sad about Amber, but their giddiness had freaked him out. At the time, he hadn't known they were ill.

Ethan heard someone call his name but didn't answer. It might have been Ava, or it might have been Ruby. He didn't care. He didn't want to talk to anyone right now, and he definitely didn't want to run into Luke. After a few more calls, whoever it was gave up. Dino lay down, stretched out in a warm patch of dirt, and slept. Ethan watched the steady rise and fall of the dog's rib cage. Before finding Cassie, his only wish had been to find another living person, and when he'd found her and her kids, he'd been so relieved. He wasn't alone. She was great. And Noah was great. Jalen was quickly becoming a better friend than he'd ever had. Crazy to think they'd only known each other weeks. Even though he liked everyone, he felt like he didn't belong. He could take Dino and leave. There was nobody to stop him.

The idea played out in his head. Him and Dino, roaming like they had before. Finding food in empty houses, taking cars or bikes whenever they needed. It was complete freedom, in a way. There had been nobody to piss him off and nobody he wanted to kill.

Sure, he'd miss Jalen and the others, but they'd probably be better off without him and his anger issues. Ethan squinted to the horizon until the sun started dipping beneath the trees in the west and the air took on a chill.

Dino lifted his head, his ears perked. A second later, Ethan heard shoes crunching over the gravel scattered in the grass.

An elongated shadow crossed in front of him. He turned to the side. "Hey, Noah."

"Ethan." He bent to pet Dino, giving a few scratches beneath the dog's chin, much to the dog's delight. Ethan shook his head. *Traitor.*

Noah sighed. "Do you mind if I sit?" He gestured to the tire. It was almost as high as a bench.

Ethan shrugged. "I don't own it."

Noah chuckled. "Neither do I." He settled beside Ethan. "Beautiful sunset."

Ethan glanced at the orange sky streaked with pink. "Yeah."

"Listen, Ethan. What happened back there—"

"I don't wanna talk about it."

"I'm a pretty good listener."

Ethan didn't respond immediately. His body tensed as he darted a look to his left. The way was clear to the goat shed. They needed to be brought in anyway.

"Jalen said he and Milo would bring the goats in after dinner." Noah glanced at his watch. "Which is right about now. We saved you some."

Ethan relaxed a tiny bit, glancing at Noah. He didn't look angry. "What kind?"

"Potato. It's made with powdered milk, but I added a little goat's milk to it. It gave it a different taste, but it was still pretty good, if I do say so myself."

Ethan's mouth flooded. He hadn't eaten for hours, and his stomach growled on cue, but he shook his head. "I... I'm thinking I should... leave."

There. He'd said it.

***

"Leave?" Noah angled his head to see Ethan's face. "Why?"

Ethan lifted a shoulder. "I... I think it would be cool to roam the country. Everything I need would be in houses and stores. I'm good at scavenging now."

"Cool to roam?" Noah clamped his lips together. It made no sense. A few months ago, the kid had been like an eager pup. He'd do everything he could to help out as though he'd had to prove his worth. "I'm sorry, but I don't get it. I thought you liked it here?"

Shock that Ethan was thinking of leaving hit Noah harder than he'd have thought possible. The pit of his stomach felt hollow even though he'd just eaten.

Ethan snapped his fingers, and Dino jumped up, took a few steps, and sat, putting his head on the kid's knee. If Ethan left, so would the dog. Noah reached out, stroking the dog's fur. Dino responded by thumping his tail on the ground but didn't take his eyes off Ethan.

"I do like it here." The kid's head dipped as he toed a stick, rolling it under his shoe, back and forth.

"Was it something we did? I know Daniel and, I guess, Luke aren't the easiest to get along with, but they'll be leaving soon."

Ethan's toe stilled. "Because of me?"

"Because of you? Oh, hell no." Noah drew a deep breath and tried to explain. "Daniel is... honestly, I don't know how they survived. He's not the sharpest knife in the drawer. So many good people died, and yet, here he is..."

"I almost hit Luke yesterday."

"Why?"

Ethan shrugged, and the stick rolled to and fro. "It doesn't really matter. I'm way bigger than him. I shouldn't have let him get to me. That's what my dad used to tell me. Only, I wasn't very big then."

"Your dad sounds like he was a really good dad."

Ethan swallowed, the sound audible in the still twilight. He nodded.

"Those things Daniel said about the people who died, they aren't true. You know that, right? Don't let someone like that taint your memories of your family. They're yours, and you know they were good people who loved you."

"I know. But what if I'm not good like them?"

As Noah wondered how to reply to that, Ethan reached down and picked up the stick and began pulling shreds of bark from it. "I have no idea why you would think that. All I can tell you is what I see. I see a young man who has overcome incredible odds. A young man who helps without question and doesn't expect anything in return. I see someone who was brought up right and has strength of character. That's what I see."

Ethan dropped the stick. "I don't know. I don't feel that good. I wanted to kill Daniel today. Seriously. It's like I was out of my mind. Do you think I could have a touch of the virus?" The fear in Ethan's voice hit Noah like a punch to the chest.

"No!" He grasped Ethan's shoulder, turning him to face Noah. "What you're feeling is normal teenage stuff. I was like that as a teen. I had different reasons, but I spent half the day wanting to punch people's lights out and the other half trying to get them to like me."

"Really?"

"Yes. And I imagine at some point, if your dad was still alive, you'd have blown up about something else, maybe even at him, and he'd be the one telling you all that emotion churning up inside you right now is normal."

Ethan's shoulders sagged. "I thought I might be crazy or stupid. Maybe both."

"No. You're not crazy, and you're definitely not stupid."

"Thanks."

"Speaking of stupid." Noah laughed. "Daniel thought we were zombies. That's what he told me, anyway. And that's why he shot at us."

"I guess I can see his point. When this whole thing began, people were acting so weird. But I don't think we were acting weird while picking blueberries."

"No, I don't think we were. I think he was paranoid."

"Maybe. Hey, Luke said his dad knew how to install solar panels. I don't know if I believe him, but just putting it out there."

"Interesting. Maybe I'll ask him about it." Noah looked out into the deepening twilight. "You're free to go and to take what you think you might need—" He broke off when he sensed Ethan stiffen, as if in shock. He didn't think the kid really wanted to leave. For some reason, he didn't think he belonged, and Noah hoped to dig for the real reason. "But if there's anything I can do to get you to stay, please tell me." He looked at Ethan.

Ethan's posture relaxed slightly, then he flicked his eyes to Noah's. "I don't really fit in here is all."

Baffled, Noah gave his head a small shake. "What are you talking about? Why do you think that?"

Sighing, Ethan glanced at Noah then rolled his eyes. "You're all family. I'm not."

"I'm not related to Dexter and Vivian or their kids."

"Yeah, but you're Milo and Bella's uncle and Cassie's brother-in-law."

"Ex-brother-in-law." Noah didn't know why he interjected that information.

"Whatever. You're still the kids' uncle. I'm nobody. I'm just a teenager who wandered in. I eat too much, and I get angry all the time for things that I can't even remember later. Like when I almost punched Luke, it was stupid. He wasn't being careful with the solar panels when we were moving them, and I called him out about it. Luke got all pissed off and said stuff like what did I care what Dexter wanted me to do. He wasn't my dad and stuff. He couldn't tell me what to do."

"What did you say back?"

Ethan shrugged. "I don't remember exactly. Something about wishing you'd never brought him here. Then Ruby said something, and I felt kind of bad, so I said I wasn't talking about her but Luke. And I poked him in the chest. It wasn't hard, but he shoved me, and I fell over some junk in the barn, and then I tackled him."

"But you didn't punch him."

"No. He looked so scared."

"Ah, so you had the self-control to stop yourself."

"I suppose, but I still felt like punching him even after I let him up," Ethan admitted, his voice grudging.

"First of all, Ethan, you *are* family. Don't ever forget that. You are just as important here as anyone else. We've all helped each other to survive—to endure during the damned end of the world."

He had Ethan's full attention, as he seemed to search Noah's face as though he doubted but wanted to believe. "And second, *eating too much*? What the hell are you talking about? When I was your age, I could eat three Big Macs, a couple of large fries, and then wonder whether to have an apple pie or milkshake for dessert, and then have both of them." Noah grinned. "I'm totally serious, though. Why do you think I went into the Army? They kept me fed. Then I became a chef so I could keep myself fed."

Ethan smiled, and Noah nudged him with an elbow. "Do I need to gather a pack for your travels, or are you willing to stay with us? We could use your help."

"Really?"

"What I'm about to say is not a joke. I am dead serious when I say, yes, your help could be crucial. I don't want to guilt you into staying, but we could really use you here. I don't know what winter will bring or if there are more people out there worse than Daniel. We have to be ready for anything. The more good men we have on our side, the better our chances of surviving."

17

A few days after Vivian had moved back to the house, Cassie caught up to Noah heading for the clinic. She balanced a tray with oatmeal and a glass of apple juice against her hip. "Hey, did you hear the good news?"

"Good news? I guess not."

"He's well enough to leave the clinic. Leona says a few more days, and he can go."

Noah didn't react as she'd expected him to. He frowned and glanced at the clinic then at Cassie. "You're sure?"

"That's what she said. He's up and walking. All traces of infection are gone, and he's hungry." She lifted the tray as proof. "This is his second breakfast."

"That's good news, about his health, but if he leaves, so does Luke."

Cassie nodded. At first, Luke had come off as a snot. He didn't like working around the farm and seemed to resent the other two boys. She had been eager to see him leave, but the last few days, she'd noted a change in him. He washed dishes without being told, helped dig potatoes without complaint, and even offered to take them down to the cellar. "Yeah. I wasn't sure about him at first, but he's kind of growing on me. But Daniel's his dad."

"I know. He and Ethan are even getting along a little better."

"Better? I didn't know there was a problem?" She shifted the tray. Let Daniel wait for his second bowl of oatmeal. It wasn't like he would even thank her for it.

She hadn't had a chance to spend much time with Ethan recently. Between the garden and the fields of corn and soybeans the farmer who'd lived here before the virus hit had planted, they had been harvesting nonstop. They weren't harvesting all of the corn or soybeans because it was obvious they were planted with the intent of selling them, and with nowhere to sell them, the time spent harvesting them would be better spent preserving food they would need over the winter. An apple orchard west of the fields needed picking. They didn't know if it belonged to this farm or the next one, but nobody was around, and the apples would rot on the ground if they weren't picked. There was always something that needed doing, and by the time she got the kids to bed, she fell into her own not long afterward.

"They had some issues, but they worked it out, it seems. I think the boys will be sad to see him go."

She hadn't thought of that. A good friend was always hard to come by, and now, friends were to be cherished. Who knew when they'd meet another person at all, let alone someone who could become a friend? "It's too bad Daniel has no redeeming qualities that I can see."

Noah made a face. "See, that's just it. He might have one. Not really a redeeming quality but a skill we could use."

"What's that?"

"Apparently he has some experience installing solar panels. He claims he worked for a small company that installed them."

"Do you believe him?"

Noah shrugged. "Dexter talked to him, and I guess Daniel was able to answer some questions that only someone with at least a little knowledge would be able to answer."

"Like what?"

Noah laughed and held up his hand. "I have no idea. I just do the grunt work. Dexter tells me what to do, and I say, 'Yes, sir.' Just like I did in the Army."

Cassie elbowed him and laughed. "Oh, please. I've seen you two. You're always giving each other a hard time."

"That's what friends do." Noah grinned. "I think the oatmeal is sufficiently congealed now for you to take it in to Daniel."

She glanced down at the solid gray mush. "Yeah. I better get going."

As soon as Cassie opened the door, Daniel bellowed, "What took you so long? Talking to your boyfriend again?"

Cassie marched to where Daniel sat at a small table they normally used for supplies but had cleared one side for Daniel to sit at for meals the last few days. "Here's your *second* breakfast."

Daniel took a bite then scowled. "What the hell? It's ice-cold."

"Is it true you know how to install solar panels?"

In spite of the oatmeal's lukewarm temperature, Daniel shoveled it into his mouth. He nodded. "Yup. I worked for a year doing it."

"Is that what you were doing when the virus hit?"

"Nah. I was between jobs. That's why I'm still alive. I was home and didn't see anyone except Luke."

"How did he manage not to get sick?" Cassie leaned back against one of the stainless steel counters, ankles and arms crossed. She might as well wait and take the dirty dishes back.

"He was skipping school and hiding out down by a creek. Damn kid was smoking pot! Only came home to eat and sleep." He laughed as he said it. "He sure does take after his old man."

"Lovely."

"Why does everyone keep asking me about solar panels? Are you gonna put some up?"

Cassie shrugged. "I don't know. I guess we were thinking about it."

"I bet you want me to help you, don't you?"

Seeing he was done eating, Cassie stepped over to the table and grabbed the tray. "You owe us."

"Owe you? No way! You guys almost killed me!"

"You shot first. We were defending ourselves—and we took care of you. Noah didn't have to bring you back here."

"Then why the hell did he? I didn't ask him to." Daniel slouched over the table, his forearms resting on top as he cast glowering looks at Cassie.

"He's a decent person. Something you probably don't know anything about." Cassie didn't stick around to argue anymore. "If you want to, you can go sit out by the fire. It's not far, and there are some chairs near it."

"I am getting sick of these four walls."

"Maybe it'll improve your disposition." Before Daniel

could answer, Cassie turned the doorknob, put her back against the door as she held the tray in front of her, and backed out. It allowed her to see Daniel's confused expression as he tried to figure out if he'd been insulted or not.

———

"HERE, LET ME SHOW YOU." Ethan held his hand out for the ax handle. Luke narrowed his eyes but handed it over.

In one smooth motion, Ethan swung the ax up and brought it down in the center of the log, splitting it neatly in two. "Let the ax do the work."

He handed it back and gave Luke a few pointers as he set a new log on the chopping block.

Luke's motion was smoother, and this time, the log split. The ax didn't go clean through but almost. It only took a little jiggle for the log to split completely.

"Good job. I couldn't do it either when I first got here. Jalen had to show me."

Ethan stayed and retrieved the split logs and set up new logs for Luke. As the pile grew, Ethan noted Luke's arms shaking. "Okay. My turn."

Luke nodded and gave Ethan the ax. He started to set up a new log, but his hands trembled as he fumbled with the log. "Sorry, Ethan."

"That's okay, Luke. We have a lot of wood stacked already. Let's go get something to eat."

They ambled toward the fire when Luke stopped. "Uh, can we go inside instead?"

Ethan had been scanning the ground for walnuts. There was a stand of black walnut trees not far from the fire, and the nuts had begun falling in the last few days. Some were bigger than golf balls. When the wind blew, sometimes one would land on the roof of the house as loud as a gunshot. He lifted his eyes from the ground, looked at the fire, and saw Daniel sitting in one of the Adirondack chairs that had been there since they'd arrived. "Yeah. Sure."

Noah and Cassie sat at the table with cups of coffee. The kitchen smelled of bread, apples, corn, and of course, coffee. He hated the taste of the brew but loved the smell. When Dexter had gone out and come back with dozens of bags from a doughnut shop, the way the adults acted, Ethan would have thought they had won the lottery.

Cassie peeled apples as Noah cleaned a rifle.

"Hey, boys. I saw you adding to the woodpile. Nice job." Noah wiped the rifle with a rag.

Ethan nodded. "Thanks. I know it's kind of early for lunch, but wondered if there's anything we can snack on?"

"Apples." Cassie nodded to a basket at her feet.

Ethan grabbed one for him and tossed another to Luke. He sat at the table while Luke leaned against the counter, tossing his apple from hand to hand a few times, as if unsure what to do about it.

"Going hunting?" Ethan asked around a mouthful of apple. Juice squirted from his mouth, and he snorted and rubbed it from the table with his arm. "Sorry."

Noah chuckled. "Yeah. Deer are getting so bold now. I saw a half dozen of them on the edge of the cornfield."

"You think you'll get one?"

"At least. I'd better, if I want to call myself a hunter. Have you ever hunted?"

Ethan shook his head. "No. My dad never did either. He was a computer programmer."

"Ah. One of the few things my dad did with us—my brother and I—was to teach us how to hunt."

"My dad takes me hunting every year," Luke added then took a bite of his apple.

Resentment stabbed through Ethan. Not because Luke had gone hunting before, but because he could talk about his dad in the present tense. Almost as soon as the resentment hit, it disappeared. Luke wasn't responsible for Ethan's dad's death, and as much as he disliked Daniel, he didn't want him dead just so Luke could feel the same loss that he did.

"What did your dad do for a living?" Ethan took the last bite of his apple and tossed the core into the bucket of scraps they gave to the goats.

Luke shrugged and nibbled on his apple. "He did construction jobs sometimes." He paused, his gaze downcast. "And, uh... he worked at a warehouse for a while... and I kind of remember him working on roofs. I think. I was little then."

"You're little now." Ethan grinned, hoping Luke took it as the joke he meant it to be.

"No, I'm not," Luke protested, but he smiled and took a bite of the apple.

"Do you know where you and your dad are going when you leave here?" Ethan scanned the counters for something else to eat. The apple only whetted his appetite.

It took Ethan a few seconds to realize the room had stilled. Noah and Cassie exchanged a glance across the table and then looked at Luke. Ethan pulled his mind from his empty stomach to follow their gaze.

Luke's mouth hung open, his eyes big. "Leave?" His voice

cracked as he said it. He looked from Noah to Cassie. "Did my dad say we were leaving?"

Noah's jaw tightened, and Ethan felt his face flush with guilt. Noah sent him a hard look, and Ethan cleared his throat. "Uh, I'm sorry, Luke. I thought you knew."

"I haven't really had a chance to see my dad. You've kept me working all the time. Where will the three of us go?"

Ethan stiffened. If Luke had ever said he wanted to go see his dad, Ethan would have told him to go ahead. But he'd never asked. He opened his mouth to say so when Noah spoke.

"It'll only be the two of you, Luke. Ruby has decided to stay here. She says she's no relation to either of you."

Ethan's gaze flew to Noah. Was it true? Ruby was staying here? She was quiet but tough. He felt a kinship with her, as they were the only kids here who had lost their parents.

Noah gave an almost imperceptible nod to Ethan before turning back to Luke. "Luke, you have to realize that your dad nearly killed one of our... own. One of our *family*. I brought him and you here because I couldn't leave him out there to die."

"Maybe you should have left us both to die. Better then than now." Luke crossed his arms. His bottom lip curled out. After a minute, his voice softened, bordering on pleading. "He didn't know what he was doing. He's never shot anyone before in his life!"

Noah tipped his head as if conceding that point but continued, "But you have to understand that he's not shown any remorse."

"What if I get him to apologize? I'm sure I can get him to."

Ethan's stomach churned as tears spilled down Luke's

face. Why had he opened his big mouth? Not that it would have changed things. Luke would have found out eventually. Still, he wouldn't have been the one to spill the tea.

Shaking his head, Noah gave the rifle one last swipe. "Look, Luke. He justified shooting at us, saying he thought we were zombies. Not only did he shoot at us, nearly killing Vivian, he started a fire that could have killed Cassie and the little kids."

"I did that. I shouldn't have, but my dad said fire would kill zombies."

Cassie sighed. "We should probably discuss this later. I don't think anything is decided for certain. Right, Noah?" She raised an eyebrow at Noah, and Ethan sensed they communicated something.

Noah looked surprised but nodded. "There's a possibility, but it's slim."

Luke swiped a hand across his eyes and sniffed. "Really? I'll work twice as hard. I swear. I'll clean the goat pen and even the chicken coop."

Ethan knew that Luke hated dealing with the chickens. He thought they were smelly and didn't quite trust the brown eggs. He'd never had a brown egg before arriving on the farm.

"I'll help you, Luke." It was the least he could do after starting this whole conversation. Forgetting about his hunger, he rose. "Is there anything you guys need us to do before we go take care of the chicken coop?"

Cassie shook her head. "No. I'm going to can some of these apples and use the rest for a few pies."

"I could use Luke's help with dinner tonight. I got a couple of pheasants that I shot this morning. He can help me create a little feast."

Luke grimaced but didn't object.

When the screen door had slammed behind them, Ethan trudged toward the chicken coop. "I am sorry, Luke. I heard Cassie and Noah talking to Vivian and Dexter the other day. I only heard that you and your dad were leaving. I didn't know it wasn't what you wanted."

Luke nodded. "It's okay."

They reached the coop, and Luke turned to Ethan. "You're so lucky. They're keeping you but probably not me."

Ethan paused, letting Luke enter first. He was lucky.

18

"I could help you, but why should I? You guys were going to shove us out with nowhere to go and no food. But now, all of a sudden, you want me to help you put up solar panels?" Daniel scoffed then hocked up phlegm and spit it in the dirt beside Noah's feet.

Noah kicked dirt over the glob and motioned to the pile of solar panels. He and Cassie had been examining the panels in the barn when Daniel had shuffled in. Cassie had seen a few YouTube videos on solar power before the pandemic, and he had learned a little bit about going off the grid when chatting with other hunters and fishermen on the internet. He wasn't sure how much he recalled from those conversations, though. Dexter's engineering background would help, and he was the one in charge of the project.

"We'll figure it out ourselves. Or we'll get by without it. We have plenty of wood. The electricity was more of a luxury than a necessity. So do what you will. But Ruby stays here."

"She came with us; she'll leave with us." Daniel's jaw jutted out, his lips a thin line.

"The only reason she was with you was because you helped yourself to her supplies at the camp she had made all by herself!" Cassie pushed in front of Noah, glaring up at Daniel. "A little girl saved you, and you don't even have the decency to say thank you."

"That's bullshit. She would have died without my protection."

"Protection from what, Daniel?" Noah crossed his arms, his feet planted wide. Ruby hadn't accused Daniel of anything inappropriate, but Noah couldn't shake off the sketchy vibe the other man gave off. Out of the corner of his eye, he saw Ruby approaching where they stood in front of the clinic. In the short time she had been with them, she had lost her gaunt look and added a few pounds. She even smiled sometimes. They still didn't know her whole story, as she couldn't yet speak of her family without breaking down.

Daniel glared at Ruby as she came closer. She met his eyes with a steady look of her own. There was a quiet strength in the girl that reminded Noah of Cassie. She wasn't going to roll over and die. Daniel pointed at her. "Tell them, girl! Tell them how I saved you from the people with the virus!"

Ruby's brow furrowed. "You mean the 'zombies'?" She made air quotes and then shook her head. "I knew enough to stay away from people. You barged in on my camp when I was sleeping. I should have sneaked away that first night. But then you took all my gear from me, and I was stuck."

"What do you mean he took your gear?" Cassie moved to stand beside the young girl, her arm around her shoulders.

"He took my tent for him and Luke, and I had to sleep under a tarp. And he took my rifle."

"The rifle he used?" Noah unfolded his arms, his hands clenched at his sides.

"Yeah. He used it to shoot Vivian." She dropped head. "I'm sorry."

Noah shook his head. "Don't even think it was even any little bit of your fault. It wasn't."

She nodded.

Daniel waved a hand at Ruby. "Aw, hell, you're lying, and you know it. But I'll let it go for now. Get your things. We're going. They don't want us here unless I put up those stupid solar panels."

"We are putting up the panels whether you stay or go, but yes, you can stay through the winter if you help. Think of it as earning your keep. While you were laid up, we've been harvesting crops, putting food up, and hunting so we don't starve this winter. Why should you get to share in it without helping?"

"Luke helped. He worked *for* me."

Noah shook his head. "Nope. Luke worked for himself, and he's welcome to stay if he wants. He's earned a place here. It's because of him that we put together some supplies to tide you over until you get your situation figured out."

He hadn't decided until right then that Luke could stay if he wanted, but the idea of sending the kid off with Daniel, even if he was Luke's father, made Noah sick to his stomach.

"Now you're trying to take my own kid from me?" Daniel took a step closer to Noah, his eyes narrowed, nostrils flaring, but Noah's only worry was that Daniel would force him to defend himself. He didn't want to hurt the man. It wouldn't be a fair fight.

"Get back. I'm not trying to take him, but he'd be better off here, and you know it."

"A boy's place is beside his dad. But you wouldn't know that because you don't have any kids, do you? You think it's so damned easy being a dad, but you never had to do any of the hard stuff."

Noah's jaw tightened. He didn't have to be a father to identify a bad one when he stumbled across Noah's path. He had firsthand experience with his own dad, and Daniel's attitude was just like his own father's, except he wasn't drunk. He had that going for him at least. "It's true I don't have kids of my own, but I feel I've kind of adopted a few in the last few months. I'd do anything for them. Sacrifice anything."

Daniel sneered. "Oh really? You'd die for them?"

Noah had no hesitation in his mind. He'd been a soldier. He'd have died for his country if he'd had to. Putting himself in harm's way to save any one of the kids on this farm would be automatic. "To save them, yes. In a heartbeat."

"You're a sucker."

"Wouldn't you do anything you could to save Luke?" Noah hated that he even had to ask.

"I raised him, didn't I? That's enough. His mom took off when he was a baby. I was the one who was always there for him."

Noah didn't know what to make of that response. "Whatever. Luke is welcome all the same. You might be welcome to stay through the winter if you help us get the solar panels up and working, and if everyone agrees. This isn't up to me alone."

"You didn't even ask us." Dexter marched through the kitchen door, his look pinning Noah to the chair.

"Wait. What did you hear? And from who?" Noah had meant to get everyone together tonight after dinner to discuss it but hadn't had a chance.

"What difference does it make? Daniel's out there smirking and saying how he's going to be here all winter. I'm about ten seconds away from going out there and smacking that evil grin right into the next county!"

"I told him it was up to everyone. That it wasn't solely up to me. He shouldn't have assumed he'd get to stay."

Dexter leaned on the table, his face twisted. "So if we say no, don't you think he's gonna figure out it was me and Vivian who didn't want him around?" He thumped his chest with his palm. "I can barely tolerate the sight of him! And you think we'd be okay with him living here?" He shook his head and straightened. "I thought you were smarter than that. I thought you'd at least ask us before discussing it with him. Don't you think we deserve that much respect?" He angled his head, still shaking it and waving his finger back and forth. "Nope. No way. That asshole tried to murder my wife." He paced away from Noah, arms crossed, turned, sent him a glare, and stalked back to the table, clearly waiting for a response.

Noah nodded. "You're right. I was wrong. I'll go out there right now and tell him he has to go." He stood, but Dexter blocked his exit. Dexter stared at him, the other man's jaw clenching as if he had something to say but was debating whether to say it or not. Noah backed up until the edge of the chair bumped against the back of his legs. "I'm sorry."

Dexter's eyes narrowed, and his head angled to the left.

He filled the space Noah had just vacated. "I just want to know how you could ever think about letting that piece of shit stay in *this house*! Sharing *our* food! Sleeping under *our* roof!" His nostrils flared as his eyes searched Noah's. "We'll move out first."

"Hold on. Don't do that. Please. Just let me explain my thinking, okay?" Noah edged forward, and Dexter backed away. Slightly.

"Now, I was totally wrong to say anything to Daniel before we had thoroughly discussed it, but I was thinking of Luke, mostly. I think the kid deserves a chance. You know that young boy leaves with Daniel, he's going to end up dead. Say what you will about the father, but the son doesn't deserve to die because his dad's an asshole. He doesn't have the common sense God gave a cockroach."

Dexter took another step back, his stance relaxing some-what. "I don't know about Luke either. Do we really want him here? I mean, I don't have much to do with him, but Jalen told me about the fight Luke and Ethan got into. I don't know if I want a kid like that around my children."

"I get it. I do. Ethan and I spoke about their situation, and I think they're getting along better now. I've noticed a change in Luke that you might not have seen since you haven't had much of a chance to get to know him."

"What's all the hollering about?" Vivian entered, her movements slow and deliberate, one hand on her stomach.

"I'm sorry, Viv, but I learned Noah here invited Daniel to stay here as his guest." Dexter moved to pull a chair out for his wife.

Noah rolled his eyes at the phrasing. "That's not how it went, exactly."

Vivian raised her eyebrows at him as she sank onto the chair. "Really? And how did it go? Exactly?"

Noah resumed his seat at the table and turned to Vivian. "Daniel knows about solar panels—he says he does, anyway —and we have the panels Dexter found. Apparently one of Daniel's jobs in the past was installing solar panels. Now, I'm sure your husband can figure it out, but having someone else there with actual experience could be invaluable."

"Is that true?" She directed her question at Dexter.

"It could be. I haven't talked to Daniel about his experience. Hell, I've avoided him as much as possible. I sure as hell didn't go and visit with him." He shot a look at Noah, as if Noah had become best buds with Daniel. "For all we know, he's full of shit. He could be making it all up just to stay here."

"Do you trust him, Noah?"

He shook his head, rubbing a hand along the stubble on his jaw. "No. But I was also going to say that he wouldn't stay in the house, so he won't be staying under this roof." Noah cast his own look at Dexter. He wasn't mad at the other man, but he also wasn't going to be cowed. "I don't want him in here any more than either of you do."

"Then where would they stay?" Vivian gave Noah a skeptical look. "As much as I don't like him, I won't kick Luke out to freeze this winter."

"You have too big of a heart, baby." Dexter plopped onto a chair across from his wife and clasped his hands behind his head, his elbows propped on the table.

Sensing that Dexter was more inclined to listen now, Noah leaned forward. "I was thinking... what if we found a camper? A trailer home would be better, but I don't know how we'd get one here."

Noah had given it some thought. Asking Dexter and Vivian to welcome the man into their home, as it belonged to them as much as any of them, was asking a lot. Most of the outbuildings were in use. Between the cow, the chickens, and the goats, the barn and chicken coop were out of the question. They'd converted the large shed into the clinic. Another was a tool shop, of sorts. It would be even more important in the winter when they couldn't work on anything outside. They had found a few woodstoves, and Dexter had installed one in there. It was a necessary building for projects, and they could heat it.

That left the grain silo, which still had enough grain in it to get the animals through the winter if they were careful, and a rickety building on the edge of the farm. It might have been the original cabin on the farm. It looked like at some point someone had made it into a guesthouse, but it had fallen into disrepair.

Noah had an idea. "We can tell Daniel if he can fix up that old cabin, he can stay there for the winter. It would give us a chance to see if he actually knows what he's doing. He can even use a couple of solar panels on it. If he can get them working, then would you consider letting him stay?"

Dexter sighed and glanced at Vivian. She shrugged, and Dexter reached for her hand. "I promise you that if he so much as looks at us cross-eyed, he's gone."

Noah nodded. "I'll send him away myself at the point of a rifle."

19

"I know it's a lot to ask, but can you stay here and keep an eye on Daniel while we're gone?"

Ethan paused, a spoonful of lentil soup halfway to his mouth, and raised his eyes to Noah. "Just me?"

He set the spoon down, trying to hide his disappointment. He'd been looking forward to hunting with Dexter, Jalen, and Noah. It was finally cold enough to be able to store meat so it would be easier to process. After bringing in all of the harvest, the attic and cellar were stuffed to the rafters with onions, cabbages, carrots, beans, squash, apples, potatoes, and even sweet potatoes. The one thing they didn't have much of was meat. They had some dried venison from deer killed earlier, and some dried fish, too, along with canned meats they'd scavenged, but everyone wanted to get as much as they could stored away. They had already seen how quickly supplies were depleted with so many mouths to feed. Their group now numbered a dozen.

They'd scoured all the nearby farms and houses, but not many people had lived with more than a week or two of food on hand. Nobody had needed to, not when a store was just at most a twenty-minute drive away. A lot of the food had been fresh and was long spoiled before they ever entered the houses. With so much food and no people around to stop them, rats and mice proliferated. Ethan shuddered as he recalled entering a house down the road. The occupants of the house had been eaten already, between microbes, maggots, and rats. All that had been left were bones and hair.

Noah sat beside him and set a bowl of soup and a sleeve of crackers on the table. "Want some?"

"Sure." Ethan took a few, dipping them into the soup. "Soup's good."

"Thanks. I made extra so you don't have to worry about lunch or anything tomorrow."

Ethan sighed. "I guess I don't have much choice in the matter."

"You know Dexter and Jalen won't stay with Daniel."

Ethan nodded. "I know. You'd come back to find Daniel's corpse." He chuckled. "I guess it won't be so bad. Luke and I can find something to do."

Noah glanced at Ethan and then ducked his head. "Luke is going with us."

"Whoa, wait a second. Why does he get to go?"

"I know it doesn't seem fair, but you're a decent shot already, and you went hunting with me last time."

"But we didn't end up even hunting."

"True. But we found the other cow. That's even better."

"Yeah, I guess, but still..." Ethan ate a mouthful of soup. "Daisy will give milk again once she has her calf."

"I sure hope so, but isn't it nice to have milk now? And cheese?"

Ethan smiled. He loved cheese. "We have goat cheese. But yeah. I get your point. I can't help being a little pissed. All there is to do here is work. Going hunting... well, it's like an adventure." He knew he was pouting, and that bugged him too.

"Next time, how about I take just you and Jalen? Or just you. Whichever way you want."

"I suppose." Ethan did his best to lose the petulant tone he heard in his voice. "I guess."

"I'm leaving a rifle with you, and Cassie has her own handgun."

"You are? Aren't you going to need it?"

"We have plenty of rifles. This is Wisconsin, after all. I've found more hunting rifles and ammunition than we'll ever need—I hope."

Ethan laughed. "That's true. I was one of the only kids in my school who didn't take off the week of Thanksgiving to go deer hunting."

Last year, his best friend Colin had asked Ethan to go with him and his father, but Ethan's dad hadn't let him. Colin would have known how to hunt. He should have been the one to live. "I guess it's your bad luck that I'm the one who survived." He ducked his head and stirred his spoon listlessly in the soup.

"*The one who survived?* I don't know what you're talking about there, but while we've all had a shitload of bad luck, having you with the group is not part of that load. You are one of the best things that's come out of all of this. For us, anyway. You're our good luck. Besides, I wouldn't trust just anyone to keep my niece and nephew safe." Noah crumbled crackers on top of his soup and dug in.

Ethan straightened. He didn't believe for one second that he was their "good luck," but he appreciated Noah saying so. "I will. I'll keep my eye on them and make sure Daniel isn't around them."

Not that Daniel had paid any attention to the kids. For the most part, nobody saw him much, just a few times a day to get a meal. Most of the time, he took it back to the old cabin. He and Luke slept in a tent while they worked on the cabin. Ethan had helped a few days. He wanted to learn how to build things on his own.

While he'd been a good student in school, he'd never felt a desire to learn anything in particular. He consumed what the teachers placed on his plate but didn't ask for seconds. Now, he felt driven to learn as much about everything as he could. He wanted to learn to hunt and forage, to build homes and plant fields, and even how to can and store food. All of it was new to him, and Ethan felt like he never knew enough. If, God forbid, something happened to the others, he'd have to survive on his own. Unlike the first time he found himself alone, the next time, if it came, he'd be prepared.

THE NEXT DAY, after taking care of all of the animals, Ethan, Cassie, and the three kids gathered up six large plastic bins of black walnuts from a grove of trees on the west side of the farmhouse. The grove stood between the farmhouse and the cabin, and Ethan noted the progress Daniel and Luke were making. Ethan had lost track of the days but figured it had been at least a week since Daniel had recovered enough to leave the clinic. Luke had moped about moving out of the farmhouse, but his dad still needed some help at times. The biggest issue was getting them to use the compost toilet Noah had rigged up for them. Daniel had balked, saying he'd just go in a field. Noah told him he'd better bury his waste every time like they had done in the woods.

"Watch out, Ethan!"

Ethan ducked as a nut flew past his head. "What was that about?"

Milo giggled. "We were playing a game. Who could get the most in the tub from here." He pointed to the bin to Ethan's right and a stick just in front of Milo's toes.

"I'm going to have to show you how to throw."

"Are you good at it?"

"Yeah. I was a pitcher in my league's All-Star game last year."

Ethan gave all the kids a quick lesson. "Ava, are you sure you never pitched before?" The girl had an arm! She covered her mouth, laughing as she shook her head.

The kids had a great time, tossing the golf-ball-sized nuts into the bins and racing around like it was an Easter egg hunt, seeing who could find the most. Every now and then, the sounds of a hammer or saw filtered through the trees to them. It was a good place to get something useful done while still keeping an eye on Daniel.

"So I may be a terrible gardener, but what I know about, I know. People would pay a premium for black walnuts in their baked goods, and I was just starting out and barely had any money for supplies. Black walnuts were expensive, so I looked at a few videos on how to harvest these guys." Cassie tossed several in the bins. "I couldn't believe how much money I was saving and how much more I was earning on those baked goods. I started specializing in black walnut desserts."

"Did you have a tree in your yard?" Ethan tossed four more into his bin. It was nearly full. Of course, the nut inside wasn't nearly as big once the thick husk was removed, but he still estimated it would be a good haul.

"No. I went to the park with the kids. That's why they're so good at doing this."

"Um, I think more walnuts are landing near the bin than in it." Ethan laughed as a few more nuts bounced off the blue plastic.

"All right, guys! Enough of the goofing around. See how fast you can fill that bin. I'm timing you!"

"What do we get if we fill it in five minutes, Mommy?" Bella held a walnut whose husk had turned dark brown. She held it between two fingers and made a face. "It smells!"

"What are you guys doing?"

Ethan whirled to find Daniel leaning against a tree. "Gathering walnuts."

"You really think you can eat those things?" He shook his head. "They're full of worms." He brought a hand up, and it was then that Ethan saw he had a bottle of whiskey. He took a long gulp.

Ethan sent a glance over his shoulder to Cassie, seeking guidance. She had her eyes locked on Daniel even as she reached for the children, pushing them behind her. Facing forward again, Ethan squared his shoulders. He wasn't going to argue about walnuts. He didn't think Daniel would listen anyway.

"How's the cabin coming along, Daniel?" Ethan stepped

toward the man. He hoped to distract him from Cassie and the kids.

"Like you really give a shit..."

"I do. I mean, I helped you just the other day."

"You helped Luke, not me." He pushed off of the tree trunk with his shoulder. "What a pretty little girl. Why didn't you introduce me to your kids, Cassie?"

"We're going inside. It's time to start lunch." Cassie swept the kids ahead of her, putting herself between Daniel and the children as she herded them back to the house.

"Are you gonna put my food on the back porch like you did last night? What? Ain't I good enough to come into the house?"

Cassie turned, her eyes locking on Ethan's. He tried to read the message in her look, but he was clueless. He did the only thing he could think of. He threw a walnut at Daniel. Not hard, but hard enough to get his attention. The walnut he used was one of the soft brown ones. Even Bella wouldn't have been hurt at getting hit with it.

"Ouch! What the hell do you think you're doing?"

"Oh, sorry. We were playing a game before you came up. We were trying to see if we could hit each other with these. The brown ones leave a mark—sort of like paintball." Ethan stooped and gathered a few more, forcing a smile. "Bet you can't hit me!" He did a mock retreat, dancing back a few steps. "Go on, try to hit me with one!"

"You hit me again, and you'll wish you never picked up one of those stinkin' nuts." Daniel still wasn't up to running, and Ethan had counted on that.

"Okay. I guess the game is over. How about I come over this afternoon and help you out again?" It was the last thing he wanted to do, but he'd do it if it got Daniel away from the others.

"Yeah. You do that. With Luke gone, I can't get nothing done. They took Luke so I'd fail and you all could kick us out."

Ethan didn't mention they could kick him out whenever they wanted. They weren't obligated to let him live near them and share in their food. "I'll bring over lunch for you. In fact, I'll bring mine, too, and we can eat together."

"Aw, isn't that nice of you to make me feel special." Daniel took another hefty swallow and turned, stumbling, but Ethan wasn't certain if he was so drunk he couldn't walk, or if he'd simply stumbled on a black walnut and turned his ankle a little. Either way, he recovered his balance and returned to the cabin.

Ethan tossed the nuts he'd gathered as ammunition into the bins. His plan had been to help Cassie separate the husks from the nuts this afternoon, but it looked like he had a different nut to deal with.

20

N oah didn't drive too far from the farm. Deer were pretty much everywhere now that people were scarce. He pulled into a state park. "This place looks good." He waited for Dexter and Jalen to park beside him. The parking lot didn't look any different than it would in the late fall just before hunting season began. It was empty, but the lot must have been resurfaced recently because it was still in great condition. Some of the less well-maintained lots and even roads where Noah had driven had begun sprouting weeds in the middle of them.

A few trees held on to their leaves still, but most were bare. The air, crisp and cleaner than Noah had ever smelled it, nipped at his nose. A light dusting of frost melted on the sun-gilded grass. The beauty reminded Noah that life went on. He pulled on his orange vest and tossed one to Luke.

"Aww, why do we have to wear this? It's not like anyone is around." Luke straightened the vest and put it on in spite of his grumbling.

"So one of us doesn't end up shooting you by mistake."

Noah put his own on and then opened the back tailgate and pulled out his backpack and a smaller one for Luke. "Here you go. I packed it with food, a first aid kit, and ammo. There's a water bottle on the side. It has a purifier so you can use it with any water you find. Keep it close. There are other things in there, but here's the next most important." Noah found the handheld radio and turned it on, showing Luke how to use it. "If we get separated, you can just call us on this." He had Luke test it a few times and, satisfied it worked, turned to Dexter and Jalen. "This seems about a good a place as any to start."

Dexter shrugged. "Sure. You're the expert."

"Hey, you and your kid are getting pretty good at all of this too." Noah gave Dexter a slap on the back. "Why don't you guys head that way a few hundred yards, and we'll go the other way the same distance? Then both of us can head due north. That way, we can be parallel to each other but far enough apart to be safe."

Noah led Luke through the woods, pausing every so often to listen. A few times, they heard something, but once it was only a squirrel dashing up a tree, his claws loud in the near silence. The second time, they found they'd startled a coyote. It took off at a sprint across a meadow and into the brush.

"Wow! Did you see that?" Luke looked at Noah, his eyes shining.

Noah smiled. "Sure did. I also know that any deer in that direction have scattered now. Let's go this way." He tipped his head to the left. "Do you feel comfortable with the rifle now?" Noah kept a wary eye on the kid. He had done well when Noah had shown him how to load, aim, and shoot, but walking for a long time over uneven ground meant fatigue, and fatigue meant the boy could get careless.

"Is it true that Dr. Leona hunts too?"

Noah smiled. "She does. Although she opted to sit this one out. She's quite the marksman."

He scanned the forest as they walked and marked their trail with neon-green tape he put on tree trunks. He explained everything he did so Luke would understand. He hoped that when he and his dad left that at least Luke would have some basic survival skills. Even if Daniel got the cabin fixed up and solar panels up and working, things wouldn't work out. The guy was just too belligerent and unstable.

As if he was reading Noah's mind, Luke broke into his thoughts with a question. "Are you really going to make us leave if my dad can't get everything done?"

Noah sighed. "I will. I'm sorry about that, but I have to do what needs to be done to keep everyone safe. Completing this project will help prove your dad is serious about wanting to help the group survive."

"I know, but my dad... he's one of those guys who doesn't like bosses very much." Luke leaped over a log, giving Noah a mini heart attack that the rifle would somehow go off. It didn't, and Luke traipsed on, oblivious of the scare he'd given Noah.

"I'm not his boss." Noah paused and held up his hand. There. A sound just ahead. Luke followed his lead as they eased through the forest.

Ahead was a small clearing, and not a hundred feet away was a good-sized buck. Beyond him were three does and two half-grown deer. They had probably been born the past spring.

Noah motioned for Luke to aim for the buck. Luke's eyes rounded, but he nodded. Noah would go for the doe who was farthest from the fawns. She probably wasn't their mother.

First Noah then Luke fired. His doe fell in her tracks, but the buck leaped in the air, thrashing. Stumbling in panic and terror, he was still very much alive. Luke dashed forward, lifting his rifle.

The buck turned toward the motion and darted straight toward him.

"*Luke! Get back!*" Noah lunged forward, grabbed Luke's backpack, and spun, flinging Luke out of harm's way, but a point from the buck's antler caught Noah in his left side along his ribs.

Luke brought his gun up like it was a club until Noah screamed at him to drop it. He brought his own rifle up and shot the buck a second time. This time, the buck's legs folded, and he keeled over.

Noah stumbled to the trunk of a tree and slid down against it, his pack getting caught on bark and twisting the straps. He kept sliding, unable to stop, as he clutched his side. He came to rest on a large root.

"Oh my God, Noah. Are you okay?" Luke sank to his knees beside Noah. "I'm so sorry."

Grimacing, Noah kept his hand clamped to his side. Blood spilled over his fingers. He wanted to look but was afraid of what he'd see. He was leaning back with his own pack stuck between himself and the tree. "Turn around."

"What? Why?"

"I gotta get out your first aid kit." He tried not to look at his bloody fingers as he gestured.

Luke drew a deep breath. "Okay, but I can do it." He

slipped off the pack and rummaged through it. "Here it is. Now what?"

"There's a couple of packs of gauze in there and tape. We need to pack the wound and tape the pack down."

Nodding, Luke opened couple of packs. "I saw you helping my dad. I think I can do this."

"Good. But before you do anything more, get Dexter on the radio. He can come and help."

"Got it." Luke called while Noah closed his eyes, trying to block out the pain of the wound.

Luke fumbled with Noah's shirt, and Noah said, "Use your knife. Cut it if you have to."

Nodding, Luke pulled out his hunting knife and slit through the flannel.

He breathed in shallow pants as every breath felt like a knife cutting through him. Broken ribs, probably. He hoped that was all it was. He sucked a breath in through his teeth when Luke put a wad of gauze against the wound.

"How... how's it... look?" Noah glanced at his side, but he couldn't see much more than the edge of Luke's hand pressed against him.

"It's hard to tell. There's a long gouge, but I can't tell if the antler went deeper." Luke tossed a wad of soaked gauze aside and put another pad of gauze on top. "Dexter and Jalen are on their way."

Noah hadn't even heard Luke radio them, but he had been focused on the pain and was only dimly aware of Luke's actions.

The pain hadn't let up, but he was getting accustomed to it. He nudged Luke's hand away. "Here, I can hold pressure. You go ahead and make sure those guys find us."

"I told them to look for our markers and the stream we crossed a ways back."

Noah barely remembered the stream. "Good detail." He closed his eyes and rested his head against the rough bark.

"I can hear them!" Luke dashed from Noah's side. "We're here!"

"*Hello?*"

Noah opened his eyes. That wasn't Dexter's or Jalen's voice.

21

C assie practically dragged Milo in behind Bella and Ava. Ruby entered behind her and shut the door.

"Lock it!"

Ruby nodded and turned the bolt. "What about Ethan?"

"When he knocks, I can let him in." Cassie made sure the other doors were also locked then returned to the kitchen. "Wash your hands, guys." She added a tiny bit of soap to Milo, Bella, and Ava's palms then a little to her own. They soaped and rinsed with the second pail that was for that purpose. The gloves had protected them for the most part. At least none of them were stained from the husks.

"Go look at books for a bit while I get lunch ready."

Daniel's behavior was probably due to the alcohol he'd obviously been drinking, but she couldn't help flashing back to the last time she'd seen her ex-husband, Dave. Unlike her ex, she didn't think Daniel had the virus, but there was something about him that unnerved her.

Ruby looked out of the window that faced the cabin. They couldn't see it through the trees, though, so they didn't know if he had returned to the cabin or if he was coming up to the house. "He's scary, right?" She looked over her shoulder to Cassie as if for confirmation.

Cassie nodded. Scary. Creepy. Weird. Frightening. It made her wonder how Ruby had managed to deal with the man in the weeks, or maybe even months, since the virus. She wasn't sure exactly when Daniel had claimed Ruby's campsite for his own. "Did he ever do anything to... scare you?"

"No. Not really, but I think he wanted to, if that makes sense."

"How do you know he wanted to?"

Ruby lifted one shoulder, looking down as she tugged her gloves off and set them on a side table that had been in the kitchen since they had found the house. "He said things when Luke wasn't around. Like how since I was the only girl left alive, it was my duty to have kids with him when I was old enough."

Cassie shuddered. "You poor, dear girl."

Ruby looked at Cassie, her bottom lip trembling. "I told him never in a million years."

"Wow, that took a lot of courage. What did he say then?" Cassie moved beside her to peer out of the window too. Where was Ethan?

"He just laughed, and it was the laugh that scared me the most."

Cassie put her arm over Ruby's scrawny shoulders and pulled her in for a sideways hug. "Don't worry. We'll never leave you alone with him. Ever."

Ruby nodded, one hand going up to swipe at her eyes. "Thank you."

CASSIE BROUGHT a tray of sandwiches upstairs to Leona and Vivian. "I hope you're both hungry."

Leona looked up from the recliner she sat in, knitting. She called it her therapy and said it had always kept her fingers dexterous, which was important when she performed surgeries. "I'm starving, but you didn't have to bring me my lunch. I could have come downstairs."

Cassie waved her hand. "It was no trouble. The kids are playing a game downstairs, and I'm caught up with my baking—can you believe it?"

Vivian held up knitting needles and a small rectangle. "Look. Leona is teaching me how to knit!"

Cassie smiled at the soft yellow square. "A baby blanket?"

Vivian's brow furrowed briefly before she gave a tentative nod. "I wasn't going to tempt fate by calling it that, but it could be a blanket."

"Vivian, my best advice is to enjoy the pregnancy—as much as any woman can, anyway—and go ahead and make dreams about this baby. If something happens, it will happen whether you make the dreams or not, and I don't think it'll be any less devastating if you try to stifle them."

Vivian tilted her head. "You know what? You're right, Leona! I've been so worried about what might happen, even before I was shot, that I haven't allowed myself to feel joy and hope."

Cassie set Vivian's lunch beside her on a table. The injured woman was still on strict bed rest except to use the bathroom. She'd been spotting a bit after being shot, and Leona was taking no chances. "Well, I wasn't even shot, and

I've had a hard time feeling joy and hope. With everything that's happened, even when I do feel happy for some achievement, I feel guilty because of the billions of people who are dead. What right do I have to feel happy?"

"Well, thanks for that ray of sunshine, Cassie." Leona set her knitting aside but gave Cassie a smile to let her know she was only kidding. "I know what you mean. I was all set to live out the rest of my life alone, but then Noah stumbled into my house, I shot him, and here we are now." She spread her hands and looked from Cassie to Vivian. "I'm in a house with wonderful people who allow me to share their food and supplies. If life is going to go on, I'd rather be here with you all than alone in my home."

"We're glad you're here too, Leona." Cassie smiled.

"I thank God every night that you shot Noah."

When Cassie and Leona burst into laughter, Vivian's eyes widened in innocence. "You know I didn't mean it like that." Then she gave them a sly grin. And they all exploded into a fit of giggles again.

Cassie chatted for a bit then gathered up the dirty dishes. "I wanted to get started husking the walnuts, but Daniel was acting weird."

"He is a strange one, I'll give you that." Leona put her dishes on the tray and tucked her knitting into a tote bag. "Well, ladies, I'm going to head to the clinic. I have some more boxes to unpack. I still can't believe how many boxes of supplies are still stacked in the toolshed."

"Watch out for Daniel. I don't know where he went after I brought the kids inside. Ethan distracted him."

"Oh, he's strange, but he knows who saved his sorry ass."

"That's true." Cassie turned back to Vivian. "Do you need anything?"

Vivian held up her knit blanket. "Nope. Just a magic potion to help me get the hang of knitting."

Grinning, Cassie left the room.

After another hour, she still hadn't seen Ethan. Cassie was beyond worried. Had Daniel done something to the boy?

"Ruby, can you keep an eye on the kids for a little bit? I'm going to go find Ethan and bring him lunch."

She made a sandwich of venison with mustard, put it between two thick slabs of bread, grabbed an apple and a hunk of cheese, and tossed them into a paper bag. Ethan might have decided to harvest some pumpkins. He'd mentioned that he'd seen a patch of them on a farm across the road.

"Lock the door behind me, Ruby. I'll knock two times then once." She wished there was a peephole in the door. Up until now, they hadn't even bothered to shut the door except at night, and that was to keep racoons or other night creatures from getting in.

Bag in hand, she headed to the farm outbuildings. "Ethan! Ethan?" Where could the boy be?

She checked the back of the barn, but he wasn't there. The children's wagon still sat in the back of the barn, so he probably hadn't gone to get pumpkins.

There was only one other place he might be, and Cassie hesitated to go there. One part of her wanted to flee to the farmhouse again. Ethan was smart. He could handle himself. But he was only fourteen. Daniel was a grown man.

Drawing a deep breath, she marched through the trees,

exiting the stand. There was no activity on the exterior of the building.

"Ethan!" She strode past piles of planks and sawhorses set up with sheets of plywood nearby.

The cabin had no door at the moment, and one glance let her know there was nobody inside. The tent was on the other side of the cabin. "Ethan!"

"I'm over here!"

She turned, craning her neck. Ethan was on the roof of the cabin. "Where's Daniel?"

"Sleeping it off, I think. I'm putting up flashing."

"All by yourself?"

Ethan shrugged, and Cassie's heart almost stopped. He was up on top with no ropes or anything holding him on the roof if he should lose his balance. "Daniel told me how to do it. It's not hard."

Swallowing warnings that make her sound like his mother, she held up the paper bag. "I thought you might be hungry."

Ethan grinned and scampered down the ladder leaning against the cabin like a squirrel after a nut. "Thanks!"

Cassie gave it to him, then they walked to the stack of plywood and sat down on it like it was a bench. "How's he been?"

"He's an ass, but since I'm helping him, he's not been too bad. Sorry I didn't come over to help with the walnuts. I figured that this was the best way to keep an eye on him."

"No apology necessary. You don't answer to me." She couldn't believe how much Ethan had grown since she had met him. While he'd grown a few inches physically, he had also matured into a young man. She was sure that his struggle to survive had a lot to do with his growth.

"This is really good." Ethan took another bite then found his water bottle on the ground near the sawhorses. "Do you think they got a deer?"

Cassie took the change in subject in stride. "I hope so. While we have a lot of canned foods, we can always use meat."

"I wish I could have gone." He crumpled the wax paper she'd wrapped the sandwich in.

Cassie imagined being out there without Ethan to distract Daniel and shuddered. "I'm glad you were here."

Ethan nodded. "The black walnuts will keep a few more days, I hope."

"They will. They're fine for now. We'll put them in a few of those big buckets, and I'll find something we can use to sort of whisk them in with water. It'll remove most of the husks. Then we spread them out to dry. I'm thinking the road out front would be perfect."

"That's all there is to it?" Ethan started on the apple.

"Yeah. That's it. We leave them in the shell until we're ready to use them. They'll last a long time like that."

"Thanks for lunch, Cassie. I'll be back before dark. I better get back to work."

"Why don't you tie yourself off in case you fall?"

"It's not that high. I can almost jump off it."

She gave him a sheepish grin. "Sorry, I can't help worrying."

Ethan was quiet for a moment then said, "It's okay. I don't mind you worrying about me."

Cassie ruffled his hair and headed back to the house. Still

restless, she wondered if Leona needed any help. She knocked on the clinic door, but when nobody answered, she turned to leave. Maybe Leona had finished and was already back at the house.

She heard a muffled sound she couldn't identify. It wasn't a scream. But it was more than a gasp.

"Hello? Leona?" Cassie opened the clinic door. With nobody using it, the room was lit only by daylight, so the corners were dark. The two beds that Vivian and Daniel had occupied were still separated by a divider, so the far bed was hidden from Cassie's view. The one she could see had crisp white linens on it, ready for the next person who might need it. Suddenly the divider shimmied a foot or so across the floor.

"*Help!*"

Cassie rushed forward. She rounded the divider and skidded to a halt. Daniel had Leona pressed onto bed, one hand pressing on her throat as the other fumbled for his pants.

"Daniel! Get away from her!"

"*Get out, bitch!*" He didn't even look at Cassie.

Cassie looked for a weapon and spotted Leona's tote bag on the table. She grabbed one of the long steel needles and pulled back, plunging it into Daniel's back. It stuck in him, and Cassie retreated.

"Oh, you *fucking bitch!*" Daniel released Leona and reached back to remove the needle, but he couldn't reach it. "What did you do to me?"

Cassie grabbed the second needle, not knowing how useful it would be, but Daniel had turned to Leona. "Get it out, Doctor!"

She rolled off the other side of the bed, clutching at her throat. Daniel lunged over the bed. Cassie took the opening and stabbed the second needle into him, feeling like she might vomit when she felt it lodge in the bed beneath him. He was pinned to it like a beetle to a corkboard.

Horrified, Cassie skirted around him as he writhed, and she grabbed Leona's outstretched hand. "Let's go!"

Daniel said something, but his voice sounded wet and gurgling. Leona clutched her hand, and Cassie half dragged her from the clinic. They headed to the house, but Cassie started screaming for Ethan as soon as she left the building.

Before they were halfway to the house, Ethan crashed through the woods, the rifle in one hand and a hatchet in the other, Dino racing beside him. "What's wrong?"

They had reached the firepit, and Leona sank onto a chair, gasping for breath.

"Daniel was attacking her. I got her away, but I don't know if he's coming after us." Cassie's hands shook as she had Leona raise her chin. "Can you breathe?"

Leona nodded. "I... I'm okay. You got there before he did any real harm." Leona trembled so hard that Cassie took off her own jacket, wrapped it around Leona's shoulders, and hugged her. At that, Leona broke into tears, sobbing.

"Shhh... it's okay." Cassie stroked the other woman's hair.

Ethan stood, his face red, his eyes narrowed. "I'll kill him."

"I think I might have already."

Ethan did a double take. "How?"

"Knitting needles. But go see. I have to know what happened."

Ethan nodded and tucked the hatchet by the head into a

case on his belt. He cocked the rifle and headed to the clinic. Cassie continued to comfort Leona, letting her ramble about what had happened. Of all the people to attack, Daniel attacked the one person who had treated him as she would any other patient. Anger at Daniel warred with revulsion at what she had done. She could still feel the resistance as the needles pierced his flesh.

It seemed like hours but was probably only about five minutes before Ethan opened the door to the clinic, the rifle no longer in his hands. "It's safe. He's dead."

22

"Hello?"

The voice came again with sounds of more than one, maybe several people, moving through the undergrowth.

Noah bunched Luke's shirt in his fist and pulled him close, whispering, "Run that way then turn to your right. It'll take you back toward where we parked, but when you're far enough away not to be heard, radio Dexter. Tell him to stand back until he hears from me."

"I can't leave you alone."

Noah shook his head, gritting his teeth. "Go. I have my radio. And take your pack!"

Luke hesitated, but as the sounds came closer, he stood and finally dashed away from whoever it was.

He rolled onto one hip and levered himself onto one knee, his left leg straight behind him. Then, holding onto the tree, he pulled himself to a standing position. He turned just as three men and a woman emerged into the clearing.

They stopped short at the sight of the downed deer. A tall

man in full camo, a pack on his back, a rifle slung over his right shoulder, gave a low whistle. "Wow. You got two. Nice work."

The other two men were shorter, one slim, the other stocky. The slim man held his rifle loosely in his right hand, the muzzle pointed in the general direction of the ground, but as the man spoke to the tall one, he let the muzzle rise, and it swung in Noah's direction. He flinched.

"Hey, a little care please." He pointed at the gun.

The slim man looked at it as though surprised at what he held in his hand and brought it up, again with the muzzle pointed at Noah. "Oops."

"Whoa, man!" Noah would have ducked if he could have.

"Dammit, Tanner. What did I tell you about carrying that thing?" The tall man looked like he might cuff Tanner upside the head, but instead, he scowled and shook his head. "Sorry about that."

Noah nodded, his own rifle held across his body, ready to use if he needed it.

"Is that your blood or the buck's?" The man motioned to Noah's chest.

"Just a scratch."

"Uh-huh." The man gave Noah a shrewd look. "My name's Russell. This yahoo"—he nodded to the man who'd been careless with the rifle—"is Tanner." He jabbed a thumb over his shoulder. "That's Grant and his wife Melissa."

Noah nodded. "Noah."

The woman, her cheeks ruddy and brown hair pulled back into a ponytail, smiled and returned his nod. Grant tipped his head, and Tanner gave a small wave. Noah pegged him for an accountant in his previous life.

Russell stepped closer but then stopped about ten feet from Noah. "Good to meet you, Noah."

If he hadn't been about to collapse, Noah would have asked them where they were from and how they were doing. But he swayed, and Russell's brow furrowed. "Easy, there, Noah. Why don't you sit?"

"I'm fine. I have to get to butchering the deer." Noah blinked when Russell grew fuzzy and the edges of his vision closed in.

"Yeah. I don't think so." Russell moved closer, and Noah leveled his rifle.

"Don't come any closer." His voice sounded weak even to his own ears.

Russell raised his arms while Grant swore and said, "Hey!"

Melissa's eyes rounded. Tanner looked like he was about to wet his pants.

"Noah, we don't mean any harm. How about if we clean these fine deer? All we want in return is half of one."

"Thanks for the offer, but no. I can manage."

"All by yourself?"

Noah remained silent.

Russell scanned the area around Noah, his eyes landing on the wads of gauze, and paused at Luke's knife lying a few feet away from the gauze. His gaze moved to Noah's waist, where his own knife still remained sheathed.

"I think someone was here with you. Do you normally carry two hunting knives?" He didn't wait for Noah to answer before he continued on, almost as though he was thinking aloud. "Although it's kind of weird that you'd put your pack back on without putting it away or without even finishing bandaging your side there."

"It slipped my mind."

Russell stared for a moment then threw his head back and laughed. Grinning, he opened his arms. "We're not looking to do any harm. In fact, I can't tell you how thrilled we are to finally see other people."

Noah lowered the rifle a fraction. "I'm happy to see others as well. But really, I don't need any help, and I'm just going to leave it at that."

"Okay. That's fine. We'll be on our way then. We haven't been as lucky as you today, but there are plenty of deer out here." He sent a scathing look at Tanner before turning back to Noah. "That is, there are plenty if they don't hear you coming first."

For the first time, Noah cracked a smile. Poor Tanner. "I do appreciate the offer, though. If you need the meat, you can have half of the doe."

Noah figured between deer, geese, pheasants, and fishing, they should be able to put away a good store for winter.

"We're okay, Noah. I mostly hunt alone, but today, I was showing the others how it's done."

Noah's legs started to buckle, and he reached blindly for the tree but missed it.

A strong hand caught his elbow before he crashed face-first on the ground. "I got you. Just relax."

Noah's tongue felt thick in his mouth, and he nodded. Or thought he did.

"Let's get this pack off your back." Russell tugged on a strap.

"No!" Noah struggled to roll away, but Russell held on tight.

"I'm not stealing your damned pack, dude. You're lying on it, but if you want to have it jabbing you in the back, fine. Jeez. If I want something, there are a million houses or stores I can get stuff."

Noah stilled. That made sense. He reached for the strap himself and tried to bend his shoulder to get it off, but wasn't able to. Russell must have realized what he was trying because he eased it from Noah's shoulders.

He spoke to someone out of Noah's limited field of vision. "Melissa, you have the kit?"

"Sure do. Step aside." A zipper sounded. Then came the rip of paper, and water gurgled. It made Noah aware of his thirst.

"Don't freak out on me, Noah. I'm just going to try to clean the wound and see what we're dealing with. It looks like you lost a lot of blood. How long ago did this happen?"

"Twenty minutes ago? Maybe?" Noah sighed as something cool pressed against his side. He should radio the others, but he didn't want to move.

"Hold it! Get away from him!"

Dexter! Noah pushed up to his elbows. He brushed Melissa's hands from his side. Dexter had moved up behind the group, who had all been focused on Noah. "It's okay! They're helping me."

Dexter didn't immediately lower his rifle, his gaze taking in the scene. It had to look damning, with all the blood. Had Luke been able to explain anything to him? And where was Jalen?

"You sure?"

"I am. Damn buck charged and caught me with his antlers." Noah rested his head back as Melissa resumed tending to him.

Russell cleared his throat. "Uh, I take it you're friends." He made introductions and then said, "Noah said we could have half of the doe."

Noah had said that, but it wasn't until Russell said it to Dexter that he heard the note of almost desperation in Russell's voice. What if they were hungrier than they let on? Noah groaned when Melissa pressed a little harder on his side.

"Sorry. Cleaning it started it bleeding harder. But while I see a small puncture, I don't think it goes too deep. If you don't get an infection, you'll probably be okay." She ripped several lengths of medical tape from a roll and taped a thick bandage over his wound.

Noah tried to sit up. "Thanks. I think we've got it from here." He stood with Russell and Melissa's help. He felt woozy and couldn't fully straighten, but for the moment, he didn't feel like he was going to pass out. He reached down for his pack, removed his water bottle, and took a long drink.

"If you don't mind, we'll get started gutting these guys—the deer, I mean," Russell added hastily, his hands up.

"Thanks. Take what you need." He'd see how much they took.

Dexter approached. "Who are these guys?"

He aborted his shrug with a wince and said, "Other survivors." He took another drink, draining it. "Where's Luke and Jalen?"

"I had them stay back about fifty yards." He put his pinky finger and pointer in his mouth and gave a shrill whistle.

Noah slapped a hand to his ear. "A little warning would have been nice."

"Sorry. That's the signal. I'm going to need their help to get all of this back to the vehicles."

"They seem okay. I mean, I was outnumbered and not in the best shape. They could have taken both deer and shot me dead, but they didn't."

"They didn't think you were a zombie?" Dexter asked with a straight face.

Noah tried not to laugh but snorted anyway, which made him clutch his side. "You asshole. Damn, that hurts."

Jalen and Luke entered the clearing, freezing when they saw the others. Dexter waved them over. "It's okay."

"Hey, why don't you go show the boys how to gut and dress the deer for the trip back to the farm? I'll get started back to the vehicles."

"Oh no. You're not going alone. Hold on. I'll send Jalen back with you."

"Noah, they're taking our deer!" Luke ran up to Noah, his eyes narrowed. "You shot them both. They're yours!"

"Settle down. I said they could."

"But what if we need it?" Luke was clearly distressed at the thought of the other group getting some of the deer. He kept casting angry glances at them.

"I think we'll be okay. We have a lot set aside already and we can go out again in a few days." Noah tipped his bottle in vain and sighed. "You should go over and learn how to field dress the deer."

"Here." Luke handed him his own bottle.

"No, you'll need it."

"I'm fine." Luke pushed the bottle into Noah's hand. "I'll go watch them, but I still won't like them taking the meat."

"Only half a deer."

"Yeah, right."

Noah ended up waiting so Jalen could get the same lesson as Luke, and rather than split the deer in the field, they transported it back to the vehicles. The water had helped with Noah's dizziness, but by the time they were halfway back, he ceased paying attention to what anyone else was saying or doing. He focused on putting one foot in front of the other.

When they finally reached the truck, he started to get behind the wheel, but Jalen nudged him aside. "My dad said I should drive."

Noah blinked a few times, trying to process that. "You're not old enough to drive."

"Neither is Ethan, but he drove before."

"What about me? I can drive!"

"Little dude, you can't even see over the wheel." Jalen laughed and gave Luke a playful push. Luke glowered but went to Dexter's vehicle.

"Where'd the other group go?" Noah craned his neck to see around Jalen.

"We're giving them a ride to their vehicles on the other side of the park."

Noah groaned. "Seriously?"

"That's not okay?" Jalen took several minutes to find the controls then opened the window and motioned for Russell and Tanner to get into the truck. Grant and Melissa would apparently ride with Dexter.

"It's fine." What else could he say with the other two men

climbing into the cab? He waved his finger toward the road. "Just follow your dad."

The ride started out with some wide turns and jerking stops, but it didn't take long for Jalen to get the hang of it. Of course, driving with only one other vehicle on the road made it a lot easier.

When they reached the lot, at least five miles around to another highway, Noah had his arm clamped to his side in an effort to protect his ribs from the jostling.

When they reached the other group's vehicle, it wouldn't start.

"I guess we're out of gas." Russell shrugged as he leaned his forearms on Noah's window ledge.

Noah sighed. "Where can we drop you off?"

"You'd do that for us?"

"We can't very well leave you out here in the dark." Although, they all had packs and a fresh haunch of venison. They'd be okay for a while. He looked at the sky. Dark clouds blotted out the sun. At this time of year, it could be rain or snow. The temperature was already cool, but a cold front could come through at any time.

"Are you okay with taking them back to their camp?" Noah asked as Dexter approached. "It looks like the weather's changing, and I don't feel right leaving them here."

Dexter glanced at the sky and then nodded. "Yeah."

"We're just a few miles down the road." He climbed in the back and waved for Tanner to do the same.

A few miles turned into at least seven, and the camp they found looked worse than Daniel's. They drove down a long driveway to the back of the house so Jalen could turn around at the end, and Noah's mouth dropped open. A tree had crashed down over the back third of the house. "What the hell happened?"

"A storm a few weeks back. It knocked over the tree and just about killed us in our beds." Russell shifted, his expression sheepish. "We were going to leave, but finding gas was so hard. We had only enough to get to the state park, and we really needed to find food since most of ours was destroyed in the storm."

"Why didn't you hunt closer to home, so to speak?"

"The park was where I shot a deer a month ago. It was the only place I hunted before." He coughed. "Except for me, nobody else has any experience with hunting. And mine is... minimal at best."

Noah half turned to look at him but grabbed his side and vowed to never do that again. He paused waiting for the pain to subside, then said, "You seemed to know what you were doing."

Jalen snorted, and Noah sent him a sharp look. "What?"

"Sorry, Noah, but you weren't watching closely, were you?"

Noah shook his head. "I guess not. Why?" He'd been too busy trying to make it back to the truck.

Jalen looked at Russell in the rearview mirror with the casualness of someone who'd driven for years. "Gonna tell him?"

"It was only my second hunt. For the others, it was their first time."

Noah digested that bit of news for a moment. "Okay, but so what? You have to start somewhere."

"That's true. And we'd better become experts in the next few weeks." Russell sighed. "It's going to be a long winter." He climbed out of the truck and moved to the back to get their half of the deer.

Grant and Melissa left Dexter's vehicle and watched as Russell dragged the doe from the bed. Russell left it there to get his pack from where he'd left it on the truck seat. Grant cleared his throat. "We better get busy, Russell, if we're going to get that meat cooked before the storm hits."

"I had to get my pack."

Noah scanned the yard. The house wasn't old, probably only twenty years or so, but it didn't have a barn or any outbuildings except a garage. A deck, half hidden by branches from the fallen tree, had a grill, on its side now, the propane tank hanging loose over the side of the deck. Noah didn't know if there was propane in it, but it didn't look safe.

Dammit. He rubbed his forehead with his thumb and fingers, pinching to ease the headache forming behind his eyes.

Dexter parked beside them, teasing his son about his driving, but then he caught Noah's eye. "Are we ready to go?"

"Can you come over here a second?"

Jalen repeated Noah's request when his dad gave him a confused look. He jumped out of his truck and rounded the front of Noah's truck. "What's up? Are you okay?"

Noah straightened as much as he could. "I'm fine." He explained the situation. "So, I don't know. I was thinking... the cabin could hold a few more people, don't you think?"

"That's four more mouths to feed. I don't know..." Dexter bit his lip and darted a look at Russell, who hacked at the deer. He winced. "He's going to butcher that."

Noah slanted him a smile. "Isn't that what he's supposed to do?"

Dexter rolled his eyes at him and then said, "Seriously, he's mangling it." After a moment he turned back to Noah. "They're like babes in the woods, aren't they?"

Noah nodded. All he wanted to do was get home and stretch out on his bed.

"And we can't leave them like this, can we?" Dexter almost sounded like he hoped Noah would say, "Yes, we can absolutely leave them out here."

Noah shook his head. "I don't feel right. There's not many of us left. We gotta help when we can."

Dexter dropped his head, giving it a slight shake. "Okay... you stay put. I'll go talk to them."

23

Cassie's ears roared. She'd killed Daniel? No. How could a knitting needle do that? They made soft, fuzzy baby blankets or hats and mittens. They weren't for killing anyone. "No..."

Ethan nodded as he approached. "Yeah. I mean, Leona might want to come and make sure, but I'm pretty sure he's dead."

Cassie released Leona and crouched, covering her face with her hands. She'd murdered a man. "I didn't mean to kill him. I... I just wanted him to stop trying to hurt Leona... oh my God. What am I going to do?"

Their roles reversed, Leona put her arms around Cassie and drew her to her feet. "Shh... you did what you had to do. You saved my life. I'm sure he was going to kill me."

"But... I could have stabbed him in the leg or just pushed him off you. I wasn't thinking... oh my God. Luke! Poor Luke!" Her hands shook as she broke away from Leona. She paced, her hand against her forehead as she tried to think. "Luke is going to hate me. I'm a murderer."

She leaned over, feeling bile rise in her throat, but she didn't vomit even though she felt like she might. "What... what do I do now?"

"Nothing, Cassie. Go up to the house and see to the children. Ethan and I will deal with Daniel."

"*How?* How are you going to deal with him?" Cassie felt a scream build in her throat but swallowed it down. What would Milo and Bella think of her? Would they be afraid of her?

"Cassie, please go back to the house. *Please*... I don't want you to see him when we bring him out." Ethan had set the rifle down on the picnic table.

She nodded and looked down, twisting the fingers of one hand with her other hand. She shuddered. "I should see what I did, but I'm a coward."

"No, Cassie. You're the bravest person I know." Ethan stood beside her, one hand on her shoulder. It looked like he was going to pull her in for a hug with the other, but then he backed off. Dear, awkward Ethan. Her champion. She bowed her head and raised her hands over her face, sinking onto the bench of the picnic table as sobs escaped.

ETHAN PATTED CASSIE'S BACK. Her sobs tore at him. He should have protected both of them. He should have kept a closer eye on Daniel. While nobody could replace his mom, Cassie had made her loss more bearable, and a small piece of his heart now belonged to her. His throat tightened, strangling any words of comfort he wanted to say, so he offered his shoulder and put his arms around her for a few seconds. He managed a quiet, "I'm so sorry," but he doubted she heard him.

Leona wasn't in much better shape. She took one of Cassie's hands in one of hers, but her other hand rubbed her throat, her gaze fixed on the clinic. "Are you okay, Leona? Can I get you anything? Like, I mean, like medicine or something for your throat?"

Leona's gaze snapped to his. "No, sweetheart. I'm okay. He surprised me, that's all. I was stupid. I should have realized that a man like Daniel wouldn't care that I saved his life."

Ethan fought to keep his anger in check. It was the last thing either of them needed, but he hated Daniel with every cell of his being. If he wasn't already dead, he'd have killed him.

"How about if I walk both of you up to the house. I can do what needs to be done."

Cassie pulled a cloth from her pocket and blew her nose. "I'm fine. Leona was the one who was attacked."

"Honey, how about we lean on each other and go back together?" Leona wrapped an arm around Cassie's waist, and Cassie gripped Leona's other hand and nodded. As they walked away, their postures straightened.

Ethan watched until they were safely in the house, although he didn't know who he was guarding them from. The only threat was dead. He turned his attention to the clinic, staring at it as dread rose up, nearly choking him. He'd seen plenty of dead bodies, of course—they all had—but the only ones he'd really handled had been his parents, and in his grief, he had been on autopilot.

He wasn't sure what to do with Daniel. He couldn't leave him in the clinic. That, he knew. And he couldn't leave him out for the animals to get at either. He looked around the farm. The only place he could think to put him was in one of the empty stalls in the barn. For now at least.

Daniel was where he'd left him. Still pinned to the bed, his arms and head dangling over one side, his feet on the other. The metallic green knitting needle only had about three inches emerging from an inch or so left of center. There was very little blood, which surprised him. Wanting to get the awful task over with as quickly as possible, Ethan grabbed a pair of gloves from a box on the counter, not caring that he was wasting them. He couldn't touch the man without them. He tried pulling back on Daniel, hoping he'd slip off the gurney so he could wrap him in a sheet and drag him out, but something anchored him to the bed. Ethan tried lifting him, but that didn't work either.

He grabbed the needle and gave it a gentle pull. It moved, but only a fraction before getting stuck. It took twisting it several times before he was able to work it free from the gurney mattress, and when he did, he saw the tip had hit the metal part of the gurney so hard, it had bent. After finally freeing Daniel's body from the mattress, Ethan slipped the body onto a sheet, rolled it up, and then rolled it onto another one to use to drag it out to the barn.

He chose the stall farthest from Daisy's, setting Daniel's body in the straw and securing the stall door after him. He tossed the gloves in a bucket and stopped by the cow's stall, but she was still out in the pasture. Ethan glanced that way. He should probably bring her in for the night and get her settled.

He did the chores after that, bringing in the goats and feeding the chickens, Dino's presence comforting him as he worked. "We have to help Cassie get through this. And Luke. We have to make sure he doesn't blame her."

Dino whined in answer.

ETHAN TURNED AWAY from the back door. "What do you think's keeping them?" He stopped for a moment to give Dino a scratch. The dog lay in front of the woodstove. Smart dog. It was the warmest place in the house.

"I don't know, sweetheart, but I'm sure they'll be here soon. Maybe they had a lot of deer to deal with." Vivian sat at the kitchen table. She had insisted on tucking Cassie into bed with one of her own pain pills, in hopes it would get her sleeping. It must have worked, because when Ethan had last checked on her, she looked peaceful, finally.

He'd given all the kids a dinner of oatmeal with dried blueberries swirled into it and an apple. Then he'd made sure they brushed their teeth and sent them all to bed, even Ava, since Vivian had already gone downstairs by then. Now, restless, he paced the kitchen, glancing out of the back door to the drive every time he came to the door.

Leona sat near them, her hands wrapped around a mug of tea that Ethan had made her over an hour ago. It had to be stone-cold by now.

"Leona, would you like some fresh tea?" Vivian patted one of the doctor's hands.

Leona flinched and blinked. "I'm sorry... what?"

"Your hands are freezing, hon." Vivian wrapped her hands around Leona's and rubbed them. "Would like some more tea?"

Ethan paused in his pacing, hoping she'd say yes so he'd have something to do.

"Oh... no. I'm fine." She released the mug and pushed away from the table. "I think I'll go to bed."

"Are you sure you don't want any oatmeal? You haven't eaten anything since lunch." Vivian gave Ethan a pleading look, seeking his help in coaxing her to eat, but Leona was a doctor. He was just a kid. She wouldn't listen to him if she wouldn't listen to Vivian.

"I can make you some eggs if you want." He could fire up the grill and use a pan on top. In fact, maybe he should make a mess of eggs for when the guys got back. They were bound to be hungry.

"No, but thank you so much, Ethan. For everything." Leona stood and approached him, put a hand on his shoulder, and gave his cheek a quick kiss. Ethan swallowed and nodded. She didn't act like a grandma, but he had never really known his own grandmothers, as one died before he was born and the other when he was five.

"I'm so sorry, Leona. I knew he was drunk. I should have kept an eye on him."

"No. Don't do that, Ethan."

He turned to Vivian, surprised at her sharp tone.

Leona nodded. "Listen to her." She patted Ethan's shoulder and left the room. They had put LED lights in every room and one in the hallway, so she didn't have to move through the dark, but her steps were so slow, it was almost like she was feeling her way.

Ethan waited until he heard her door close and turned to Vivian. "But—"

Vivian shook her finger at him. "No! No buts. He was a grown-ass man. He knew right from wrong."

Ethan nodded. That was true.

"Nobody here would ever harm another, right? We are a tight group. What was the first thing you did when you heard Cassie screaming?"

"I took off to see what was wrong."

"Of course you did. Because you care about everyone here. We are a family. Daniel would never have fit in here."

"That doesn't mean he should be dead."

Vivian tipped her head. "Granted. I was never a big fan of capital punishment, but this wasn't the same thing. Cassie did what she had to do to save Leona."

"Oh, I know. I'm not saying she shouldn't have. I'd have done the same. I just wish..." He didn't know what he wished. He wished Daniel had been a good person. He wished Luke wouldn't have to learn that his father had died. He wished he had billions of wishes so that he could wish back the lives of everyone who had died.

Frantic horn honking caught his attention, and he spun to the doorway, grabbing the gun from where he'd leaned it behind the door. Why were they honking like that? Dino barked, and Ethan hushed him. "Shh... it's okay. Don't wake up Cassie."

It was almost completely dark, but he saw Luke riding shotgun with Dexter. Noah's truck bounced on a bump, going entirely too fast for the potholed gravel drive, and it skidded to a stop only inches from the back of Dexter's bumper.

Jalen hopped out of the driver's side, and Ethan did a double take. Jalen driving?

"Get Leona, Ethan!" Jalen moved around to the other side

of the truck and opened the door but not before Ethan saw two more people exit the back seat of the cab on Jalen's side.

He raised the rifle across his chest. "Who are they?"

Dino stood beside him, hackles raised, a growl rumbling continuously in his throat.

"They're okay, but Noah's been hurt."

He hesitated a second, but when he saw one of the men help Noah to stand, he grabbed the door handle and raced through the kitchen. "They're back, but Noah's hurt. I have to get Leona."

Vivian struggled to her feet. "I'll get Leona. You help with Noah."

"No. You sit." Ethan raced down the hallway. "Leona!"

"I'm coming. I heard." She looked like her usual self. "Can we take him to the clinic?"

Ethan nodded. "I cleaned it up."

She averted her eyes, her hand going briefly to her throat, before she nodded. "Okay."

Vivian stood, despite Ethan telling her to stay.

"I heard a lot of voices outside."

"There were some other guys out there." Ethan turned to leave the house, but Vivian caught his sleeve.

"Guys? What guys?" Vivian struggled even harder. "Why are they bringing even more new people here? Those damn fools."

"I don't know, but keep Dino here with you. He'll protect you."

24

Noah clenched his teeth. Sitting in the car had caused him to stiffen. His side felt like someone was jabbing him with a dull knife, but his head was clear. The wooziness had subsided. That had to be a good sign. If he was dying, he'd probably have been a lot less aware of how much his side hurt.

Leona came outside just as Noah managed to put both feet on the ground and stand up with Jalen and Dexter's help. Russell and Tanner stood to the side.

"Who are these men?" Leona waved a hand toward them, her voice harsh.

Noah froze at her tone. She'd never spoken like that before. Not even when he'd brought Daniel back.

Dexter lifted a hand. "It's a long story, but they're decent guys."

"And gals." Melissa had joined them, and Leona's eyebrows went up. "Are you the doctor they were telling me about?"

Dexter shrugged. "I mentioned you on the way back."

"I am, but before we go into this anymore, let's get Noah to the clinic." Leona shepherded them down to the clinic as the newcomers marveled that they had an actual clinic on-site.

Once Noah was settled on a bed, Dexter excused himself to go start the generator. Melissa helped Noah get settled while Leona washed her hands with water from a bottle marked Sterile.

As Melissa gave Leona the rundown, Noah zoned out, exhausted. Luke entered and hovered at the end of the bed.

"Hey, Luke. You did a good job out there today."

Before Luke could reply, Leona's head whipped toward the boy. "Luke!"

Noah didn't know who was more startled, him or Luke, at the outburst. He flinched, and Luke took several steps back until his back was against the wall.

"Wh—what, Leona?"

Leona's hand went to her throat, and she started to say something, then shook her head. "Nothing. You surprised me, that's all. I didn't know you were there."

"Where's Ethan?" Noah had seen him come out behind Leona but had lost sight of him.

"He was helping with the deer," Luke said.

"Oh, you got a deer?" Leona's voice sound almost normal, but there was still something off. She didn't look at Luke but had turned her attention to Noah, gently removing the bandages.

"There was a lot of blood when we got there." Melissa took the soiled bandages from Leona and dropped them in the trash bin.

"From Noah or from the deer?"

Noah sucked in his breath when she pressed on his side. "We got two deer."

"One and a half, actually." Luke chuckled.

Leona's gaze raised to Noah's eyes. "How did you manage half a deer?"

"I can answer that. He gave it to us." Melissa handed Leona a fresh square of gauze.

"You seem to know what you're doing," Leona said as she took the gauze and wiped off smeared blood.

"Ten years as a paramedic."

Leona glanced at her. "That's excellent."

"Thank you, Doctor."

"You can call me Leona." She raised her hands to shoulder level, bloody gauze and all, and looked around the clinic. "This isn't exactly the Mayo Clinic. We don't need to be so formal."

Melissa chuckled. "Yes, ma'am. Leona."

Leona did a full exam, listening to his lungs, pressing her fingers against his skin, saying she was feeling for crepitus, whatever that was. Apparently she didn't find it because she finally straightened.

"You have bruising over the left side of your chest, and it looks like the antler entered just under your seventh rib, in the intercostal space. It probably cracked both of the ribs, but it looks like it slid along the top of your seventh rib instead of penetrating too deeply. When it came out, that's what gave you this gash."

"So what's the verdict?"

Leona gave him a wan smile. "You should live. I'm going to give you some antibiotics to prevent infection of the wound. Rest for a few days, then do whatever feels comfortable. Nothing too strenuous for a couple of weeks, though."

"I'm getting good at chopping wood, Noah. I can do your share." Luke had nearly disappeared into the shadows after Leona had shouted his name, but he stepped forward now, a grin on his face.

"I won't argue with that." Noah smiled.

"Also, I'm going to stitch up the gash but leave the puncture alone, except for a light dressing. We'll need to check it every day to make sure it's not getting infected."

Was it his imagination, or were Leona's hands shaking as she readied the suture kit to stitch him up? She gave him a smile, and he relaxed, except for when she gave him a couple of shots of Lidocaine to numb up the area. He didn't feel the stitches at all, and Melissa seemed to have been Leona's right-hand aid for years instead of for the first time ever. Luke watched in fascination.

"Does that hurt, Noah?"

"No."

"Wow, it looks like it would. That's cool."

"Yeah. Glad I can provide you so much entertainment."

Luke just grinned at him, and Noah chuckled. "So, Leona, does this mean I don't need to stay in the clinic?"

Leona shuddered before shaking her head. "No. You can go back to the house." She cut the suture, and he wasn't imagining it this time when her hands shook. "Melissa, can you apply the dressing? There's tape and other supplies right over there in a drawer." She pointed to the stainless steel cabinets.

Noah searched Leona's face. Her eyes welled. Something was wrong, but he was certain she wasn't going to speak in front of Melissa and probably not in front of Luke because of his age.

"Hey, Luke, can you go see if Cassie can get us something to eat? I bet you're hungry."

Luke nodded. "Starved."

"Why don't you go with Luke and get something, too, Melissa?"

"Are you sure? What about the dressing?" She gave first Leona then Noah a confused look.

Leona shook her head and smiled, but it looked forced to Noah.

"I think Leona wants to do it after all."

Leona nodded.

The second the other two had left, Noah sat up and swung his feet to the side of the gurney. "What's going on, Leona?"

She looked at him. "Something terrible happened while you were gone."

25

E than wanted to follow Dexter and Jalen to the clinic to see how Noah was, but he didn't want to leave the house unprotected. He'd already failed in that regard one time today.

The men left behind had introduced themselves as Tanner and Grant, and they seemed nice enough, but he wasn't about to trust them until he talked to Dexter and Noah. He wasn't about to let them into the house.

Ethan had Vivian lock the door behind him while he helped raise the deer up to hang from a couple of trees. It was cold enough at night to keep the meat until it could be properly butchered. He supposed he and Dexter would do it in the morning. Good thing Noah had shown him how with the last deer he'd taken down a few weeks before. That meat had to be processed right away so they could smoke it. They'd salted it, drained it, and packed it in barrels covered in a brine. He was pretty sure he remembered all the ingredients for the brine. However, they had eaten some fresh for a few days too. His mouth watered at the thought of a venison steak.

"This is a pretty nice place you have here. Was this your house before?" Grant asked as he helped Ethan get the second deer up into a tree.

Ethan shook his head. He didn't want to reveal too much, so he only said, "We've been here about three months now, I guess. Maybe a little longer. It's hard to tell."

"Yeah. I know what you mean. I have no idea what month it is. Do you?"

Ethan leaned down and wiped his hands on the dew-wet grass. He wanted to go inside and wash his hands with soap and water but resisted the urge. He had to keep an eye on these guys, especially since both seemed to be looking around with a lot of interest.

"Did they say they were taking him to the clinic?"

Before Ethan could reply to Tanner, Grant asked, "You have enough people here to have a clinic? How many are here, anyway?"

Ethan straightened his shoulders and looked Grant in the eye. "How many deer did you guys get?"

Grant shuffled his feet and shrugged. "We didn't have much time to hunt. Almost as soon as we reached the forest, we heard the shots fired by Noah, or maybe it was the kid. Anyway, we headed toward the sound."

Ethan climbed the few steps to the porch and turned. "Why did you head for the sound?" Had they planned to get the deer for themselves?

"We heard gunshots that weren't our own. Of course we were going to investigate. Damn, kid. What do you think? Wouldn't you?"

Ethan narrowed his eyes. He didn't like this guy—even if he had a point. He didn't answer the question and instead asked, "Where do you all live?" See if they liked answering questions. "How many of you live there?"

Tanner approached and stopped beside Grant. "Do you mind if I sit on the steps here? My legs are killing me."

Ethan rolled his eyes. "The ground is a fine place to sit."

Grant snickered at Ethan's reply. "Yeah, Tanner. Sit down."

Tanner scowled at Grant, but to Ethan's surprise, he did sit down. Remembering how wet the grass was, Ethan felt a pang of guilt.

"And to answer your question, we had a place about ten miles from here." Grant pointed toward the east.

"What do you mean, *had*?"

"A tree fell on it. I guess we're staying here for now."

"Wait... who said that?"

"Dexter and Noah said we could. And if you don't mind, we're tired and hungry. Any chance of getting a bed and dinner?"

Ethan looked to the clinic. Dexter had come out with Jalen, but he couldn't see them anywhere. Had they gone in while he and the guys were stringing the deer up? Dexter probably wanted to check on Vivian, so he guessed that was where they had gone. He wished Dexter had stopped by to give him some direction, though. "I have to see what's going on. We're not exactly a bed and breakfast, you know."

"Yeah. Sure. I know. I only thought you might have something you could give us. We have some provisions, and Noah said we'd get half of the doe too. I could hack off a few chunks of meat. Can I use that grill?" He nodded to the gas grill on the other end of the porch.

"No. And don't touch the deer. I'll bring you out some scrambled eggs I made a little while ago."

"Eggs? You have eggs?"

Ethan ignored the question and tried the doorknob. It opened. Dexter must have gone in already. When he entered the kitchen, nobody was there, and when he went to knock on Dexter and Vivian's door, he heard Jalen and Dexter's exclamations of disbelief about Daniel. Ethan closed his eyes and backed away from the door. He checked in on Cassie, relieved she still slept, scraped a helping of eggs onto a couple of plates, and added a slice of bread for each of them.

"Here you guys go. You can sit on the steps to eat or go down to the firepit. Stir it a little. It should still be burning a bit, and you might be able to get the fire going. There are logs piled on the other side of those trees." Ethan pointed to the firepit. A few embers glowed in the dark.

When the men headed that way, Ethan headed to the clinic. He had to find out what was going on and tell Noah, if he wasn't hurt too badly, about Daniel.

"WHAT HAPPENED?" The local anesthetic Leona had injected before stitching him had helped with the pain for now.

"Daniel... he was drunk and frightened Cassie and the kids earlier this morning, but Ethan got him to go back to his tent."

A knock sounded on the door, and Noah snapped in irritation at the interruption. "Who is it?"

"Sorry, it's just me, Ethan."

Noah glanced at the door then at Leona. "Is he part of it? Is it okay if he comes in?"

"No... I mean... yes, he's part of it, but it's nothing he did. He knows what it's about. He can come in."

"Come in!"

Ethan entered. "Are you okay?"

Noah waved his hand. "Yeah, I'm fine. Did you need something?"

Ethan stepped forward until he was in the circle of light instead of in the shadows. "Who are those men, and where are they supposed to go?"

Noah rubbed his forehead. "They helped. Sort of... after my accident." He sighed. "But as far as sleeping arrangements, they can sleep in the cabin. It's finished enough for them to sleep in it. Wasn't the fireplace cleaned out the other day?"

Ethan's eyes opened wide, and he shot a look at Leona, who gave her head a slight shake. "Um, yeah. Me and Luke did our best cleaning it. Got an old bird's nest out. It doesn't smoke inside anymore."

"Good. Direct them there. If Daniel gives you any trouble, he can come and see me or Dexter."

"That's what I wanted to talk to you about, Noah."

"What happened? What aren't you telling me?"

Leona drew a deep breath and closed her eyes briefly. "Daniel's dead."

"What? How? Did something happen with his wound?" Noah looked first at Leona then at Ethan. "Hello?"

Leona brought her hands up, as though protecting her throat. Her mouth worked, but no words emerged.

"Are you okay?" Noah stood and reached for Leona's

shoulder. She flinched away. He had an inkling of what had happened. He shot a look at Ethan. "What did he do?"

"He attacked Leona here in the clinic when she was out here working on something. Cassie was looking for her for some reason, and she caught him trying to... trying to—he was attacking Leona and—"

"Oh my God! Cassie! Is she okay?"

Noah wanted to bolt for the house, but Leona caught his arm.

"She's okay. Physically, anyway."

"What does that mean?" He pushed his hands through his hair, pulling it taut.

Ethan cleared his throat. "Cassie did it. She killed Daniel to save Leona."

Noah stared at Ethan and then took a step back, sinking to sit on the edge of the gurney. "How? Did she shoot him?"

Leona shook her head. "I... I had been knitting earlier with Vivian. I'd been teaching her. Well, I wanted to practice in here so I could surprise her with a scarf. I brought my bag of knitting here so I could hide it. I was thinking Christmas is coming and I could start making gifts..." She gave a muted sob.

"I'm so confused." Noah glanced at Ethan.

"Cassie stabbed Daniel with Leona's knitting needles."

Noah blinked. "Are you kidding me?"

Ethan shook his head. "Nope. I didn't see it happen but came running when Cassie started screaming for me. He was dead when I checked on him."

"Shit." Noah blew out a breath. "Where is he now?"

"In the barn. I wrapped him up and put him in a stall."

Ethan looked down, shuffling his feet. "I'm sorry, Noah. I was trying to keep an eye on him, but he got by me."

"Where were you when it happened?" He didn't mean for the question to sound accusatory, but Ethan's head jerked up, and he looked at Noah.

"I... I... was helping Daniel with the house." His eyes slipped away from Noah's, as if ashamed. "Well, I mean, he was sleeping in his tent—sleeping it off, actually. He'd been drunk earlier and kind of harassing us while we were gathering walnuts, so I told him I'd help him today since Luke was gone."

"You have nothing to be sorry for, Ethan."

"Yes, sir. I know. I still wish I'd seen him leaving his tent."

"I shouldn't have left. Either me or Dexter should have stayed behind." He rubbed the back of his neck. *Dammit.* "It won't happen again, Ethan."

Ethan nodded. "Cassie's pretty shook up."

"I better go to her."

"She's sleeping. I just checked on her before I came out here."

"I gave her something to help her sleep tonight." Leona sighed and pinched the bridge of her nose. "It's been a long day."

"Leona, are you okay?" It had just occurred to him that Leona had suffered an attack, and here he hadn't even asked her if Daniel had hurt her. He swore if Daniel had done the unthinkable, he'd raise him from the dead and kill him all over again.

"I'm okay. Just a bit shaken." She gestured to Ethan. "This young man took care of everything while Cassie and I went back to the house."

"That had to have been difficult. I can't imagine doing anything like that when I was your age. Hell, I was practically a delinquent at that age. You're more of a man than Daniel ever was." Noah searched for the remnants of his shirt.

Ethan slipped out of his jacket. "Here. Take mine."

Noah took it. "Thanks." The fit was a bit tight, but it would do to get back to the house without freezing. "Does Luke know?"

Ethan shook his head. "I don't think so."

"Okay. I'll tell him."

"Will you allow him to stay?" Ethan shoved his hands in his pockets.

"Of course. I wouldn't ever put a kid out. Even if Daniel hadn't fulfilled his end of his deal, I would have still welcomed Luke to stay." He tried to zip the jacket, but it would only go up a few inches. His shoulders stretched the material too much for the teeth to meet. It would have to do. "Poor kid."

26

E than trudged behind Noah and Leona as they returned to the house, but Ethan swung by the firepit where all four of the newcomers had gathered. It looked like the other two, the man and the woman, had also eaten plates of eggs. He hoped there was some left for Noah. Vivian was the only one who could have offered it to them, so he was sure she had set a plate aside for Noah.

It was a good thing they had so many eggs on hand. Usually they didn't, but with the abundance from the garden, and Cassie working so hard to can as much as possible, she wasn't baking except bread. That meant extra eggs. If only they had more chickens. He'd heard a rooster crowing somewhere the last few days. It would be worth it to find him and bring him back to the flock to make new baby chicks. Eventually, they'd have enough to eat fried chicken every once in a while. And to think a year ago, if he wanted fried chicken, all he had to do was go to the nearest fast-food fried-chicken restaurant and order up a whole bucket of the stuff. He pushed the image out of his mind before he started drooling and stood on the outskirts of the firepit's glow.

"Noah says you all can sleep in a cabin we've been renovating on the other side of the stand of trees west of the house."

"Thanks. That's really nice of you all. We were thinking we'd have to bed down in the barn." The man Ethan hadn't met yet, who had helped Noah to the clinic, laughed. "I thought I'd have to share my bed with a pig."

"It wouldn't be the first time, I bet!" Grant elbowed the woman and smirked as if he'd told the most hilarious joke. The woman shook her head and gathered the plates set on the rocks near the fire. She yelped and dropped one.

"Sorry. I hope I didn't break it. It was hotter than I expected."

Ethan shrugged. "It's fine. We can get plates pretty much anywhere. Do you have sleeping bags or anything?"

"We have a blow-up mattress," Grant said as he wrapped an arm around the woman.

"I threw a bunch of blankets and quilts in the back of Dexter's truck." The man stood and started to head back to the house.

"I'm sorry... I don't think we've met." Ethan stepped in front of him and stuck out his hand. "I'm Ethan."

"Oh... sorry. I'm Russell."

The woman, the stack of plates in her hands, stopped beside them. "Hi, Ethan. I'm Melissa. Grant said he'd met you already. Grant's my husband, by the way. Thank you for the eggs. They were delicious."

"You're welcome. They were just plain eggs." Ethan took a

few steps back, unused to the attention and uneasy with the strangers approaching so closely.

"I'm not joking when I say it was the best meal I've had since this whole thing hit. Man... fresh eggs."

"We got chickens. And goats." He clamped his lips shut before he gave too much information away.

"Wow! That's amazing! How did you guys do all of this?" Melissa spread her arms and looked around. "We had a house and some land we took over, but we chose for isolation, not for long-term."

"We're isolated." Ethan wanted to kick himself again for giving too much away but then mentally shrugged. Everyone was isolated now, and it wasn't like they could call 911 if there was an emergency.

"Yeah, I guess so, but I mean that we assumed we'd all get the virus eventually, so why bother with preparing for long-term, you know?"

Ethan recalled his thinking early on. He, too, had figured he'd die any day and had wandered the roads waiting to die. Then he'd found Dino and had a reason to keep going, but he still had assumed he'd get the virus eventually. Knowledge that he'd saved Dino from a gruesome death had kept him going for a while, but it wasn't until he found Cassie and the kids that he found hope.

He shrugged. "I get it. I guess once all of us came together and none of us had died from it yet, we couldn't sit around just waiting for the virus to get us. We had to make plans in case we did survive." He waved toward the house. "Come on. We can put the dishes in the sink, and then I'll show you all the cabin. We'll have to grab a lantern."

The farmyard angled up to the house, and roots and the

occasional rock made the terrain uneven, but Ethan navi-
gated it easily in the faint light from the dying firepit and a
half-moon overhead. The farm had become a true home. He
imagined how it looked to someone who had only seen the
death and decay wrought by the virus over the last six
months. Compared to most places, the farm was heaven.

"WE HAVEN'T MOVED any wood for the fireplace over to the
cabin... yet." Ethan didn't know how or if he should explain
what had happened earlier today. When they had put the
dishes away, Noah and Dexter were asking Luke if they could
talk to him on the front porch. They seldom used that porch,
as you couldn't see the other buildings, but it did have a
bench and a couple of rocking chairs and was private. Luke
had sent Ethan a questioning look, and it was all Ethan could
do to act like he didn't know anything. Poor Luke.

"That's okay. We all have sleeping bags." Russell walked
beside Ethan as he led them down the back steps.

"That's great, but what I was going to say is that you guys
can grab some wood or come back and get some. We have a
lot chopped."

Russell held up his pack and rolled sleeping bag. "I'll
have to come back."

Ethan nodded and didn't point out that the sleeping roll
could be tied to the pack and the pack worn, leaving their
arms free. They could even keep their rifles over their shoulders that way and carry an armload of wood. They'd learn
eventually.

As they neared the cabin, Ethan leading the way with a

flashlight that he would leave for the group, he shined the beam on a small tent set up to the west of the cabin. "That's the bathroom."

"A tent for an outhouse?" Russell sounded skeptical. "That's gotta reek."

"Not exactly. I mean, yeah, it's a tent, but there's a table inside, and there's a pitcher for water and a big bowl for cleaning up. It has a compost toilet inside. We just set it up the other day, so it shouldn't smell." Ethan slanted him a look. "What have you been using?"

Russell shrugged. "Nothing. Just going out in the yard."

Ethan wrinkled his nose. "Uh yeah. We don't do that here." Not that he had room to talk. He ducked his head as he recalled that's what he'd done, too, before coming here. What else was he supposed to have done? Noah had told them all how important it was that they make sure their waste didn't come anywhere near their drinking water, which was the stream. When he'd wandered, he'd been on the move for the most part, except when he was at the veterinary hospital and taking care of Dino until he was strong enough to go. He'd gone outside to pee and had just done the other on the edge of the parking lot behind a tree—not that he even needed that much privacy. He'd been drinking out of the jug of water from the water cooler in the waiting room, though, and not relying on a stream.

"Anyway, here's the cabin. It's not done yet. We think this might have been the original home on the farm. It's pretty cool." He shined the light on the wall, illuminating several pegs in the wall. "That was where they hung their clothes."

Russell looked around. "It's pretty primitive, but I guess if we get a fire going, it'll keep us warm and dry for now."

"We filled in a bunch of holes between the logs and put glass in the windows. It wasn't easy to get the right measurements from nearby houses. I mean, there aren't many houses nearby, so..." Ethan wanted to go into the details of all the work that had already gone into the little cabin, but the subject made him think of Daniel and his body, cold and lifeless out in the barn. Nausea gripped his belly, and he quickly pointed out how to work the flue in the fireplace and left them to figure out the rest.

On his way back to the house, he slowed and gazed up at the sky. The Milky Way showed so bright and clear, like he could reach up and grab it. He'd never seen it like it was now before the virus hit. To think it had always been there but he'd never seen it before. Ethan sat on the edge of the back stoop, unsure if he should go in or if Luke was still being given the news. Everything seemed quiet, but he needed time to think. The day had started so promising until Daniel had ruined it. Men like Daniel had always been around, but he'd never been aware of them. In their case, they hadn't been obscured by light pollution but had hidden in plain sight, pretending to fit in. It was an awful thought, but he couldn't help wishing that Daniel was the last man like that. Wouldn't that be something if all the bad men had died from Sympatico Syndrome?

27

"Luke... I'm afraid I have bad news for you."

Noah sat on the edge of the good, solid chair. He imagined the former owners had sat in it often. It afforded a beautiful view of the northwestern sky and was a wonderful place to witness a sunset. They hadn't had too many evenings when they'd had times to relax and witness one over the last few months, but in the times before, it must have been peaceful.

Dexter leaned against the porch pillar, a lantern hanging on a nail they'd pounded into the post. Luke sat on the other chair. Dexter had already heard the news from Vivian. He wasn't exactly broken up about the news and admitted he was probably the worst person to tell Luke about it. While Dexter had always been kind to the boy, it was no secret that he'd loathed Daniel for what he'd done to Vivian.

"What's wrong?" Luke glanced at Dexter and back to Noah. As if sensing the news, he asked, "Where's my dad? Did he go somewhere?"

"There's no easy way to say it. Your father... he attacked Leona—"

Luke stood and looked out over the dark countryside. "And they sent him away? I'll have to go find him."

"No... Luke. That's not what happened. Look at me."

Luke's gaze met Noah's. "What happened?" He sounded like a small child as he sank back onto the bench.

Noah closed his eyes briefly and drew as deep a breath as his ribs allowed. "Cassie walked in on him trying to strangle Leona, and in trying to save her, she... well, she accidentally killed your dad."

Luke stared at Noah. The lantern light shimmered in his wide eyes. "No... no! My dad wouldn't try to hurt anyone."

Dexter cleared his throat, and Noah shot him a warning glance. Now was not the time to point out Daniel's faults. He was gone, and even if he didn't deserve it, Luke had loved his dad.

Dexter gave a small nod. "We don't know why he did what he did, but he sneaked up on Leona in the clinic and attacked her without provocation."

"How do you know?"

"Leona told me, and she has the bruises on her throat to prove it—although I don't need proof other than Leona's word. She wouldn't lie."

"She has to be lying." Luke bit his lip and twisted his fingers clenched in his lap. A tear dropped onto the back of his hand, glinting for an instant before rolling down his wrist.

"I'm sorry, Luke. We all are, but it's the truth. I wish it wasn't."

"Luke, you did a fine job out there today." Dexter moved from the pillar to squat down in front of Luke. "We talked it over, and we'd like you to stay with us. Nobody feels worse about what happened to your dad than Cassie."

"Where is she?" There was a hard edge to Luke's voice. "Why didn't she come out and tell me herself? Was she too afraid?"

Dexter stood. "Listen here, Luke. Cassie didn't go out looking to hurt your dad. He didn't stop even though she yelled at him to and tried to pull him away. He pushed her. She grabbed the first thing she saw and stabbed him. Even that didn't stop him. He went back to attacking Leona until Cassie stabbed him a second time."

Luke wrapped his hands around the back of his head and leaned forward. "Stop! I don't want to hear any more!"

Dexter stood back, arms crossed. "I'm sorry. I had to tell you how it happened. Cassie and Leona both told Vivian, and Ethan walked in right after it happened. He had the rifle and probably would have shot your dad if Cassie hadn't already stopped the attack. We have to defend our own."

"Why'd you even bring us here?" Luke shot off the bench, nearly colliding with Dexter as he stared at Noah. "We'd have been just fine on our own!"

"You know your dad would have died without Leona."

"You don't know that. I could have helped him. Ruby could have helped him."

"Why the hell would Ruby help him?" Dexter shot off then raised his hands. "I'm sorry, Noah. I'm not making this any better." He turned and paced to the far end of the porch.

Noah stood, putting himself between the two. "Luke, I know how you're feeling—"

"No, you don't! How could you?" Luke put his hands on Noah's chest and shoved.

Noah gasped and staggered backward, catching his balance with one arm hooked around the pillar.

"Hey!" Dexter crossed the porch in three long strides. "Keep your hands to yourself!"

"Cassie didn't! Why did she get away with it?" Luke's fists balled at his sides, his body stiff. "It's not fair! You've always hated us! All of you! I've tried so hard to make you like me, but you never will!"

Noah gritted his teeth, sucking in until the pain subsided. "That's not true. We all like you. You've grown a lot in the last few weeks. We know you're hurting right now, so we're not going to take anything you say personally. Think about our offer of staying with us."

Luke didn't reply. He sat on the edge of the bench, gripping the edge of it, his feet braced as if trying to ward off a hurricane.

"If you want to talk—tonight or tomorrow—I'll be there for you." Noah reached over and put his hand on Luke's shoulder. When the boy didn't flinch away, Noah gave his shoulder a gentle squeeze. "Again, I'm sorry for your loss."

After a moment, Dexter gave a gruff condolence, and he and Noah went into the house.

Dexter sighed and rubbed the back of his neck when they got into the kitchen, lit by one LED light stuck on the wall. "That didn't go well, did it?"

"No. I don't know how something like this is supposed to go. Was it bad? Good? Who knows?" Noah scrubbed his hands through his hair. His stomach growled.

"You didn't even eat yet, did you?"

Noah gave a soft chuckle. "You heard that?"

"I'm pretty sure the whole house heard it." Dexter moved

over to the woodstove. "Vivian saved you a plate of eggs. They're cold now, but there's a slice of bread here too."

"I'll eat them, cold or not."

The kitchen door opened, and Ethan entered.

"Did you get them settled?"

Ethan set the flashlight on the counter and shrugged. "I guess. How did they manage to survive so long? That's my question." He glanced at the plate Dexter handed Noah. "Oh, good. You did get some. Do you want me to warm them? I can start the grill. It wouldn't take long."

"No. They'll be fine. I don't want to waste propane on one serving of eggs." Noah scooped up eggs, pushing them onto his fork with the edge of his bread. The eggs were great.

Ethan glanced around and looked from Dexter to Noah. "How's Luke?"

Noah shook his head. "He didn't take it well. Not that I'd expect him to."

"Yeah. Poor Luke." Ethan plopped down a chair opposite Noah. "What's going to happen now?"

"We told him he's welcome to stay, so it's up to him, really." Dexter cut a few slices of bread from the loaf wrapped on the counter and lifted one up for Ethan, raising an eyebrow in a silent question. Ethan took it and reached for a jar of jam that always seemed to be out on the table. Dexter grabbed the butter knife and handed it to Ethan. The whole exchange had been wordless. Noah watched the interplay. They really were like a family now. He hadn't been lying when he'd reassured Ethan that he was part of the family.

Dexter set a couple more slices of bread on a plate beside Noah, and Ethan slid the jam to Noah's end of the table, pushing the slightly sticky knife along with it.

"Thanks." Noah took a bite of the bread. He'd already wolfed the first slice down. He coughed when the bread started to lodge in his throat.

Ethan jumped up and poured him a glass of water. "Here, Noah."

"Thanks. Damn... I should get injured more often. I could get used to being waited on." Noah sipped from the water, doing his best to keep the pain out of his voice.

Ethan gave him a wan smile, then he picked at his bread for a few moments, pulling bits of crust off and eating them. "Hey, Noah, does Luke know where I put his dad's body?"

Noah shook his head. "We didn't get that far. I guess in the morning we'll have a funeral."

"What about the new people? What do we tell them?" Ethan looked from Dexter to Noah. "Do we tell them that one of us killed a man?"

28

C assie awoke slowly, stretching, luxuriating in the feeling of being fully rested. When had she last felt so good? She closed her eyes, wondering what the twins were up to. Had anyone given them breakfast? The sun slanting in the window hinted that it was almost midmorning. Why hadn't the kids awakened her? Had something happened? As if wading through thick fog, yesterday's event forced its way into her mind. Her eyes snapped open. She'd killed Daniel.

The muscle memory of the knitting needles sinking into him made her clench her hands. If she kept them tight enough, the feeling would go away. It had last night.

She heard Milo's sweet voice down in the kitchen. He was laughing about something. The sound washed over her, soothing her nerves. Everything was okay if her children were okay. Then Luke's voice reached her. He wasn't laughing, and his tone wasn't soothing.

She jumped out of bed and pulled her clothes on. She had to apologize to Luke. *Dear God*. He must hate her. Tears sprang to her eyes, and she rubbed them away. All feelings of rest and rejuvenation drained away in the space of a few heartbeats. She'd murdered Luke's dad.

Raking her fingers through her hair, she pulled it into a ponytail then slipped a band over it from her dresser top. She kept a bowl and a pitcher of water on the dresser just like people used to do before indoor plumbing. It made sense to have water to wash handy, and she scrubbed her face, poured a little water from the pitcher into her bedside glass, and squirted toothpaste on her toothbrush. As she brushed, she tried to think of what to say to Luke. What could she say? She rinsed and spit into the bowl and opened the window. After making sure nobody was below, she dumped the water onto the flower bed below, only there were no flowers in it.

When she rounded the corner into the kitchen, Vivian and the kids were sitting around the table, snapping green beans.

"Hi, Cassie." Ruby gave her a shy smile. "We're getting these ready for canning."

"Oh. Yeah. I almost forgot." They'd been canning for weeks. Today they were supposed to be getting the walnuts processed too. She shouldn't have slept so late.

Every scavenging expedition included getting mason jars, and they never passed any by. As a result, the pantry and basement shelves were full of beans, corn, apples, berries, and even fish and meat. She'd only canned a few times in her life before arriving at the farm, but Noah had some knowledge from culinary school, and they found information in old recipe books on the shelf in the den. They'd figured it out.

"Hey, Cassie, can I have a minute?" Vivian pointed out a few beans that Bella had missed and motioned for Cassie to follow her outside. "We'll be right back, guys. Just keep doing what you're doing until that basket of beans is empty."

The kids groaned, but soon Cassie heard their laughter as she and Vivian went out the back door.

Cassie looked around. The baskets of walnuts were still where she had left them yesterday. It didn't seem possible that only twenty-four hours had passed. "Where's Luke? I heard him not long ago."

She caught sight of the deer hanging in the tree. "Oh. Nice. They got two." She knew she should feel more excitement about the kills. After all, the meat along with everything they'd scavenged and harvested meant they would make it until at least next spring, but she couldn't even muster a smile. She'd have to remember to smile when she saw Noah and congratulate him. Or maybe Dexter had made the kill. Or one of the boys.

Even her ever-present worry about what they'd do between then and harvest time seemed distant. Her mind was still foggy. She remembered Leona giving her something last night. *Leona.* Cassie searched the farmyard for her. "Where's Leona? Is she okay?"

Vivian patted the stoop, where she had taken a seat. "She's okay. She's tough."

Cassie nodded. "That's good. I'm glad she's okay. Is she sleeping?"

"No. She's changing a bandage on Noah's side."

"Noah's side? What happened to him?"

Vivian tilted her chin up toward the deer hanging in the tree. "The buck got him with an antler. And before you ask, he's fine. Banged up and probably a few cracked ribs, but Leona said he should heal up just fine."

"I'm glad we have Leona with us."

Vivian patted her stomach. It was decidedly more rounded than it had been the week before. "You and me both."

Cassie gave Vivian a sideways hug. "It looks like the baby is growing?"

Vivian smiled and dipped her head. "Yep. He or she has started kicking."

Tears sprang to Cassie's eyes, and she shook her head. "I'm a regular sprinkler today. What in the world?" She ground her fists into her eyes, embarrassed.

"Aw, hon, you're fine. You've earned those tears." She glanced at Cassie. "I wanted to let you know that Luke... well, he was pretty upset last night when Dexter and Noah told him about Daniel. It was what we expected, but we hope he'll decide to stay with us. Him going off on his own will never set well with me."

"Maybe I should take the twins and leave."

"Damn... that is not happening. I'll tie you up myself and force you to bake bread for me before I let you leave."

Cassie gave a strangled laugh.

"Oh, you think I'm joking?" Vivian chuckled. "Seriously, we need you, and Ava would be lost without Milo and Bella. Ruby would be pretty torn up too. She's lost her whole family. We can't let her lose anyone else."

"But I killed Daniel. She probably hates me too." Cassie's feet dangled, and she stared at her socks. She couldn't even remember where she'd taken off her shoes.

"Oh, hell no. You know that man had his eye on her. He was no good." Vivian shook her head, her lips pursed. "Nope. You did the world a favor—and God will probably strike me down for saying that—but with the billions of innocents who died, his death is one few would mourn. I feel bad for Luke. I do, but otherwise, good riddance."

"What do I say to Luke?"

Vivian sighed. "I don't know. He's hurting and angry, but he has to know deep in his bones that his dad was wrong, and you were justified in doing what you did."

Voices she didn't recognize sounded like they were on the side of the house. "Vivian... get inside. Get the rifle." She scrambled to her feet.

"What? What is it?" Vivian couldn't scramble with her wound still healing. She held out a hand, and Cassie grasped it, bracing to help Vivian stand.

"Shhh... I heard men, and they weren't Noah, Dexter, or even Ethan, Jalen, or Luke."

Vivian made a face. "Oh... yeah. I forgot you were already sleeping when they arrived. We have four folks who apparently helped Noah out in the woods staying with us."

"Staying? For how long?" Cassie thought of their stored food. They had been doing well, but could they stretch it to feed four more mouths?

Hopefully, they'd find more canned foods. Being out in the country meant there were only so many houses and stores they could scavenge from. They'd definitely need to broaden their radius, but she knew Dexter was worried about how good the gasoline would be driving a year from now. Finding it wasn't a problem. They were already having to strain it sometimes.

"You don't sound too enthusiastic. Is something wrong with them?"

"No. I don't know." Vivian shrugged, darting a look at

Cassie. "They seem okay, but look what happened with the last man we let stay." Vivian grimaced.

Revulsion washed over Cassie as she thought of Daniel. These people could be monsters, and now they were going to be living in close proximity to her children? "Who said they could stay? Did anyone ask us?" Cassie's lethargy washed away as fury rose inside.

"Noah and Dexter. Dexter told me these people could barely feed themselves, apparently."

"So that makes them our responsibility?" Cassie wanted to hunt down Noah and ask him what the hell he was thinking.

Vivian opened her arms, palms up. "Hey, I'm just telling you what I was told. I've been stuck on this farm since we got here, and lately, I've not been in a position to have much of a say in anything."

Cassie's anger cooled slightly. "I'm sorry, Vivian. I didn't mean to direct my wrath at you."

The voices moved away from them, and for the moment, Cassie pushed them from her mind. She had too much to think about right now without worrying about strangers in their midst.

"I know. I get it. These men of ours—"

"Hold on. I have no man. You have Dexter. I have no man." Cassie shook her head.

"But Noah looks at you—"

"He's my ex's brother. That would be weird." Cassie contemplated her feet and wiggled her toes. It would be weird. And confusing.

Vivian chuckled. "I'm just saying. It's practically the end of the world, and you're still young." She pantomimed a growing belly, sending Cassie a knowing smirk. "Somebody's gotta repopulate the globe."

"*Vivian!*" Cassie couldn't help laughing. "You're terrible." She nodded to where Milo and Bella were playing on an old seat torn from some car the farm's owners had left in a pile of junk beside the barn. "Besides, I've done my part already."

"Well, you already know you'd make cute babies with Noah, because his brother's babies sure are adorable."

Cassie tipped her head in acknowledgement. "I did make cute babies, no matter who the father was." She grinned, for a few moments pushing aside the weight of what had happened the day before. Even as she thought of Noah in the way Vivian suggested, all she could see was Daniel attacking Leona. Sighing, she stood. "I need to find my shoes and then have a chat with Noah."

29

"Luke?" Ethan found the other boy behind the barn in Ethan's usual thinking spot. Ethan bit his lip, wondering if he'd found his father's body. It was on the lower level of the barn. But as the barn was built on a hill, the ground sloped down, and the stall with the body was only steps away if Luke went down the hill and entered the barn down there.

"What do you want, Ethan?" Luke didn't turn to look at him, but Ethan saw him furtively wiping at his eyes and nose.

"I'm really sorry about your dad."

"Yeah. Sure you are."

"I am. I mean it."

Luke made a noise that sounded like a cross between a grunt and a sob. "Quit lying. I know nobody liked him."

"Okay, I'll admit that I didn't like your dad, but I like you, okay?" Ethan moved in front of Luke, ignoring Luke's effort to turn and hide his face. Hands on his waist, Ethan used the toe of his boot to hammer a rock from the dirt. He stole a glance at Luke. "I don't care if you cry. I cried when my parents died."

"I'm not crying!" Luke spun and slid on his butt, his feet now on the other side of the old tire.

"Okay... well... if you *were* to cry, that would be normal. Anyway, I'm sorry you're going through this. If there's anything I can do, let me know." Ethan sat on the spot Luke had slid away from, leaving them back-to-back.

They sat in silence for about five minutes as Ethan watched Dino chase a squirrel in the pasture before Luke's voice broke the quiet. "How do I know he's really dead? What if he just left? He said he might."

Ethan drew a deep breath. "I saw him, Luke. He's dead."

"Well, then where is he?"

Ethan glanced at the slope, wondering if he should tell Luke or ask one of the adults first. Noah was injured, Dexter was talking to the new people, and Cassie was still sleeping when he left the house. Leona was the last person he wanted to ask, and Vivian had been taking care of all the kids. Noah had said he was a man now. That made him an adult.

"Luke, do you want to see your dad?"

What if there were bugs on him? Ethan swallowed hard. He doubted Luke was a stranger to seeing a dead body. Nobody was anymore—not even the little kids—but seeing your own father crawling with bugs wasn't a sight anyone should see. However, if Luke wanted to see him, Ethan would show him. They had to bury the body very soon anyway.

"You know where he is?" Luke's shoulder bumped Ethan's as Luke turned to look at Ethan.

"I'm sorry to say that it was my job to remove his body from the clinic."

"Oh."

Ethan glanced at Luke. "I was real careful with him. I tried to be gentle. He's wrapped up in sheets in the empty stall downstairs."

Luke jumped up and looked at the ground as if his father was reaching through it to him. "He's right down there?"

"Come on. Maybe you need to see him for yourself." Ethan slung an arm over Luke's shoulder and led him down the slope.

"Wait here a second." Ethan wanted to go in first and unwrap the body instead of fumbling with the sheets with Luke right there. Plus, if there were any bugs, he could warn Luke.

Thankfully, the cool air had kept the body from decomposing much, and Daniel just looked like he was asleep. Sort of. Ethan uncovered only his face and shoulders, leaving his torso covered for the most part. Even though there wasn't a lot of blood, there was still a stain, and it was bigger on the front than the back.

"Okay. He's ready." Ethan opened the stall. Eyes huge, Luke's gaze darted from Ethan to beyond him, into the stall. "Do you want me to leave?"

"No. You can stay." Luke entered, and for a moment, he only stared at Daniel's body. "He looks... weird."

Ethan glanced at Daniel's face. Luke was right. There was something different. Daniel's sneer was gone. In death, his face looked peaceful and serene.

"I don't think he suffered."

Tears flowed unchecked down Luke's cheeks, but he seemed less upset than he had earlier. "That's good, I guess."

He sniffed, then he gave Ethan a questioning look. "Where did Cassie shoot him?"

"She didn't shoot him."

"Then how did he die?"

"You see, Leona had been knitting and had her stuff in a bag with her. Those knitting needles are long, and they're made of metal. Or at least, these ones were."

"Cassie killed my dad with *knitting needles*? That's... I don't know. Crazy, I guess." Luke shook his head. "She must have been desperate to attack with those. My dad's a pretty big guy compared to her."

"I imagine she was scared, and Leona's throat is all bruised. I'm sorry to have to tell you that your dad almost killed her."

Luke's head dropped, his chin almost touching his chest. "I'm sorry he did those things. I could have stopped him if I was here. He wasn't so bad when he wasn't drinking."

"You don't have to apologize. Kids aren't responsible for how their parents act."

Luke nodded, so at least Ethan's words were getting through to him.

"We'll have a funeral. Probably today, in fact. I'll talk to the others, and we'll have a service. Dexter can say a few words. He's good with Bible stuff." As soon as he suggested Dexter, he remembered how Daniel had almost killed Vivian, so he probably wasn't going to be up for eulogizing the man. Ethan moved to rewrap Daniel, first giving Luke a look to make sure it was okay. Luke nodded.

"I don't want a service."

"But... how come?"

"I don't think he deserves it." Luke turned and fled the stall.

Ethan hesitated but quickly made sure Daniel was covered again. "Rest in peace, Daniel, because you sure didn't live in peace."

"I FEEL FINE, Leona. You should be the one resting after what happened to you." Noah pulled his shirt down and pushed off the table, doing his best to hide a grimace.

Leona's raised eyebrow let him know he'd been unsuccessful. "The wound looks good, but you can't get complacent. An infection these days could mean a death sentence." Leona moved over to a side table, washed her hands in a basin, and dried them on a towel.

"I know, but I also know that PTSD is a real thing. We've all had our share of traumas lately, but yours was less than twenty-four hours ago."

"I'm fine." Leona continued drying her hands.

Noah moved over to her and gently took the towel away, hanging it on the rack on the side of the table holding the basin. Leona simply looked at her hands.

Noah gestured toward the door, careful not to touch her. "Why don't we see how Cassie's doing?"

Leona nodded. "Poor Cassie. I gave her something to help her sleep. She should be waking pretty soon if she hasn't already."

"I know. I haven't had a chance to talk to her since I've been back."

"She's a strong woman. I mean that literally."

Noah smiled. "She's strong in many ways. I know my brother put her through a lot of shit." His smile broke as he recalled what he knew about Dave. It mystified him how his brother could have ever been abusive toward Cassie.

"How is Luke? That boy has had a rough life even before the pandemic. Did he ever tell you about his life?"

"Not that I can recall." Noah noticed Leona still avoided talking about what had happened to her and instead redirected to others who'd been affected. He guessed her next question would be about Luke.

"It's not a pretty story. His mom died of a drug overdose, and he's been in and out of foster homes. Finally, his dad got clean long enough to get him back, and then the virus hit."

"Damn." Noah shook his head. "I thought I had it bad."

"You mentioned your dad a few times. I look at you and wonder how you turned out so well." Leona walked with Noah as they headed back to the house.

"I didn't. I'm really good at hiding the bad, damaged side. Inside, I have a heart blacker than the night sky." Noah meant it as a joke, but Leona stopped and looked up into his face, searching his eyes.

"Hmm... I don't think so. You and Cassie, and even me, we're survivors. We do what we need to do to survive."

"What about Dexter and Vivian?" Noah looked back toward the house, uncomfortable under the close scrutiny.

Leona shrugged. "Vivian for sure is a survivor. And Dexter? He's different. I think he's probably a creature of habit, and this was hard on him, but he's happy to have something to work on, like my clinic. He's the kind you point in the right direction and get out of his way."

"Definitely. The solar panels were his idea, and I think we

can still make them work. We need to find some kind of battery storage, I think. But I don't know the details. The wiring part is the tricky part anyway, and Dexter knows how to do that."

"So, what about these new folks? Melissa is a good addition, but what about the others? How will they fit in?"

Noah sighed. "I don't know. I'm having regrets. They had next to nothing saved up for winter. I mean, seriously. What were they thinking? They were eating canned foods, which is fine, but they scavenged as they needed food, apparently. Like a weekly shopping trip, instead of planning ahead. They had a huge yard but didn't plant a damn thing, according to what Dexter told me this morning."

"Well, they're here now, and we'll have to put in more supplies."

"I know. I'll do it. I agreed to letting them come here. I think we can get a few more deer before it snows hard, and there's a little town down south of here we haven't visited yet."

As they crossed the farmyard, Noah saw Cassie and Vivian sitting on the back stoop. The new people were rounding the corner of the house, heading toward the women. He hurried his steps. "I'm going to talk with them a minute."

"I'll come along. I'd like to see how much Melissa knows."

"Hey, there he is!" Russell pointed at Noah and closed the distance between them. "It's good to see you up and about."

"Thanks. How was the cabin?"

"Great! Ethan got us settled in. Want to see? We opened a few cans of beans for breakfast. Do you want some?"

He felt Leona nudge his elbow and tried not to crack a smile. "No, thank you. I had breakfast already."

"We couldn't help but notice the solar panels nearby. Are those from you or the people who were here before?"

It took Noah a moment to grasp that they were talking about the previous owners of the farm and not Daniel and Luke. "We brought them here. We're hoping to get them up and running. The cabin seemed like an easier place to start, with its low roof, than the farmhouse. Before we could do that, though, we had to get the cabin livable. We were just about done with it."

"Excellent. Grant has some construction experience." Russell motioned to Grant, who stood back, his hands in his pockets.

"Russ, I painted houses. I didn't construct them."

"And I'm a chef by trade." Noah grinned. "We're all learning new trades."

"Okay. I'm game. I just didn't want you to think I know what I'm doing."

Noah nodded. "And what about you, Russell? Or should I call you Russ?"

"Either. I'm a lawyer. Or, I was. Melissa's my cousin. Tanner is a friend. We went to college together."

As they spoke, Noah walked toward the cabin, bringing the group along with him. He had hoped to speak to Cassie before they met the new people, but maybe she had already met them. As they moved out of the narrow band of trees that separated the cabin from the house, he pointed at the roof of the cabin. "We have the frames up and were about to add the panels in the next few days."

Dexter exited the trees, giving Noah a wave. "There you are. I'm trying to find Luke. Have you seen him?"

"No. We just left the clinic. He's not in the house?"

"No but neither is Ethan."

"Where's Jalen?"

"I sent him to build the fire up at the firepit. I figured we'd need a good fire to boil water for helping to process the deer."

"Oh yeah. I almost forgot about them." Noah rubbed the back of his neck.

"Yes. We're hoping you'll help us butcher our half, too, Noah. If you're up to it."

Noah glanced at Russ, distracted by the request. "Yeah. Sure. There's just something we need to do first."

"What's that?"

It was on the tip of his tongue to tell the man that it was none of his damned business, but Leona spoke up. "We, unfortunately, had one of our own pass away yesterday while you were out hunting."

Russell backpedaled and pulled the collar of his shirt up over his nose. "Was it the virus?"

Leona shook her head. "No. It was an accident with a sharp object."

Dropping the shirt, Russell stepped closer. "Like, a knife?"

"Something like that. It was Luke's dad."

"Aw, the poor kid." Russell sounded sincere, and Noah nodded.

"As you can imagine, he didn't take it well. We need to find him, and then we'll have some kind of burial."

"I'm very sorry to hear about this. I'll keep our group away out of respect for your privacy in this trying time."

"Thank you. We will be butchering the deer later, though. We don't want the meat to go bad."

Leona motioned toward the cabin. "Is Melissa inside?"

"She was a few minutes ago," Grant said. "Why?"

"I would love to have a chat with her. She did a good job with Noah."

"Well, sure. Come on in." Russell put a hand on Leona's back, and Noah saw her give the tiniest flinch.

"Hey..."

Leona looked over her shoulder. "It's fine, Noah. Go find Cassie and talk to her. Remember?"

"Okay." With a wave, Noah turned back toward the house and motioned for Dexter to walk with him. "Other than being incompetent in the survival skills, these guys seem nice enough. So why do I feel so uneasy?"

"I feel the same, but I think I'm feeling like that because of Daniel. He was the first person we met after all of this who was a bad person, and we let him live here. I guess I'm questioning our judgment." Dexter ambled beside Noah, his hands in his pockets.

"That's it. I thought Daniel had been just afraid and misguided, but it went far deeper. I didn't sense it, and it almost got Leona killed."

"None of us sensed that he was truly evil. He acted like a jerk, but he seemed okay with his kid."

"That's true." Head down, Noah walked beside the house, noting the damp weeds beneath Cassie's window. The rest of them brushed their teeth in the bathroom, even though there was no running water there either. The septic tank wasn't full yet. He didn't know what they'd do when it did fill. Find a truck that emptied them?

"Hey, Noah. I want to talk to you." Cassie marched toward them.

Dexter stepped to the side. "See you in a bit. I'm going to go check on Vivian." He veered off the walkway around the house, even though it would take him right to the back door. It was clear he'd picked up on Cassie's body language too.

Cassie stabbed a finger in Dexter's direction. "Don't run far, Dexter. You're as guilty as Noah, from what I've heard."

Dexter froze and shot Noah a look. "We're dead."

Noah couldn't help chuckling.

"Oh, you think this is funny?" Cassie stopped in front of them, crossing her arms, one foot slightly ahead of the other. "What's the meaning of bringing strangers here without even asking if anyone else agreed? Since when did you two become the king and president of this farm?"

"Wait... are we a monarchy or a democracy?" Noah grinned as Dexter shrugged.

Cassie shook her finger at Noah, coming dangerously close to his nose. "I'm serious. Look what happened when you let Daniel stay here!"

Noah sobered. "I'm sorry. You are absolutely right to be upset." He cast a look over his shoulder as he heard voices from the cabin. While he couldn't make out what they were saying, he didn't want to take a chance that they would overhear his and Cassie's conversation. "Can we talk inside?"

Her eyes narrowed, but she nodded.

The three of them entered the kitchen, and Noah grabbed an apple. He was starving, having gone right out to the clinic with Leona. The bruises on her neck had shocked Noah. Last night, he hadn't noticed them as much, but today they'd stood out in stark relief on Leona's pale neck.

After sitting, he motioned for Cassie to sit opposite him, and Dexter took a seat at the end of the table. "I'm so sorry about what happened yesterday—both here and when we asked the new people to come back." He set the apple aside and reached for Cassie's hands, which were lightly clasped in front of her on the table. Taking them in his own, he caught her eye. "I'm so sorry."

At first, she stiffened, pulling her hands away. Immediately, he released them from his grasp, but he maintained eye contact. "Are you okay?"

Her shoulders wilted, and she nodded and shrugged at almost the same time, her actions in conflict with each other.

"You're not okay." Noah stood and moved to her side of the table. Impulsively, he bent to give her a hug but held back at the last second, switching his action to an awkward pat on the back when he processed that only seconds ago she'd pulled her hands from his. "What do you want me to do?"

Vivian, after her initial distrust of him, had become someone he thought of as a sister. Leona was like a favorite aunt. His easygoing relationships he had with the other two women differed from what he had with Cassie. It was confusing.

He was her former brother-in-law, and when he'd thought of her before, it had always been in that context or as simply the mother of his niece and nephew. Now they lived in the same house, and he saw her every day. He knew things about her that only family knew about each other. There wasn't much to do in the evenings after the kids were put to bed. The adults and the teens tended to sit around either the firepit or the kitchen table now that it was cooler and talk for a few hours until they got tired and people drifted off to their rooms. Often, he and Cassie would be the last ones talking. He'd have to be dead to not be aware of her as a woman.

"I'm afraid I'm the guilty party, Cassie. Noah was half out of it when I said I didn't feel right about leaving those four to try to survive on their own. You should have seen the place." Dexter shook his head. "I already caught hell from Vivian. Go ahead and give it to me." He took a deep breath. "I'm ready."

Cassie looked between the men. Normally, Noah was sure that Dexter's stoic acceptance of his punishment, whatever it might be, would have had Cassie at least smiling, if not outright laughing, but today, her lips didn't even twitch.

"What happens if one of those men try to attack one of us? Are you two going to be around twenty-four seven to protect us? Do you know what I had to do yesterday?"

Noah swallowed. "Yeah. We heard."

Tears formed in her eyes and spilled down her cheeks unchecked. "I hated what Daniel was trying to do, and I hate what he'd already done to Vivian, but I never meant to... to... *kill* him. I just wanted him to leave Leona alone."

"We know, Cassie. Nobody blames you for what happened."

"Oh really? You don't think Luke blames me?" She angrily smeared the tears from her cheeks and sniffed. "I will forever wonder if there was something more I could have done. Like, I should have had my gun on me. I got complacent. I should have known better after what happened with Dave." She cast Noah a look that might have been regret, but he wasn't sure. "I'm sorry, Noah, but your brother should have prepared me to recognize the signs. I sensed something off in Daniel, but what do I know about how people act at the end of the world? Maybe his behavior was entirely normal in that context."

She splayed her hands on the table, studying the backs of them as if looking for instructions on what to do next. "I can't believe I fucking killed a man."

Noah heeded his instincts this time and rushed to her side, enveloping her in a hug. The top of her head pressed against the side of his neck as he circled her shoulders. "I'm so sorry I wasn't here to protect you and the kids. From now on, either me or Dexter will remain on the farm at all times."

Dexter cleared his throat. "And I can tell those folks they'll have to move along and figure it out on their own."

Cassie's shoulders shook in silent sobs, but Noah felt her shake her head as the sobs subsided. She leaned back and drew a deep, shaky breath. "I'm okay, guys."

"Are you sure?" Noah moved back to his seat and picked up the apple. "What happened is a lot for anyone to handle, on top of what you've already been through."

"It is a lot, but there's not much I can do about it. I'm not sorry about saving Leona, so…"

"Of course not," Dexter said. "Any one of us would have done the same—probably not with knitting needles, though."

Cassie lasered a look at Dexter. "Really, Dexter?"

He gave her a weak smile. "I hid Vivian's knitting needles, if that means anything."

Her lips twitched as she gave her head a little shake. "You know what? Let them stay for a few days. You guys had no way of knowing what was going on here while you were gone."

Noah nodded. "We had no clue."

His input wasn't appreciated as she raised a finger at him,

her voice stern. "Yes, it would have been best if you'd come back and asked if it was okay, but with you being injured, and them helping out, I understand how you felt you owed them something. Besides, we can teach them a few things first, I guess. Also, there's half a deer with their name on it, right?"

Noah chuckled. "Yeah. That's true."

30

In a far corner of the farmyard, Daniel's coffin, built by Dexter, sat beside the grave Ethan and Jalen labored to dig. It was late morning, and Noah wanted to hold the funeral around noon so they could get to processing the deer.

Ethan couldn't help but remember that the only other graves he'd ever dug had been for his parents and his sister. If he closed his eyes, he could still see Amber's face and almost hear her cute giggle. She'd only been walking for a few months, but in that time, she'd loved to follow him around the house. Sometimes, he'd complain to his mom. *Mom, she's trying to follow me into the bathroom!* He'd acted annoyed at the time, but now he'd give anything to have his little sister chasing him around.

An ache in his chest deepened with every shovelful of dirt he tossed out of the hole. He thought he'd been over their deaths, but he'd been fooling himself. He'd simply learned to not think about his family. If he didn't think of them, then it didn't hurt, but as Amber toddled around in his mind's eye, the ache intensified. He missed not only his family's physical presence but their place in his thoughts. Keeping them in his memories was the closest he could ever have to having them alive. Why did they all have to die?

"I think it's deep enough, Ethan." Jalen grabbed Ethan's arm, keeping him from scooping another shovelful of dirt.

Ethan shook him off. "Stop!"

The jolt back to the present was like waking from one of the dreams he'd had recently of being with his family. As the images slipped away, he wanted to chase them and bring them back.

"Hey, man—you okay?" Jalen tossed his shovel up onto the side of the grave and rested his palms on the ground, lifting himself out of the hole. He extended a hand to Ethan.

Ethan drew his forearm across his brow. "Yeah. I'm fine. It's hot down here." He took Jalen's hand, sad to leave his memories but glad to get out of the grave.

The service for Daniel, such as it was, was brief. Everyone was there except for Cassie and Luke. Ethan wasn't sure where he'd gone.

He'd scanned the edges of the woods as they'd buried Daniel, only half listening to the words Noah said about Daniel, although he was glad the focus was on how Daniel had tried to be a good father to Luke. None of them really knew if that was true, but he had managed to keep his son alive, so he must have been doing something right. Ruby stood at the graveside, her eyes dry, but she dropped a purple wildflower on the coffin as it rested in the grave.

After a few awkward prayers, that was that. The funeral was over. In all, it had taken less than fifteen minutes to bury Daniel, but that was more than most had received.

Cassie had stayed in the farmhouse, ostensibly to make

dinner, but they all knew how torn up she'd been over what had happened. Ethan hoped she knew that if she hadn't killed Daniel, he would have seconds later, but it might have been too late for Leona by then.

The new group had been told by Dexter of the death, and he'd given them a few general details of what had happened. With no laws, or rather nobody to enforce them, it made the disclosure uncomfortable for everyone.

Ethan wanted to tell them exactly how it happened because he caught a few looks they gave each other and the way they watched Cassie as if worried she was about to go on a rampage any minute.

If Cassie had defended Leona back in the time before, there would have been a homicide investigation, according to Jalen, who seemed to know what he was talking about because his life goal before had been the NBA, and if that didn't pan out, then he'd wanted to be a police officer. With no television, Jalen had been excited to find true crime books on the shelf of the den in the farmhouse. Somebody had been an avid reader of them. Ethan had tried reading them, but the references to modern life before the virus made them too painful for him to read. He found a few westerns that he preferred to read. The simple life then was more in tune with how they now lived.

The new group had retreated to the cabin after lurking at the edge of the funeral, their curiosity too strong to resist the morbid pull. He imagined they thought the farmhouse group was full of homicidal maniacs. He wanted to tell them that the only one who had fit that description had been the one who'd died.

In the afternoon, the weather threatened to turn stormy,

so it was all-hands-on-deck to get the deer butchered and processed. Noah showed the newcomers how to pack the meat in barrels of salt and said they'd change it out for new salt in a day or so.

In spite of all that had gone on, the dinner had a festive air. Ethan stabbed a bite of his venison steak and sighed as he chewed. So good. Potatoes and green beans rounded out the meal, but there was blueberry pie for dessert. That must have been what Cassie had been making when she skipped the funeral.

"Cassie, this pie is amazing." Ethan lifted his fork with the last bite on it. "Thanks for making it."

Cassie smiled then nodded as Russell added his praise. "I think I can truthfully say that this is the finest meal any of us"—he gestured to Tanner and the couple, Grant and Melissa—"have had since before all of this happened."

Melissa nodded. "It was. I'm so stuffed, I could pass out right here in my plate. Thanks, Cass."

Cassie gave her a tight smile. "You're welcome, Mel."

If Melissa was aware of the slight sarcasm in Cassie's reply, she didn't show it but instead started collecting dirty plates. "You folks cooked, so it's only fair that we do the dishes."

Ethan stood, gathering his own dirty dishes. "Here, I'll show you how we wash them."

"This is a cool setup." Melissa swirled the plates through the soapy water and scrubbed them with a sponge before dropping them into the pot of clean rinse water. "I have to confess that we've either been eating out of packages, like crackers and peanut butter, or off paper plates, just throwing them on the ground when we're done."

"Paper plates?" Ethan shrugged. "I guess we never looked for many of them, but that's not too bad of an idea, except for what to do with them when you're done." Ethan fished a dish from the rinse water and dried it with a towel. He motioned around the yard. "As you can see, we try to keep the grounds clean because anything we don't eat or can't be given to the goats or chickens has to be disposed of by us. We don't want rats hanging around, so we haul our garbage away from here."

Melissa nodded. "Smart. I wish we'd have found you guys sooner. I've seen enough rats to last me a lifetime. It's really nice of you all to let us stay with you. We'll do our best to earn our keep."

Ethan bit his lip. He hadn't heard they were staying, but apparently she seemed to think they were. "That's great. Everyone here is really great."

"Who's in charge? Noah or Dexter?"

Ethan set the plate in a milk crate, where they kept them between meals. "Neither? I mean, nobody really decided that one person was in charge. Vivian or Cassie might be in charge as much as Noah. Vivian makes all of us do a bit of schoolwork every day. She's our teacher. The little kids have more school than I do, but all the adults make sure I get time with schoolwork every day."

"Really? School? Why?"

"*Why?*" Ethan gave her sideways look. "I'm only fourteen. I'd be a freshman in high school if the virus hadn't hit."

"Yeah, I get it. You're still a teenager, but the world we knew is gone. What's the point of a kid your age studying more? It's not like you can go on to college."

"Thanks for reminding me." Ethan glared at Melissa

before throwing the towel over his shoulder. "Maybe your husband can help you finish."

"Wait!" Melissa stepped in front of him. "I'm sorry. That was thoughtless of me. Of course education is important."

Ethan looked her in the eye. "It is. I want to learn how to get things going again. How am I going to do that if I don't know how things work? We don't know exactly how many people have died, right? Maybe there are places where more people survived."

"You mean creating a new society?" Melissa raised an eyebrow at him.

"What else can we do?" Ethan returned to the rinse bucket and pulled another plate out.

"Survive. That's all we were trying to do. We were taking it one day at a time, but I don't know what we'll do when winter comes. Russell suggested heading south."

"We have everything we need right here. Or almost everything. Eventually we'll need to find more supplies, but for now, we're okay." Ethan's pride at what they'd accomplished warred with his anger at Melissa for her skepticism.

Melissa scanned the farm. "I'll have to admit that I was impressed with that little clinic you all have. It's like a mini hospital."

Ethan smiled. "Leona's the best."

"I'm a paramedic. I could help her if she needs it." Melissa sounded like she was applying for a job.

"You'd have to talk to Leona about that. I don't know anything." Ethan clammed up. Whether these people stayed or not wasn't up to him.

Despite threatening rain, it only sprinkled, but Ethan shivered hard when a gust of wind brought a cold front in.

The temperature must have dropped at least twenty degrees in fifteen minutes. It almost felt like it could snow.

When he and Melissa had finished the dishes, they found that the little kids and the women had gone back to the house. He shivered and started to head that way, too, but paused when Dexter mentioned his name.

"Jalen, you and Ethan get in a load of wood. Russell, you guys better grab some too. It's going to be a cold night." Dexter motioned to Luke, who sat on a log beside the dying bonfire. "Luke, you're welcome to sleep in the house tonight. The tent might be a little too cold."

Luke barely glanced at Dexter, but he nodded.

"Come on, Luke. Help me carry in firewood." Ethan went over and nudged Luke's shoulder. The other boy sighed but stood and followed him to the woodpile.

"Hold out your arms." Ethan piled as much wood as he thought Luke could carry then did the same for Jalen, who joined them. He took a load as well.

"That's a nice fire." Jalen held his hands to the flames several minutes later after they had stacked the remaining logs in a neat pile on the hearth.

"It does feel good." Ethan turned to get his backside warm too.

"Where am I supposed to sleep?" Luke sat on an ottoman, staring with a forlorn look into the flames.

Ethan waved to the sofa. "Until we get a bed for you, the couch isn't bad. I think we have extra blankets in the closet."

He gathered the blankets and an extra pillow and handed the stack to Luke. "Try to get some sleep."

31

Noah heard voices yelling, but his eyes felt glued shut. *"Wake up!"*

Someone shook his shoulder, hard enough to send a sharp pain through his ribs. His eyes finally snapped open to find the beam of a flashlight shining in his face. "Hey! What the hell?" He bolted up in bed, swinging his feet off the side.

"Get up! *Fire!*"

In the second it took Noah to realize Russell had been the one to wake him, he was already following him, snagging his coat from a hook beside the door. As soon has he hit the hallway, smoke engulfed them.

"Get down on the floor. Follow me!" Russell crawled, a flashlight gripped in one hand. Noah dropped to all fours and followed the bouncing beam of the light but stopped in front of Cassie's door, pounding on it. *"Fire!"*

Her room, shared with Leona, was beside his own.

Russell reached back and tugged on Noah's arm, but Noah shook him off. "We gotta get the others!" He couldn't see a thing and could only go by the feel of the carpet runner in the middle of the hardwood floors.

"I already got Cassie and her kids. They should be outside already. I don't know where the others are." Russell coughed. "I've never been up here before."

Cassie's kids had beds in other rooms but often ended up in their mom's room. He hoped Russell was right on that count.

Noah tried to make certain but was overcome with a bout of coughing. He rose to a crouch and rushed around the corner of the hallway. "There are three more bedrooms this way."

He banged on the doors, yelling as loudly as he could. *"Fire! Get out! Jalen! Dexter! Ethan!"*

Russell echoed Noah's calls, and Ethan and Jalen joined them in the hall, both boys coughing.

Smoke poured from the hallway they had left only seconds before. Thick and black, it threatened to cut off their escape down the steps. "Go, everyone. Get downstairs and get out!"

Vivian ran from her room across to the girls' room. Dexter followed her, carrying Ava in his arms. Vivian pushed Ruby in front of her as Russell and Noah shooed them all downstairs. Ethan tapped Noah. "Leona? Where is she?"

"I don't know." Noah assumed she must have gone out with Cassie and the kids, but Russell hadn't said so. He started to move toward her room, but Russell grabbed the hem of Noah's T-shirt.

"She's outside already." Russell coughed. "Hurry, or we'll never get out of here!" He raced down the stairs. Noah ushered Ethan ahead of him. Suddenly, Ethan stopped.

"Dino! He always sleeps with me." He bolted back to his room.

Noah dropped to his hands and knees again, clutching his chest, caught in a spasm of coughs. There came a loud thump and something hitting the floor close by.

"Help, Noah!"

Noah edged forward, sweeping his hand in front of him until he felt soft fur but also Ethan's hand.

"You got him?"

"Yeah, but I can't see anything." Ethan's voice sounded weak and hoarse.

"Follow my voice." Noah turned and crawled back to the stairs, but Ethan wasn't behind him. Panic shot through him. "Ethan!"

"I... I can't hold him and crawl."

Noah felt Ethan's shirt and grabbed it as he half shoved, half tossed Ethan toward the stairs. "Get down! I'll get Dino."

Ethan, coughing, stumbled down the stairs. Someone shined a light up from the bottom. "Hurry! This place is going up!" It was a female voice—Melissa?

Noah's eyes burned as he strained to see through the dark, the smoke stinging his eyes. He lifted the collar of his shirt over his mouth and nose, not that it helped much. He scooped his arms beneath the dog, the animal's limpness worrying him, but he couldn't stop to see if the dog was breathing. He lifted the dog and struggled down the stairs with him, his ribs screaming in pain, the air so hot and thick, he felt like he was walking through the gates of hell.

Someone grabbed the dog from him when he reached the bottom, and someone else put their arm around his waist, dragging him to the back door and down the porch steps. He fell to his knees and then face-first onto the ground. Cold, damp grass tickled his cheek as he fought to draw a breath.

Melissa's face loomed in front of his, and somehow, the farmyard was bathed in bright lights. Headlights. He closed his eyes. "Here, Noah. I'm putting this mask on you."

Somehow, he was now on his back, although he didn't remember rolling over.

Something pressed tight against his face and smelled of plastic and chemicals. He turned his head and tried to pull it off, but someone grabbed his hands.

"Leave it on, Noah."

Cassie. He relaxed.

Voices swirled around him and he heard someone calling out to the dog. He wanted to ask if Dino was okay—if everyone was okay—but his mind couldn't seem to force his mouth to work.

"Here are the blankets, Leona."

Noah recognized Jalen's voice, and other voices started filtering through. He shivered, his back cold even as his lungs burned. A blanket was dropped over him. He heard Dexter and Vivian calling out the names of the girls, and he tensed. Ava? Was she okay? Dexter had carried her out. Everyone spoke fast, their voices loud and harsh. He struggled to sit up. He had to help.

"Lay down, Noah." Cassie pressed a hand to his chest.

"You're okay? The kids?" He didn't recognize his own voice.

"Yes, I'm fine, and Milo and Bella are with Vivian, Ruby, and Ava. They're sitting in the truck to stay warm. Everyone but you and Ethan are okay."

"*Ethan?*" Noah resisted Cassie's hand and sat up. Ethan

lay several feet away, wearing a similar mask to the one Noah had on, attached to an oxygen tank. He was so still, Noah's heart almost stopped.

"Is he okay?" Noah's question came out like a croak as he tried to crawl to him, but Cassie held him back by the shoulders.

"Give them room. Leona's helping him."

Noah turned to look at her. "But... how bad is he?"

"He's breathing."

Noah coughed, exhausted from the effort of trying to reach Ethan and sank back. "What happened?" He meant how did the fire start, but Cassie must have thought he was confused.

"You were in the house, and it caught fire. Do you remember?" Cassie had a few smudges of soot on her face but appeared unharmed.

"Yeah... yeah, but how?"

"Melissa said they saw flames coming from the chimney."

They had cleaned the chimney in the cabin because they knew that one was bad. The farmhouse had a clean fireplace, and the other fires they'd burned in it hadn't caused any problems.

"I was stupid. Should have checked the chimney."

Grant walked by, offering Cassie and Noah bottles of water. "We had these in our supplies."

Cassie thanked him and took the water. "Yeah, well, you'll have to share the credit for this one with all of us." Cassie opened her bottle, took a long drink, then poured water onto a face cloth and began wiping Noah's face, lifting the mask just enough to get underneath it. He closed his eyes and sighed.

"You're a mess."

"Yeah. You are too. But damn, you look great."

Cassie tilted her head. "It must be lack of oxygen making you hallucinate."

Noah gave her a tired grin. "Maybe. But I like the hallucination, so let me enjoy it."

He took the cloth from her and finished wiping. It felt good. He opened his water and sat up. This time, Cassie didn't try to stop him. He heard a sob to his right and found Jalen holding oxygen tubing up to Dino's nose, petting the dog. "Come on, boy. You gotta be okay. What's Ethan gonna do without you?"

He stood, his legs wobbling. He pulled the oxygen mask off entirely and let it drop. Leona pointed at him. "Turn off the tank. We have to conserve it."

Noah nodded and bent, trying to figure it out, but Melissa rushed over and turned it off, wheeling it over to Ethan.

A cough came from Ethan's direction, and Noah turned to look. He sagged with relief as Ethan's legs moved and he flailed at the mask. Leona made him stop. Noah knew exactly what Ethan was going through. He'd be all right.

A loud crash made Noah jump, and he turned around to see the farmhouse engulfed in flames. "Oh shit!"

After everything they had survived—everything that they had endured—now this? "Damn it!"

Cassie stood beside him, her hands steepled over her nose and mouth in horror.

Almost all of their food was stored in the house. He watched as part of the roof collapsed. No fire department was going to come and save them. Noah couldn't watch anymore. He turned away, his focus landing on Dino. The dog twitched, and Jalen buried his face in the fur. "Good boy, Dino. *Good boy*."

Dino whined, his tail thumping the ground. Noah smiled. He didn't want to have to tell Ethan that his dog had died. Not after everything else.

Russell sat a few yards away, his knees raised, arms draped over them, coughing from time to time. Noah's head started spinning as he moved toward him, so he had to stop and get his balance. Cassie's arm went around his waist, and he recognized it as the same arm that had led him to safety as he'd come down the stairs. He looked down at her. "It was you."

She tipped her head. "What?"

"You saved me from the fire."

"No. I was only there at the end. Ethan came out and said you were still inside... then he collapsed."

"He almost died trying to save the dog." Noah shook his head. "Damn kid."

Cassie nudged him and smiled. "So did you."

EVERYONE WAS SPLIT the rest of the night between the cabin and the clinic, with the men in the cabin and the women and children in the clinic, but Noah wasn't sure anyone got a good night's sleep. Just as dawn started lightening the eastern sky, he heard Dino stirring. He slept beside Ethan, but when he saw Noah awake, Dino scurried around Jalen's and Luke's sprawled legs and raced to greet Noah. "Come on, boy. I'll take you out."

Dino bolted for the door, looking back at Noah as he found his shoes, his eyes begging him to hurry.

"I thought you were a goner last night." Noah gave the dog a good scratching around his neck. "I'm so glad you're okay."

Dino licked Noah's nose in response. Noah laughed and stood. Part of him wanted to exult in the pink-and-orange sky as the sun peeked over the trees. He'd lived to see another sunrise. The other half of him felt defeated as he watched the smoking embers of what remained of the house. He whispered an apology to the former owners of the farm. "Your beautiful home sheltered us when we needed it most. I'm sorry we weren't better caretakers."

The house had continued to burn after they retreated to the other buildings for sleep, but the long-threatening rain finally came and doused the flames. Now, it was a smoldering mass of ruins. He couldn't tell one room from another. The stench of wet, burned wood stung his nose and made him feel nauseated. He turned and headed to the clinic. He had to know that everyone was okay there.

After a soft knock, he poked his head in.

"Is everything okay?"

Noah squinted in the gray light, finding Cassie sleeping on a pallet on the floor, her kids curled beside her.

"Yeah. I'm just checking on everyone."

Cassie eased out from under her blankets. "We're fine, but I want to see what's left of the house."

"Not much, I'm afraid."

Vivian had one of the gurneys and rose on her elbows. "How are you feeling today, Noah?"

"Decent. It could be worse." His ribs hurt, and his wound still pulled when he moved certain ways, but he could draw a breath, and he wasn't dead. That had to count for something.

Vivian got off the gurney and tiptoed across the floor. "I want to see too."

Melissa waved a hand from her corner of the floor. "You ladies go ahead. I'll keep an eye on the little ones."

"Thanks, Melissa," Cassie whispered.

When Noah and the women returned to the house, they found Ethan and Dexter standing in the driveway. They wore sweatshirts Noah didn't recognize, and Ethan said, "Grant lent us his."

It reminded Noah that they literally had only the clothes they'd slept in. They were starting from worse than before the virus hit. He sighed.

Dexter pulled at the back door then jumped back when a piece of wood fell from the frame. A strong wind could blow what little was standing right down.

Noah's throat still hurt from the smoke. "I guess we'll have to start over."

"We'll never find a place as good as this." Dexter brushed the soot from his hands.

"Sure we will, hon." Vivian took his hand, soot and all, and folded her own around it. "Won't we, Noah?"

Noah's throat threatened to close, and it had nothing to do with the smoke inhalation. He could only nod. Finally, he coughed and said, "Yeah. Of course we will."

Cassie leaned against him. "We have to. Our kids depend on us."

"Yeah." None of the kids were biologically his, but they were all his children. "We'll figure it out."

"Today, we'll salvage what we can. Get as much gasoline in the vehicles and head out tomorrow or the next day. We have to find somewhere to spend the winter."

"But where?" Ethan scratched Dino behind the ears, the dog looking none the worse for the wear. He was quiet for several seconds. "I came through a town after I left home. It might have a place. If I can find it again."

Noah put an arm around Cassie, and the other rested near Ethan's neck. "We make a good team."

Ethan nodded. "The best."

Breakfast consisted of venison and leftover potatoes from the night before and beans supplied by Russell's group.

Noah took his plate over to where Russel sat on the floor of the cabin, where everyone had congregated to eat since they could heat the food in the fireplace. It was crowded, but at least it was warm. Noah dropped to sit. "I owe you... again."

Russell shook his head. "You don't owe me anything. I did what anyone would do. We were in the clinic, me, Melissa, and Leona. Melissa was Leona were talking shop. I got bored and was going to head back to the cabin, but we only had the one flashlight. I didn't want to leave Melissa or Leona in the dark, so I waited. I almost fell asleep on a gurney."

"I'm glad you didn't."

Russell smiled. "Yeah. Me too. As we were heading back to the cabin, we saw the flames just shooting out of the chimney like a Roman candle. It was crazy."

"And you ran into a burning building to save almost complete strangers."

Russell's brow furrowed as he turned to Noah. "No... we went in to save new friends."

The End

AFTERWORD

If you have a moment, a review of this book would be fantastic and greatly appreciated. It would help other readers decide if this book is something they might enjoy.

I had a lot of fun writing Isolation, especially the scenes where the characters were scavenging for supplies. Imaginary shopping is almost more fun than real shopping!

Please join my mailing list for the latest information on book releases.

M.P. McDonald's New Releases & Newsletter,
It's easy to join the list. Just go to my website at: www.
mpmcdonald.com

ABOUT THE AUTHOR

M.P. McDonald is the author of supernatural thrillers and post-apocalyptic science fiction. With multiple stints on Amazon's top 100 list, her books have been well-received by readers. Always a fan of reluctant heroes, especially when there is a time travel or psychic twist, she fell in love with the television show Quantum Leap. Soon, she was reading and watching anything that had a similar concept. When that wasn't enough, she wrote her own stories with her unique spin.

When not writing, she works as a respiratory therapist, hangs out with her kids and grandkids, and loves to swim.

Contact Me:

Website: www.mpmcdonald.com

Email: mmcdonald64@gmail.com

Made in the USA
Middletown, DE
27 January 2023

23264107R00182